A BLAST LIFTED
BLOWING I

He flew through the doo̶̶̶̶̶ ̶̶̶̶̶̶̶̶̶against a wall, stunned. Shaking his head, he got to his feet. He felt a wetness running down his arm, but he ignored it.

The Able Team leader could still hold his piece, so he raised the Colt and fired toward the gunners to cover his retreat. He had seen his Gadgets and Pol go down, and his first inclination was to charge the enemy and kill as many of them as he could. But the big ex-cop knew it would be a suicide play.

He had to get to Bolan.

DON PENDLETON'S

MACK BOLAN®

STONY MAN™

BREACH OF TRUST

A GOLD EAGLE BOOK FROM

WORLDWIDE®

TORONTO • NEW YORK • LONDON
AMSTERDAM • PARIS • SYDNEY • HAMBURG
STOCKHOLM • ATHENS • TOKYO • MILAN
MADRID • WARSAW • BUDAPEST • AUCKLAND

First edition March 1999

ISBN 0-373-61923-5

Special thanks and acknowledgment to
Michael Kasner for his contribution to this work.

BREACH OF TRUST

Printed in U.S.A.

BREACH OF
TRUST

CHAPTER ONE

Berlin, Germany

The guard at the east door of the old flak tower in what had once been East Berlin came completely alert and stepped out of the deeply recessed doorway where he had sought shelter from the bite of the spring wind. The big man who had parked his car on the corner and was approaching him looked like bad news. The guard himself was a big man, bigger, in fact, than the smiling stranger. But something about the man's purposeful stride and his cold blue eyes set off alarm bells.

The guard's hand slid into the pocket of his overcoat, wrapped around the grip of the 9 mm Makarov PM pistol and flicked off the safety.

The stranger had a Berlin guide book in his left hand and held it out, open to a street map. "Speak English?" he asked with a decidedly American accent. "I'm looking for the Hohenzollerndamm..."

"Buzz off, Joe," the German snarled as he exhausted his English vocabulary.

The stranger's facial expression didn't change at the rude rebuff. But his ice blue eyes grew even colder as he triggered the silenced Walther PPK concealed in his right hand. The subsonic .380 hollowpoint slug punched through the guard's upper face and drilled into his brain. Like a puppet with his strings cut, the guard slumped forward into Mack Bolan's arms.

"Mine's down," Bolan said, tilting his head down and speaking into the mike of the com link clipped out of sight under his coat collar as he dragged the body back into the alcove.

"Copy," David McCarter replied in his ear.

"So's mine," Rafael Encizo reported.

"Are we go?" McCarter asked the rest of the team.

"Copy, rock and roll," T. J. Hawkins responded.

"I'm go," Calvin James called in.

"Wait one," Gary Manning cautioned. "I've got a... No, it's okay. I'm go."

"What was it?" McCarter questioned the Canadian demolitions man.

"I thought I had a stray bandit, but it was just a guy in a leather jacket running to catch a bus."

McCarter radioed to Yakov Katzenelenbogen at their mobile command post parked several blocks away. "We're a go."

"Copy all go," Katz sent back. "Wait for Gadgets to kill the surveillance system."

"Roger."

Hermann Schwarz's voice came on the line a moment later. "You're go for entry."

"Phoenix is go," Katz responded.

"Let's do it, mates," McCarter said.

On the Briton's command, the six men slipped through the doors leading into the ground floor of the tower. Bolan and Phoenix Force were on the move.

HEINZ BLATZ PULLED the German-made 85 mm RPG-7 rocket round out of its plastic shipping canister to check that the somewhat fragile nose fuze was intact before repacking it and putting it into the nylon bag on the table. Normally he wouldn't have needed to inspect the rockets, but these particular rounds hadn't come to him directly from an arsenal. They had been in the hands of black marketeers since the fall of the wall and could have been damaged by improper handling before they came to him.

Blatz was intimately familiar with the Russian-designed RPG-7 antitank rocket launcher. Before the fall of the Berlin wall and the collapse of the German Democratic Republic, he had been a sergeant major in the once-feared East German Border Police. The Communist forces had been armed with

Russian weapons, and he had fired the RPG launcher hundreds of times in training. It was good at what it did, and he liked it.

The RPG was not only a superb weapon for busting armored vehicles, it was useful for opening bank vaults, as well. A single shot was all it took to blast a hole through up to three feet of concrete, and vault doors were a snap. He and his men had an appointment with a bank in a few hours, and he wanted to be ready for it. This would be their fourth bank job in the past six months and the last one before they took a well-earned vacation in Spain.

Blatz's comrades in the bank business were all ex-East German border guards as well. The Border Police had been an elite unit and had attracted many of the same kinds of men who had enlisted in the earlier Nazi SS. It could be said that the border guards had been very good at following orders and not very good at considering human life to have much value.

That decided lack of regard for human life made Blatz's gang as good at their new profession as they had been at their old one. Anyone who was unfortunate enough to get in the way during one of their bank jobs simply ended up dead. Blatz had killed so many East Germans trying to flee the now-defunct worker's paradise that adding a few West Germans to his body count was no big deal.

As soon as the RPG round had been checked,

Blatz turned to the man loading 7.62 mm rounds into AKM assault rifle magazines. "Are you done with those, Dieter?"

"Yes," Former Corporal Dieter Glantz answered. "Four magazines each."

"The radios check out," Franz Beckmann reported to his old sergeant major. Of all the gang members, he had been with Blatz the longest. They had served together for many years and, as far as he was concerned, the banking business, as Blatz called it, was almost as much fun as what they had done with the Border Police. Gunning down runners, as they had been called, had been fun, but it hadn't paid very well. At the most, they had received a small bonus for every man, woman or child they blew away in the wire, and maybe a party for the unit.

Reaching around for another RPG rocket from the open wooden ammo crate, Blatz's eyes swept past the bank of video monitors mounted on his workbench. All of them were blank. Cursing the vagaries of the electrical power supply, he figured that the surveillance system had gone down again from a power surge and punched the reset button. When the cameras didn't come back on, he reached for the handheld radio.

"Conrad?" he called to the guard in the east door. "Conrad?"

He checked to see that the battery indicator on

the radio was lighted before trying again. "Conrad? Gunther?" he shouted. "Dammit, where are you bastards?"

Listening to his boss, Glantz stopped loading magazines, reached for his AKM and pulled back on the charging handle to chamber a round. He had served with Gunther and Conrad for a long time, and if they weren't answering the radio, something was wrong.

Blatz quickly followed his subordinate's cue and reached for his own weapon. "Send Mannie and Heinrik down there and find out what in hell is going on."

"Yes, sir."

THE GROUND FLOOR of the old flak tower was being used as a service station and parking garage. Left over from the dark days of World War II, the antiaircraft artillery structures still dotted Berlin. They had been built so well that they had withstood the storm of bombs and artillery shells that had obliterated so much of the Third Reich's capital. Because of the thickness of their reinforced concrete walls and floors, good use had been made of them after the war.

A dozen cars were parked against the walls by the maintenance lifts and the gas pumps were positioned by the main door for drive-in service. Leading up from the garage area was a spiraling ramp that provided access to the upper floors and more parking places. Katz had been able to secure a plan of the massive structure, so the Stony Man team knew that there were three floors above them as well as two below ground level. The plans also indicated that there were office spaces on the upper floor and that was where the strike force was headed.

As well as the ramp, an elevator shaft connected the floors, but that wasn't the optimal avenue of approach to the upper floors. Getting trapped in an elevator was a good way to die.

After making sure that the ground floor was clear, the commandos shucked their thick civilian overcoats, freeing themselves for action.

Calvin James and T. J. Hawkins led the way up the spiraling ramp. They were making the turn onto the second floor when they heard the sound of booted feet running down the ramp. Any chance they'd had of surprising the gang evaporated.

Whispering a warning into the com link, James and Hawkins pressed themselves against the walls on each side of the ramp, their silenced MP-5 SD submachine guns at the ready.

The two men descending the ramp carried Paratroop AKM assault rifles, but they weren't held in immediate firing position. With the two Phoenix Force commandos hidden in the shadows, the Germans didn't spot them until it was too late. The gunmen were still trying to bring their rifles into play when two silenced bursts of 9 mm lead cut them down.

"Two down," James whispered into his com link.

"We're right behind you," McCarter sent back. "Keep going."

Stepping over the bodies, the two point men raced up the stairs. The element of surprise was lost, and it was time to go to work.

HEINZ BLATZ THOUGHT he heard a muffled noise from the ramp and reached for his radio. "Mannie? Heinrik?" he said.

When there was no immediate answer, Blatz signaled for his men to take cover. Somehow, his hideout had been betrayed and their only chance to survive was to fight.

Snatching up one of the RPG launchers, he quickly stuffed a grenade into the front and thumbed back the hammer. Firing an RPG in an enclosed area was risky, but if this was a police raid, he might need its firepower before it was over.

THE PHOENIX FORCE COMMANDOS knew that the tactical advantage always lay with the guy holding the high ground. That axiom of war was as true when you were fighting in a building as it was in open ground combat. The way to overcome that advantage was to attack.

Slipping grenades from their harnesses, James and Hawkins opened the assault. Pulling the pins, the two men tossed the grenades around the corner of the ramp wall into the top floor. Even before the bombs detonated, a storm of AK fire slashed down the ramp at them. Because of the angle, however, the rounds went over their heads before ricocheting off the concrete.

"Flash bang," McCarter warned. "Cover us."

James and Hawkins stuck the muzzles of their MP-5s around the corner and emptied their magazines in long bursts. Right before their bolts locked back on empty, McCarter and Encizo lobbed two flash-bang grenades.

The detonation echoed off the concrete walls as if a thousand-pound bomb had gone off, and the reflected flash illuminated the dim ramp like an arc light. The Phoenix Force commandos charged the last few steps up the ramp, their MP-5s blazing silenced fire.

The Germans were stunned by the grenades and firing blindly. Even so, an unaimed AK bullet would kill as quickly as an aimed one.

The gunman closest to the ramp was on his knees, hit by an earlier burst. Hawkins put a trio of slugs into him to finish the job and ran on.

A long burst of AK fire cut through the air close

enough to Encizo's face for him to feel the heat. Cursing in Spanish, he went into a crouch, spinning as he triggered a spray of lead. The AK gunner took most of the hit and collapsed behind the workbench.

"That one!" McCarter shouted over the roar of gunfire and pointed at Blatz, who was bringing up his RPG launcher.

Manning drew the CO_2-powered dart pistol from the special holster under his left arm and took aim.

When the German saw the long pistol aimed at him, he dropped the RPG and tried to dive for cover. The dart caught him while he was still in the air. Slamming into his back, the auto-injector flooded his system with enough tranquilizer to instantly knock him out. He fell to the floor like a side of beef and skidded to a halt against the wall.

Seeing his leader go down, the last gunman called out something in German. McCarter wasn't in the mood for a language lesson right at that moment and took him out with a short burst to the upper body.

In the sudden silence, Manning crossed the floor and knelt beside the unconscious Blatz. After checking his pulse, he quickly pulled his arms behind his back and slipped plastic riot restraints over his wrists.

"Is he ready to go?" McCarter asked.

"We're go," Manning answered as he jerked the

unconscious man to his feet and draped him over his shoulder.

"Let's get out of here."

Leaving the bodies in place, the Phoenix Force commandos hurried back down the ramp. Even with the tower's thick walls, someone would have heard the grenades, and the efficient Berlin police would be on the way.

JACK GRIMALDI SAT behind the wheel of a Mercedes van parked at the corner of the block. The tower took up most of the block, but a ring of small stores and shops had been built around its base. Grimaldi's white van bore the elaborate red, pink, yellow and green advertisements of a local flower supplier on the sides. The markings were printed on magnetic plastic sheets that could be removed easily and replaced with another logo.

Grimaldi was Stony Man's resident ace pilot; if it was designed to travel through air, he could pilot it. This time, though, an aerial extraction wasn't possible. The German government was touchy about who it let fly through its skies. And, since the Germans had no idea that a Stony Man operation was being run on their turf, that made it twice as difficult. So, the flyboy was behind the wheel of the van for the getaway today.

James had said that the gaudy van looked like a pimp's delivery wagon. But, in a flower loving city like Berlin, dozens of vans exactly like it could be seen on the streets almost any time of day. It was the perfect getaway car.

"I sure wish you were standing by somewhere with a chopper," Hermann "Gadgets" Schwarz muttered as he listened to what was coming over the Phoenix Force com links. "I'd sure as hell rather fly out of a situation like this."

"Not in Berlin you wouldn't," Grimaldi said. "They've got the most restricted air traffic control in all of Europe. We'd never be able to get out without a chase."

"Looking at the traffic in this damned town, I don't see how in hell we're going to get through it on time."

"This is nothing." Grimaldi grinned. "You should try driving in Athens. That's some real traffic, man."

"We're ready for pickup," McCarter said over Grimaldi's com link.

He hit the starter. "On the way."

CHAPTER TWO

Stony Man Farm, Virginia

"Striker has just reported closure." Yakov Katzenelenbogen's face on the video monitor in the Stony Man Computer Room wore a big grin. "Grimaldi made the pickup, and they're headed out of town now."

For this operation, the Stony Man tactical adviser was running a mobile command post out of a van emblazoned with prominent CNN markings. Since the equipment and antennas he needed to talk to the Farm were the kind of things one would expect to see on a TV van, it was a perfect disguise.

"The target was neutralized," Katzenelenbogen reported, "and the Berlin police have been tipped off, anonymously of course. They should be closing in on the flak tower anytime now."

"Good work, Katz," Barbara Price said simply.

As Stony Man's mission controller, she always felt a deep sense of satisfaction when one of her plans went off without a hitch. This had been a little more difficult than their usual mission and had carried risks the Stony Man teams usually didn't have to deal with. Conducting a raid in broad daylight in one of Western Europe's largest cities without the knowledge of the local authorities always raised the stakes.

Had the Berlin police stumbled onto the Phoenix Force's operation, it would have been all over for the Stony Man commandos. They would have been incarcerated as terrorists until high level behind-the-scene negotiations could free them, and the political fallout would have been catastrophic. Headlines about U.S. secret operatives being caught committing a terrorist act in a NATO nation wouldn't have been helpful. Nonetheless, the President had decided that it was an acceptable risk.

"Did they make the snatch?" Hal Brognola asked around the stub of the well-chewed cigar clamped in a corner of his mouth. He had quit smoking a long time ago, but he still had to get his nicotine fix somehow and had developed an addiction to chewing cigars.

"They sure did and I've made contact to initiate the transfer," Katz stated.

"Very good," Brognola said. "Hopefully they'll be able to find out what the hell is going on over there and give us more leads to follow up."

On the rolls of the federal civil servants, Brognola was listed as a high-ranking official of the Justice Department. In reality, he was the man responsible for the activities of the covert organization known as the Sensitive Operations Group.

Being in charge of the nation's most closely guarded secret operation was no easy job. Balancing the realities of Sensitive Operations, as they were called, with Washington D.C.'s political wishful thinking played hell with the lining of his stomach. Particularly at a time like this when he had to wait for information from halfway around the world so he could pass it on to the President, who would then let the Russians know what had gone down.

The irony of his situation this time wasn't lost on him. The Stony Man teams had been formed to fight international terrorism that, more times than not, had been sponsored by the old Soviet Union. With the fall of the Communist regime in 1991, however, America's cold war opponents had become their new allies. Since then, the struggling new government had asked for American assistance several times. In particular, they needed help dealing with the fast-growing criminal element born out of the democratic reforms.

Under the Soviet Union, criminal activity had been a monopoly of the Communist government. However, with the transfer of power to the Russian people, the opportunity to do evil had been given to them as well. Unfortunately certain elements of the new Russia had taken advantage of this opportunity with a vengeance. Every vice of the Western World could now be found in any small Russian town and, since most of those vices were the same crimes as those in the West, they were supplied by criminals. Also, since the transition to a capitalistic economy wasn't going well, there was money to be made in the control of scarce commodities and goods. That meant price gouging and smuggling, two more enterprises where criminals excelled.

While the DEA and FBI worked closely with the Russians providing training and advice, they had come up against something they couldn't deal with even with that help. This time, the Russian Mafia, as these criminal gangs had come to be known, was taking its operation to new heights. All of Europe, not just Russia and the new Eastern nations, was suffering from a Russian-sponsored crime wave surpassing anything ever seen in the West. Even in a Russia where fighting gang turf wars with car bombs and AKs has become commonplace, the government was helpless against this new onslaught.

When intelligence indicated that the Russian Mafia was actively expanding its operations into Eastern European states from Latvia to the Ukraine, Russia decided to ask the United States for more active assistance. The President had turned that request for action over to Stony Man Farm.

"You know," Brognola said thoughtfully, "I never thought I'd ever see the day when we'd ever be fighting alongside the Russian government against a Russian-backed Euro Mafia. This is just a little too weird for me."

"Well," Aaron Kurtzman said, "no one ever said that the Russians aren't an imaginative people. They looked around, saw how well organized crime was doing in the West and decided to try it themselves."

"But it's not just a Russian problem this time," Price reminded them. "All of the old Eastern Bloc nations are having problems with organized crime right now."

"How long are Striker and Phoenix going to stay in Munich?" Brognola asked.

"As long as it takes for the Russians to interrogate the prisoner," Price answered. "Then, we'll reevaluate the situation and see what we can do next for them."

"There'll be something," Brognola said. "You can take that to the bank. They won't be able to get a handle on this themselves. According to Minister Vallinsikov, the Russian agencies are riddled with spies that let the gangs know every move the government tries to make against them."

"Nothing ever changes over there, does it?"

"No, unfortunately."

Russia

GREGOR ROSTOFF, ex-colonel of the 105th Guards Regiment, sat in his office complex several miles outside Moscow going through a stack of reports. Rostoff was a dynamic man, tall and fit, and his rugged good looks had served him well both in the Red Army and his new civilian career. Watching him in action, it was easy to believe that he would do anything he said he would, whatever that might be. While he had never spelled out his long-range plans, they included becoming the most powerful man in what had been the Soviet Union and its eastern satellite nations.

Though he was still a few years away from meeting his goals, he was already one of the most powerful men in the criminal underground of the new Russia. As he had discovered, gaining power in a democracy required thinking on one's feet while taking risks, and Rostoff was a well-known risk taker with an agile mind. The men he had gathered into his organization were also quick-witted, but their greatest value was their loyalty to him and his plans.

He put down the report he had been reading when a knock sounded on his office door. "Come," he answered.

"We may have a problem, sir." Former Major Boris Detlov came to attention as he reported to his old CO and now his civilian boss. Like Rostoff, he, too, had been dismissed from the Red Army and had loyally followed his colonel into his new venture.

"And that is?"

"I believe the Americans are sticking their long noses into our business."

Though Rostoff ran his organization like a military unit, he insisted that his men always refer to themselves as businessmen and what they did as a business—which in a way it was. But their business was what other people usually called organized crime. By whatever name the business was called, it paid well and Rostoff was quickly becoming one of the new Russia's wealthiest men. His followers were becoming wealthy right along with him, which served to cement their loyalty even further.

"What happened?"

"The scheduled operation in Berlin was intercepted. A strike force hit Blatz's headquarters and wiped it out completely. It's all over the German TV news."

Rostoff pushed back his chair. "Let's have a look."

The converted SS-22 ICBM missile launch complex Rostoff called his business headquarters hadn't been stripped of its military electronics before it had been offered for sale on the civilian market. One of the disgraced colonel's old Red Army contacts had been the officer in charge of demilitarizing excess military property before offering it for sale. As a result, the facility retained all of its military computer and communication equipment.

Even more important, this particular complex had been what the old Soviet military had called a Mother Center. Not only was it an ICBM launch command post, it was also a military satellite communications facility and a computer control center. It had been built to command other launch sites if their links to central control were broken. With this sophisticated equipment intact, Rostoff owned a facility unmatched by anything in civilian hands anywhere in the world. Only major military forces operated the kind of equipment that Rostoff had been able to purchase for next to nothing. One of his mainframe computers alone was worth more than he had paid for the entire complex, and three such powerful mainframes had come with the deal.

Entering what had been the launch control center, Detlov seated himself behind one of the computers and punched in a command. The monitor clicked on and started running a tape of a Berlin TV station's coverage of the shoot-out at the flak tower in the old Eastern sector. Rostoff spoke German as well as English, French, Arabic and the major Afghan dialect, so he had no trouble following the reporter's comments.

According to the report, persons unknown had

raided a flak tower being used as a garage and auto-repair facility in what had been East Berlin and had killed seven men. What made the story, though, was that the police had discovered a large cache of loot from a recent string of bank robberies in Western Europe. The tape showed officers loading sack after sack of currency and securities into armored cars parked on the street in front of the tower.

"We needed that inventory," Rostoff said, using the business vocabulary he insisted that all of his people use as part of his overall security plan. He headed a business now and the use of military terminology wasn't compatible with business activities. It set the wrong tone when he had to deal with civilians. The brutal reputation of the old Red Army hadn't faded yet.

"Why do you think that it was our American competitors who blocked this transaction?"

"It was certainly not the German police," Detlov stated. "I would have heard about it from our representatives."

As an ex-GRU, Military Intelligence, officer, Detlov ran Rostoff's network of "representatives" as they were referred to. But, by whatever name, a spy was someone who supplied needed information. With Rostoff's wealth, he could afford to hire as many representatives as he needed, and to make sure that they stayed loyal to him, he paid them well.

"What do our Rome and Paris representatives have to say about this?" Rostoff asked.

"They were just as surprised about it as I was."

"Then you don't think that it was a move by one of our European competitors?"

In Rostoff's lexicon, Europe's old-line criminal enterprises, the Italian Mafia, the Union Corse, the French narcogangs and others were his friendly competition. They, however, didn't quite see things that way; there was nothing friendly about what Rostoff was trying to do. The established European gangs had long agreed to a live-and-let-live mentality that gave everyone a cut of the pie, and turf wars were rare. Rostoff didn't hold to such gentlemen's agreements and was crashing the party.

One thing that made Rostoff's criminal enterprises different from the norm was his eagerness to rush into any venture, no matter how dangerous, that could turn a profit. Where the old-line European gangs had been reluctant to deal in matters that might bring them to the attention of NATO or other military forces, Rostoff didn't care. Since many of his operatives were veterans of the Afghan War, they had an expertise in weaponry that most of Europe's underworld didn't have, and he wasn't shy about unleashing it. The military nature of Rostoff's operation had created a level of criminal violence beyond anything ever seen in the West.

Fighting turf wars with RPGs and AKs had become a trademark of his operations.

"It was not our European competitors," Detlov stated flatly. "They would not have left the inventory behind. Apparently nothing was missing and the police are saying that they recovered almost eight million dollars worth."

Though Rostoff's operation hadn't yet crossed the Atlantic, he conducted all of his business in U.S. dollars rather than having to jump back and forth between some two-dozen European national currencies. It made the bookkeeping much easier, and he didn't have to adjust his numbers to take constantly fluctuating exchange rates into account.

"You are completely convinced that it was the Americans who did this?"

"Yes, sir," Detlov replied. "If you remember, I predicted this when I learned about Vallinsikov's secret visit to the White House. And this is not the first time that they have cooperated with the government in this manner. As you know, the FBI, the DEA and other agencies have been advising Moscow on so-called crime issues for some time now."

The ex-intelligence officer shook his head. "It's a sad day when we Russians cannot govern ourselves without having American big brothers watching over our shoulders."

"What branch of the American intelligence apparatus do you think is most likely to be the one involved in this action, the CIA?''

"This was not a CIA action," Detlov stated confidently. "They simply do not operate that way. Had they been planning an operation against us, they would have coordinated with the German government and the Berlin police before they did anything. They would not have struck without warning as was apparently done."

"So you think that it is some deep cover, clandestine organization?"

"Yes, I do. I have heard rumblings of a group known as Phoenix Force."

"What do you think we need to do to protect our operations?"

"I think that we should devote some of our resources to eliminating these particular competitors."

"That's what I think too. Start planning it and put out the word that we want everything we can get on these men. No matter how undercover this Phoenix Force is, someone has to know something about them."

"I think that some of our new associates may be able to help us with this," Detlov suggested. "Many of them have come up against this group in the past and they may have information we can use."

One of the things that made Rostoff's operation

different from all of the other Russian Mafia organizations was that he recruited followers from outside Mother Russia herself. Using his old Red Army and ex-KGB contacts, he had invited the IRA, the Red Brigades and various other terrorist groups to join his plans to dismember the new Eastern democracies. With these groups providing experienced foot soldiers to back up his Red Army veterans, Rostoff had more firepower than many of the emerging national armies he was targeting.

"Good idea," Rostoff said. "Get right on that."

"At once, sir."

CHAPTER THREE

Berlin, Germany

As Jack Grimaldi had predicted, he'd had no difficulty weaving his way through the congested Berlin traffic. The number-one rule of the road in Germany seemed to be that the bigger vehicle automatically had the right-of-way. In the van's passenger seat, Hermann Schwarz kept a death grip on his seat-belt harness until they reached the Stadt Ring, the freeway that circled the city. From there, it was a fast trip to the entrance to the Frankfurt—Berlin Autobahn.

Once westbound on the Autobahn, Schwarz relaxed a little. "This isn't so bad," he said as a solid stream of cars zipped past them in the fast lane. "It's just like the Santa Monica Freeway."

Grimaldi glanced at his kilometer-marked speedometer and translated the kilometers. "Except that we're going ninety-five miles an hour in the slow lane."

"You had to tell me that, didn't you?"

At the first roadside rest stop in what had been East Germany, Grimaldi pulled into the parking lot and stashed the van between two long-haul rigs to wait for the arrival of Katzenelenbogen's CP van.

When Katz showed up half an hour later, the still-unconscious Heinz Blatz was transferred to the larger vehicle. As the team's medic, James checked him over and gave him another shot to keep him out until the Russians arrived to take him off their hands. In the meantime, the team slipped into the rest-stop canteen one at a time to get coffee and something to eat.

When the black Mercedes sedan finally arrived, Blatz was transferred to the custody of the Russians and they drove off with him. In accordance with the agreement the President had made with the Russians, they would handle the interrogation of any suspects who survived the Stony Man operations.

As soon as the Mercedes was out of sight, Grimaldi took the removable Berlin florist shop markings off the van and replaced then with the logo of a Frankfurt chemical company. That would be their stopover destination while they prepped for the next mission.

Stony Man Farm, Virginia

HAL BROGNOLA WAS GLAD to hear that the transfer of Blatz had gone off without a hitch. He might not enjoy working with the Russians, but this wasn't the first time that the Stony Man teams had undertaken a mission in cooperation with the new democratic Russia, and he knew that it wouldn't be the last.

This operation had been kicked off when Vallinsikov, the Russian Minister of the Interior, made a secretive, unofficial visit to the Oval Office. After providing the President hard evidence of the threat posed by the criminal gangs, he asked him to help his country put an end to this threat to the democracy they both wanted to survive. As Vallinsikov had pointed out, the Russian Mafia had gained so much power that the government could no longer control it. Moscow's fear was that if the Russian military command felt that the nation was slipping into anarchy, it would take over and impose a new dictatorship.

Since America's best interests were for Russia and Eastern Europe to become strong democracies and join the West, this wave of criminal violence represented a clear and present danger to U.S. national security. In the spirit of democratic cooperation, the President offered the Russians the services of America's most experienced covert action agency.

The President's offer had been gratefully accepted, and Phoenix Force, as well as Able Team, who usually operated domestically, were dispatched to Europe to follow up on the one lead Vallinsikov had provided. Now that the bank-busting gang had been eliminated, they would wait and see what leads came from the interrogation of the prisoner. Brognola knew that the one raid wouldn't put an end to the problem. The Stony Man warriors would have to fight again before this situation was turned around.

But, for the time being, he had good news to take back to 1600 Pennsylvania Avenue.

Russia

AFTER PUTTING Boris Detlov to work finding out what had gone wrong in Berlin, Gregor Rostoff went into his private office. The room in the launch complex reflected his old occupation as a combat soldier more than it did his new one as a wealthy criminal. It was sparse to the point of being little more than a small room with a desk, lamp and chair. While the rest of Rostoff's complex had state-of-the-art communications gear and computers, this office had only a single military field phone on the desk. As humble as it was, this simple brown plastic instrument was probably the most important telephone in all of the new Russia.

Rostoff's field phone was hooked up to a single user line, and the phone on the other end sat on the desk of an old Red Army comrade of his, General Pavel Belislav. In forced retirement since the abortive coup attempt that had put Boris Yeltsin in office, Belislav hadn't been content to sit in his dacha and drink himself to death. Instead, he had put together a clique of other dissatisfied officers who intended to overthrow the faltering civilian government and install army rule to halt the slide of Russia to Third World status. So far, they had done little except plan and recruit while they waited for the right opportunity to make their move.

Though he was running an independent criminal organization for his own benefit, Rostoff was an integral part of the Belislav group as well. In fact his criminal enterprises were the major source of support for the general's plans. With the Russian economy as bad as it was, it was difficult for anyone to acquire enough money to support something like a government takeover except through criminal activities. For this reason alone, the Americans had to be dealt with quickly. The Berlin raid had been a major setback, and it would take several months for him to make good the losses.

Heinz Blatz and his unit were particularly valuable assets for his operation. They had the discipline that most of the terrorist units lacked, which was why he had given them the mission of acquiring bank assets. Now he would have to train another unit to take over their assignment—maybe one of the Irish teams.

But, to insure that something like this didn't happen again, his priority had to be eliminating these Americans as soon as possible.

While the Americans needed to be taken care of immediately, their actions might be the triggering incident General Belislav had been looking for. For the Russian government to have invited in a covert American military strike force to deal with a domestic problem was an affront to every Russian. The modern Russians might be pale imitations of the heroic men and women who had struggled to bring their nation out of the dark ages under Lenin and Stalin, but they still had pride.

Sometimes that pride was hard to see in the ragged people who walked the streets of Moscow nowadays, but Rostoff knew that it was still there. In the breast of every Russian beat the heart of the same men who had beaten the Nazi hordes to defeat the Third Reich. The Russian people could be great again, but the soul-sucking democratic government had to be put down before that could happen.

Rostoff knew that Vallinsikov had invited the Americans in to deal with his organization because he couldn't trust his fellow Russians to do it, and he was right. Between Rostoff and Belislav, they had an interlocking web of spies and informants that reached into every nook and cranny of the government. Their access into the police and military was almost as good.

When sole power eventually fell to Belislav's military clique, Rostoff wouldn't claim a spot in the general's new government. He had no need to massage his ego through the accolades of others. He would be in the heart of government, but he would never be in the spotlight, any spotlight. He had seen the fate of others who chased after public acclaim; they either died or their efforts were stymied by the jealousies of others. He would let General Belislav and his cronies bask in the glow of public worship while he ruled an empire larger than Napoleon's.

First though, he had to brief the general on the failure of the Berlin operation. He wouldn't tell him about the Americans until he had worked out a plan to deal with them. Belislav tended to get excited when Americans were mentioned, and he didn't want to deal with that right now.

Reaching for the field phone on his desk, he rang through to the general's dacha. As always, the phone was picked up on the second ring.

"Comrade General," Rostoff began, "we have a problem."

As WELL As being Gregor Rostoff's right-hand man, Boris Detlov was also his in-house computer wizard. Unlike the United States, the new Russia wasn't living in the Internet. Few computers existed outside the government and the military, and even there, there weren't many except in the rocket and space forces. And, of course, the GRU, the Military Intelligence service.

As an ex-military intelligence officer, Detlov had been well-trained in the use of cyberspace to gather information. The facilities of the launch complex Rostoff had procured had been designed to function as the center of a Russian version of the Internet. From there, he was able to access almost any computer in Russia, including those in use by the Russian offices of Western companies.

When he logged into the computers of the Interior Ministry, he was shocked to learn that there had been a survivor of the Berlin flak tower shootout and that he had been turned over to the Russian government. Since all of the former East Germans knew enough about Rostoff's operation to be dangerous, he wasted no time. Without bothering his boss with the details, he called up one of their spies within the Moscow metropolitan police force and issued termination orders in Rostoff's name. As soon as that was done, he reported to Rostoff.

Rostoff wasn't concerned that Detlov had ordered Blatz's death without consulting him. He trusted all of his top men to make decisions when they were needed. He only reserved the right to make the ultimate decisions, like how to deal with the Americans.

"Have you come up with any ideas on how to deal with this American commando team?"

"Actually I have," Detlov replied. "But I came to the conclusion that it might be better for us in the long run if I did not have them all killed outright."

"I am listening," Rostoff prompted.

"As I thought would happen," Detlov said, "several of our new associates were able to give me bits and pieces of information about this unit. After going over it, I started thinking that it might be a mistake to have them all killed. It would take care of the problem for now, that it true. But it might invite more attention to our activities than we need at this time, attention from the CIA.

"If, however, a few of them were to be killed under circumstances that point to their having been sold out by the Russian government they are supposed to be helping, it might get the Americans out of our business completely. Regardless of what their President says about his willingness to cooperate with Moscow, they do not trust us any more than we trust them. If he loses valuable assets because the government can't keep a secret, he might change his mind."

Rostoff smiled. "I like the way you think, Detlov."

Stony Man Farm, Virginia

HAL BROGNOLA'S SENSE of satisfaction about the Berlin operation quickly faded. No sooner had he returned from reporting to the White House that the Stony Man team had pulled it off than he was informed that a problem had come up during interrogation of the prisoner.

"The prisoner from the Berlin mission died in custody," Brognola told Barbara Price.

"What happened?"

"The results of the autopsy aren't in yet, but it looks like he was poisoned."

Brognola shook his head. "Vallinsikov wasn't kidding when he said that the Russian Mafia has their people planted everywhere. This guy was in a high-security cell and they still got to him."

"Does that put us back to square one?" she asked.

"Not really," Brognola replied. "The Russians have come up with another lead that may prove to be even better. The team will have to go to Prague to check it out, but it should be well worth the trip."

"What's there?"

"The headquarters of one of the biggest drug distribution operations in all of the Eastern countries."

"That sounds like an interesting proposition."

"It should be, because we were given the names of a couple of the major Czech players there. The team should be able to make contact with them and then play it from there.''

"Give me the particulars, and I'll start putting the operation together.''

Russia

"THEY'RE GOING for it,'' he said. "My contact says Vallinsikov has been notified that this Phoenix Force is headed to Prague to follow up on the 'lead' they were given.''

"Good work,'' Rostoff said. "One thing, though, when you take them out, I want you to capture some of them if it is at all possible.''

"Like they did with Blatz.''

"Exactly. Since these people have made themselves my enemy, I need to know as much as I can about them. But I want it done in a way that keeps them from learning that I am onto them.''

"That should be no problem,'' Detlov promised. "My team is well-trained, and we can easily change the plan enough to incorporate that additional task.''

"When are you leaving?''

"This afternoon.''

CHAPTER FOUR

Stony Man Farm, Virginia

This time, the gathering of players in the Farm's War Room didn't have the sense of urgency that the premission briefings usually did. This wasn't crisis management, merely a skull session with the Farm team to go over the last few points of the Prague operation with Hal Brognola so he could bring the President up to date.

Having Yakov Katzenelenbogen in the field with a mobile command post was working out well. Since the vehicle was equipped with full data uplink capabilities, the Computer Room staff was able to get data to him almost as soon as they got it. By the same token, Katz could keep them instantly abreast of any changes on his end.

"Okay, people," Barbara Price said, opening the meeting, "here's the drill. We are go for the attempt to infiltrate the Russian Mafia's narcotics operations in Prague. We have the names and contact numbers for two of the biggest Czech players, and Able Team will make the initial contact. They'll be posing as overseas agents for an American Mafia group that wants to make a connection to the Afghan pipeline.''

''Why not try for the Iranian heroin connection?'' Brognola asked. ''That's a bigger network, isn't it?''

''It is,'' she agreed. ''But we chose the Afghans because they're starting to figure prominently in the European drug trade. Even with the country in the hands of the Taliban fundamentalists, they realize they need cash flow, and it makes sense that U.S. dealers would want to get a piece of that action. Our 'buyers' will know that means making a connection with the Russian Mafia, since they have a monopoly on the Afghan hash production. Even with the bad blood between the two nations, the Afghans know the Russians and are used to dealing with them.''

When Brognola nodded his understanding, she continued. ''The way Katz has set up this scenario, Rosario will be playing the role of the Mafia capo with Gadgets as his moneyman and Carl as the muscle.''

Everyone smiled at that lineup. Rosario Blancanales, known as ''The Politician,'' was perfect as a modern Mafia front man, and Carl Lyons was as tough as any gunman ever needed to be.

"What's Phoenix's role going to be in this?" Brognola asked.

"Katz wants to hold them in reserve this time," she answered. "He doesn't want to have too many people exposed at one time. But they'll be standing by and ready to support Lyons if anything goes wrong. And even though we're not expecting trouble, Striker's going along with Able Team as their wheelman. He'll be their instant backup."

"What's the follow-up plan?"

"After they make the trial buy, they're going to wait a couple of days, as if talking to their principals, and then try to set up a major transaction, a million dollars' worth or more. Katz figures that the Czechs will have to call on their Russian partners to supply that much product, and that's when we'll use Phoenix to grab the lot of them. We're hoping that will net us a couple of the major Russian players."

She shrugged. "If it works, we'll turn them over to Vallinsikov again. Hopefully this time they'll be able to keep them alive long enough to find out what they know."

Brognola was satisfied. Since the Berlin raid had only been partially successful, the White House was very anxious to see this go down to help the Russians. Anything that would make that happen was welcome. This was a good plan, nothing too flashy, but one that should produce for them. "It sounds good to me," he said. "Tell them to proceed."

"They'll make the initial contact within the hour."

Czech Republic

THE PRAGUE OPERATION went well right from the beginning. It didn't take long for the Stony Man team to learn that the information Brognola had received from the Russian minister was right on. There was a drug ring operating within the Czech capital city. Unlike some of the other Eastern European nations, the Czech Republic was doing very well with its transition to a capitalistic economy. They had never been good Communists anyway, and were well out in front of their old socialist brothers when it came to making money. As a result, the Czechs had a lot of it to spend and much of that was being spent on drugs.

Most of the drug transactions were small buys made to freelance entrepreneurs who then smuggled their purchases into the neighboring Western nations for marked-up resale. More and more, though, major deals were being made as the word got out that Prague was the place to buy at Eastern discount prices. Even drug dealers liked to get a discount.

Able Team's initial contact with the Prague connection went well. The Czech gangsters were a little surprised to learn that the American criminal brotherhood had learned of their success. But business was business, so they were ready to deal. They had a good source of supply for hashish from the Russians, and they wanted to turn over their inventory as quickly as possible to maximize their cash flow. After all, when all was said and done, dealing drugs was simply a business and, in any Eastern European city, American greenbacks were always welcome.

A meeting place was set up for the first buy.

CARL LYONS DIDN'T look out of place on the streets of Prague. There were a lot of tall blond men in the city, and the Stony Man team had gone shopping for European clothing during their layover in Frankfurt. The one thing that always marked Americans visiting Europe was their distinctive Yankee clothing. Everyone had packed away their blue jeans and gone in for a complete makeover.

Gadgets Schwarz was also dressed in Euro clothes, but he had insisted on wearing his cowboy boots with his new threads, thus defeating the camouflage effect.

"Dammit," he said when Lyons pointed that out, "we're supposed to be Americans, right?"

Lyons nodded.

"Okay then," Schwarz asked. "What's more American than Western boots?"

Lyons just shook his head.

Rosario Blancanales was a clotheshorse anyway and now he looked like he had just flown into town from Rome or Milan. When they had outfitted themselves, he had gone for the Armani look all the way, with footwear by Gucci. But, since he was supposed to be the capo, he had to have that expensive look. American drug dealers weren't shy when it came to flash and spending money on clothing.

None of the Able Team trio was wired for this meeting. Checking for wires was now a standard security measure throughout the world's professional criminal underground, and they couldn't risk it. Plus, if their information about ex-Russian military personnel being involved in the European gangs was true, they could also expect to be swept for electronic bugs.

However, each of them did have a panic button, a one-shot device that stayed electronically dormant until it was activated. Bolan had insisted on that much protection, and Schwarz had been able to put them together from his little bag of electronic tricks.

On the day of the buy, Able Team stopped by Katzenelenbogen's CP van for a last-minute briefing. "Are you guys ready for this?" Katz asked.

"As ready as we're ever going to be," Lyons replied. "Let's do it."

Katz handed Schwarz a thin, black briefcase.

"Brognola wanted me to remind you not to lose that on the way to the meeting. If you do, it'll come out of your allowance."

"That's two hundred big ones, right?"

Katz nodded.

"That's a lot of allowance."

"Plus, he says he'll charge you interest while you're paying it back."

"Bummer."

David McCarter was in the CP van to see Able Team off. The rest of Phoenix Force was waiting in their rented van four blocks from the meeting place, ready to go into action if they were needed. The fact that McCarter had left them to watch the operation with Katz, however, meant that he didn't think there was going to be a problem.

"Remember," he told Lyons, "if you don't like the way it looks, Carl, hit the panic button and find a place to hide. The lads are only four blocks away, locked and loaded, and we can be on them in a minute and a half."

"Unless they get greedy, this should work," the Able Team leader replied. "And I'll have Striker waiting in the car as instant response if they want to argue."

McCarter grinned. "That should do it."

WITH MACK BOLAN behind the wheel of Able Team's leased Mercedes sedan, they drove to the east of the town to the empty factory building that was the designated meeting place. With the rapid pace of economic reengineering in the Czech Republic, it was cheaper to abandon older factories instead of trying to modernize them to fit a new industry. In time, it would be torn down to make way for new construction, but for now, it stood and it made a good place for a clandestine drug deal.

Bolan drove into the factory compound and parked the car so that they could make a quick getaway if necessary. "If anything goes wrong," he reminded them, "hit the emergency transmitters and get out of there. I'll come in to cover you until David can get here."

"You got the briefcase?" Blancanales asked Schwarz.

"I'd never forget the cash."

"Let's get this on the road, guys." Lyons's eyes swept the abandoned site, looking for snipers or any signs of a setup.

Since he was posing as a Mafia bodyguard, he was wearing his Colt Python pistol openly; gunmen were supposed to be armed. When he stepped out of the car, he pulled back his coat to expose the butt of the big Colt riding in his shoulder rig. Three speed loaders full of .357 Magnum hollowpoint rounds rode in his jacket pocket just in case.

Schwarz and Blancanales were both packing Walther PPKs in shadow holsters in the small of their back. The Czechs would expect that because everyone who watched the movies knew that the Mafia never left home without being strapped.

Two Czech hardmen with subguns stood outside the door. When they saw that Lyons was carrying a weapon, they stiffened, but they let him pass. They didn't try to pat down Schwarz or Blancanales.

One of the guards showed the trio into a room that had to have been the main office when the factory was in production. All that remained of its furniture was a single table that stood in the middle of the room. The two Czech contacts they had met with previously were standing behind the table with a third man they didn't know. Three more armed guards occupied the corners of the room.

"Do you have the goods?" Blancanales asked, opening the conversation.

"We do," the man replied. "Do you have the money?"

Blancanales turned to Schwarz. "Show 'em the green."

As if his words were a signal, the Czechs opened fire. Dozens of rounds hit them, and the blood was flying with each hit. They went down like puppets with their strings cut.

Lyons cleared leather almost too fast for the eye to follow. The first .357 round out of his Colt Python took the Czech in charge right between the eyes, blowing out the back of his head. The second shot doubled up one of the submachine gunners. He was tripping the big Colt's hammer for the third time when a blast lifted him off of his feet and blew him backward.

He flew through the door and slammed against a wall, stunned. Shaking his head, he got to his feet. He felt a wetness running down his right arm, but he ignored it. He could still hold his piece, so he sprinted back into the cloud of dust obscuring the meeting room. A burst of AK fire sent him back into cover.

He hadn't seen any AK gunners, but there was no mistaking the sound of the assault rifles. Bringing up the Colt, he emptied the cylinder toward the gunners to cover his retreat. He had seen his teammates go down, and his first inclination was to charge the enemy and kill as many of them as he could. But the big ex-cop knew it would be a suicide play. He had to get to Bolan.

BOLAN HEARD the authoritative roar of Lyons's big .357 Colt Python and brought up the Beretta Model 12 subgun from the seat beside him. As he sprinted for the door, he saw Lyons stagger out, firing back into the factory as he came.

"Where's Pol and Gadgets?" Bolan yelled over the roar of his Beretta as he dumped half a mag into the door.

"Go! Just go!" Lyons yelled as he jammed a speed loader full of .357 hollowpoints into the empty cylinder of the Python.

Knowing that Lyons never would have left his two partners behind unless they were dead, Bolan emptied the rest of his magazine and followed Lyons back to the car. Slipping behind the wheel, he slammed the Mercedes into first and dropped the clutch. The howl of the big V-8 under the hood smoked the back tires as they bit into the cobblestones.

Reaching out the open passenger-side window, Lyons emptied the Python again to cover their escape.

Bolan twitched the wheel, throwing the Mercedes sideways to round the corner at the end of the block. Checking the slide, he powered the vehicle down the almost deserted street, backing off only when it was apparent that they weren't being followed.

"What happened?" he asked.

"We were set up." Lyons stared out the windshield of the car. "When Gadgets opened up his case to flash the money, they cut loose with their weapons. There was no warning at all, no argument, no nothing. They just started shooting at us."

Lyons's voice was tightly controlled, but Bolan could hear the raw pain in it. The big ex-cop was suffering the greatest loss of his life, but he knew that he had to keep it under tight control. Only later, how much later he had no way of knowing, would he be able to let that control slip and grieve for his friends.

"I was standing by the door, playing the bodyguard," Lyons continued. "And by the time I could get my piece into play, they were both down, shot to pieces."

He blinked as if to shut out a vision. "They both took over a dozen rounds. I saw the hits, and they went down. Then someone touched off a couple of grenades, and I was blown back out the door."

He turned to Bolan, his face a controlled mask. "Jesus, Mack, they're dead."

Bolan remained silent; there was nothing to be said.

Keeping the Mercedes to the legal speed limit of fifty kilometers, he punched the speed dial on his cellular phone to connect him with the CP.

"We were ambushed," he said when Katz picked up on the first ring. "Gadgets and Pol didn't make it out. Carl picked up a round, and I'm bringing him in."

Bolan could hear the catch in Katz's breath. But since they were still on the clock, his next question was mission-related. "You want me to roll Phoenix?"

"I don't know what's there for them to deal with, but I want to try to recover the bodies, if at all possible. Tell them to be ready to pull back, though, if they see any police presence. We were set up, and the Russians may have called the cops in.''

''I understand.''

CHAPTER FIVE

Prague, Czech Republic

Inside the Prague factory, Boris Detlov smiled as he looked down at the motionless figures of the two American secret agents on the floor. He loved it when a plan came together. Especially a plan against men as good as these were supposed to have been. He was a little disappointed at how easy the takedown had been. He had expected it to be a little more difficult, but they had completely fallen for the trap. If it hadn't been for the reaction of the big blond man, it would have gone without a hitch. Even so, the only casualties were the Czechs, and they didn't count.

If these three were the best covert operatives the Yankees could put in the field, Rostoff had nothing to worry about. He didn't know what had gone wrong in Berlin, but Blatz had to have really screwed up to have been taken down so easily.

"Get them out of here," he told the ex-Red Army sergeant, "and get ready to blow the place."

"What about the Czechs?" The sergeant nodded at the four other bodies. The American who had been allowed to get away had been a crack shot with his big pistol.

"Leave them for the police to find in the rubble," Detlov said as he reached down to pick up the black briefcase containing the money that had been intended to make the buy. "And make sure that you leave the hashish behind. When the police investigate this, it has to look like a drug deal gone bad."

Detlov didn't mind the loss of the Czech gang members at all. They had been good foot soldiers, but men like them were a dozen to the kopek. He would have replacements for them before the night was over. In a place like Prague, there were always dozens of street-level pushers who were eager to move up in the organization.

As soon as the two Americans had been loaded into the back of his Mercedes, Detlov slipped into the front passenger seat. "The soccer field," he told the driver. "And be sure to watch the speed limits here."

"Yes, sir."

Three blocks away from the factory, Detlov hit the switch on the small radio transmitter. A muffled crump followed, and, looking into his side mirror, he saw the column of smoke billowing into the air over the factory. The demolition charges should have dropped the walls of the building, and the police would have to dig out the rubble before they could start their investigation. But, with the police there, the Americans wouldn't be able to learn that the bodies were missing.

AT THE SOCCER FIELD, a Russian army Mi-8 helicopter with Czech military markings was waiting, its rotors spinning. As soon as the two bodies were loaded onboard, Detlov slid the door shut and jerked his thumb upward.

At the controls, the pilot pulled pitch and the chopper rose into the air. Feeding a little tail rotor control, he turned the nose of the ship to the north, toward the border with Poland. Twisting the throttle up against the stop, he stayed at low altitude all the way.

As soon as the Mi-8 crossed the border, the pilot set down on the ground long enough for the copilot to jump out and strip off the bogus Czech tricolor markings to reveal the red-and-white Polish army insignia underneath.

The rest of the flight to the small airfield in southern Poland was uneventful. There, the two Americans were loaded into an An-26 turboprop transport with civil markings and flown the rest of the way into Russia.

WHEN PHOENIX FORCE reported that they couldn't get to the site because of the Czech police, Yakov Katzenelenbogen recalled them. There was no use throwing away their lives as well. Lyons had seen his teammates fall. For now, all they could do was go on the defensive while he reported the incident to Stony Man Farm.

Katz sat in the CP van and stared at the blank video screen in front of him. He didn't want to make the call to the Farm and report that Hermann Schwarz and Rosario Blancanales had been killed. He was no stranger to death; the Black Angel had visited those close to him many times, and, many more times, he had delivered death himself. But these weren't common deaths.

In their long careers, the Stony Man warriors had lived charmed lives. They had brushed against the dark wings of Death many times and bore the scars proudly. But it had been a long time since one of their number had been killed. Every time they went on a mission, they were very well aware that it was just a matter of time before the odds caught up with them and one of them met his fate.

Katz knew that it was the lot of every man to die and men like the Stony Man warriors didn't often die at home in their beds. To lose two of them on the same operation, though, was difficult even for Katz to accept.

Even worse was that they hadn't been able to

recover the bodies. By the time Phoenix Force had arrived on the scene, the factory had been swarming with Prague police and emergency units. While they owed it to their fallen comrades to recover their remains for burial in the States, that would have to wait.

The thing that had to be done now was to inform Stony Man. As difficult as it was, it was always the job of the commander to make the death notifications, and Katz was fulfilling that role. He had made death notifications many times before, and he would do it this time. But it was never an easy task.

Feeling very much alone, Katz reached out and punched in the code for the satcom video link to Stony Man Farm. "Aaron," he said when Kurtzman's face came on the screen, "I need to talk to Barbara."

Kurtzman saw the look on Katz's face and knew that bad news was coming. He also knew that Price had been chosen to take the burden first this time. "Just a second."

He reached out and punched the intercom for Price's office. "Barbara," he said, "Katz is on the line for you."

"What does he want?"

"He didn't say."

Price clicked on the monitor on her desk and one look at Katz told her that he bore bad news. "What happened?"

"I regret to inform you that Hermann Schwarz and Rosario Blancanales have been killed in action."

Price felt her heart sink. "Oh no, Katz."

"I'm afraid so, Barbara. We haven't been able to recover the bodies yet and confirm, but both Striker and Carl believe them to have been killed."

That was all the confirmation she needed. They would have never left the two behind if they hadn't been certain that they were dead.

"How is Carl taking it?" she asked.

"About as well as can be imagined," he replied.

Price knew what he wasn't saying. There was no way that Lyons could be taking the loss of his two teammates well at all. The three of them had been a team for a long time, and their deaths would cut him deeply.

"How did it happen?"

"Somehow, our cover was blown before they even walked in." Katz's voice was hard. "According to Carl, the meeting was going well when the Czechs suddenly started shooting. Schwarz and Blancanales were gunned down immediately, and Lyons received a minor wound before a grenade blew him out of the room. That's the only thing that saved him. Striker went to his aid, but they were both driven off and had no choice but to retreat. I sent Phoenix in, but by the time they got there, the police were on the scene and they had to withdraw as well.''

''What's your next move?''

''Since we're obviously more than finished here,'' he said bluntly, ''I'm going to pull them back into Germany while we try to figure out what happened. Then, we'll have to see if there's anything left that we can do. At this point in time, I cannot make any predictions.''

''I understand.''

Stony Man Farm wasn't known for leaving its work undone, but it also wasn't known for taking unnecessary chances. If someone was on to them, it didn't make any sense to continue the mission.

''We'll be standing by if there's anything we can do for you,'' she said.

''Thanks,'' he said. ''We'll be in touch.''

Price sat back in the chair for a moment to gather her thoughts. She was the mission controller, and one of the things she was paid to do was to pass on bad news. Nonetheless, it had been a long time since she had heard news this bad. Usually the bad news was that some part of an operation hadn't gone off as planned. This was different.

The worst thing about her job was that she couldn't allow herself the comfort of doing something human, like crying. Instead, she punched her intercom button to connect her to Brognola.

"Hal," she said when he answered, "there's been an incident in Prague."

"What happened?"

When she told him of the shoot-out, there was stunned silence on the other end of the line. "They have confirmed that they're dead?"

"Lyons saw them killed."

"Get the chopper ready. I need to inform the President immediately."

"It's being cranked up right now."

"I'm sorry, Barbara." Brognola knew how inadequate that sounded, but he had to say something.

She took his condolences in the spirit that they had been offered. Members of her family had died. "So am I."

Even a place like the Farm, where all business was conducted on a strict need-to-know basis, news got around fast, particularly bad news. And, there hadn't been any news this bad in a very long time. A sense of sadness almost thick enough to see fell over the entire operation.

With the sadness, however, came a grim determination to do everything possible to get revenge for their friends. It wasn't only the field teams who burned to see payback, direct and final, delivered to whoever had killed Schwarz and Blancanales. Everyone from the blacksuits to the kitchen staff had payback on their minds, and they were willing to do anything they could to make it come to pass.

Since everyone was accustomed to looking to Barbara Price to call the shots, they turned to her to offer their help. One by one, they came to her, offered their condolences, asking them to be passed on to Carl Lyons, before offering their services if there was anything they could do. All she could do was thank them and say that she would call on them if she could use them.

The problem was that there was nothing they really could do. The decisions that would be made would all be made by the men in the field. All she and the rest of the Stony Man team could do was stand by and wait for developments.

YAKOV KATZENELENBOGEN took the Able Team tragedy as a call to action. It was obvious that they had been set up, and whoever had betrayed them would pay for that betrayal. But that would have to wait until adequate measures had been taken to protect the rest of the team. Right now, they had to get out of town and find a safe haven to regroup. Nürnberg was only a three-hour drive away, and it made sense to go there.

"We need to ditch this truck," Lyons said when Katz told him where they were going.

"We can't do that just yet," Katz replied. "We still need it for our CP."

"But," he quickly added, considering Lyons's frame of mind, "we do need to change its appearance. Get rid of the CNN logos, and I'll take the antennas off the roof.''

When Lyons left, Katz turned to Bolan. "Mack," he said seriously, "I think we need to have a conference."

"With the Farm?"

Katz shook his head. "Not this time. I think that we need to talk this through among ourselves. We've suffered a serious loss, and we need to regroup before we go on from here. If, that is, we do decide to go on with it."

"Are you thinking of abandoning this mission?"

"I honestly don't know." Katz's dark eyes flicked back to lock on Bolan's blue ones. "I really don't. Something has gone wrong here, bad wrong, and we need to find out what it is. We got sucked in and chopped up like amateurs. But since we aren't amateurs that means we were shopped."

Being "shopped" was intelligence jargon that meant they had been sold out, betrayed. This was a serious allegation, and, if it was true, it meant that the Farm had been compromised as well. If that was the case, continuing the mission would only bring more deaths.

"You don't think that it was simply an act of God?" Bolan asked to clear the other option.

Katz's eyes flashed. "You and I both know the god of war a little too well, Striker. He's capricious at best and brutal all the time. But we also know that he has favored us for a long time now. And he's favored us because we're damned good at what we do. All of us have gone into the fire countless times and have come out whole.''

He tapped his artificial right arm with his left hand and smiled grimly. ''Not completely whole, granted. We all bear the marks of a warrior's life.

''But—'' Katz's eyes went cold ''—this wasn't a capricious act of a brutal god of war. This wasn't a time when our two comrades were in the wrong place at the right time as we so often put it to keep from admitting that someone has made a stupid, fatal mistake. Able Team was set up and cut down. It's as simple as that. And before I put the rest of you on the line again, I want to know what the hell is going on here. And I want to make sure that everyone knows the situation. Then, and only then, will I get back in contact with the Farm.''

Bolan realized that there was a lot to consider in what his old comrade-in-arms had said. He needed no reminding that they were in a brutal, nasty business. But, even considering the fact that the god of war was fickle, he usually favored those who fought for the betterment of humanity. And, in almost any fight, he favored the more skilled combatant. That had always been the Stony Man ace in the hole.

Every man on both Phoenix Force and Able Team were among the best who had ever put their lives on the line for a cause. This tragedy hadn't come down because they didn't know what they were doing. But, as he well knew, even the best men in the world could be betrayed.

"You're right," Bolan said. "Let me gather everyone and we'll continue this when we've reached Nürnberg."

CHAPTER SIX

Stony Man Farm, Virginia

"Barbara," Aaron Kurtzman called over the intercom, "is Hal back from Washington yet?"

"He just got back in, why?"

"I think you two need to come down here immediately."

"What is it?"

"Just come down here, please."

When Price walked into the Computer Room, she saw that Kurtzman had a very serious look on his face. "What's going on?"

"Wait until Hal gets here so he can hear it too."

Brognola entered the Computer Room a few seconds later and noticed that everyone seemed to be waiting for him. "What's going on?"

"Katz and the mobile CP have gone off the air. But," he said, raising a hand to forestall all the questions, "they sent us a message before they signed off."

He reached out and punched in a code on the keyboard. When Katz's face flashed up on the monitor, every eye in the room turned in that direction.

"In light of the Able Team ambush," Katz announced, "we have decided to stand down until we can determine how and why this event happened. Since our cover's blown here in Prague, we're pulling back to Nürnberg to get out of the line of fire. Then we're going to discuss this incident, review everything we have on it and make a recommendation on how and where we will proceed from here. Until that time, we will be out of communication."

His face faded from the screen.

"I tried to call him back," Kurtzman said, "but all of their lines are dead."

"Oh shit," Brognola said as his hand automatically went into his jacket pocket for the roll of antacid tablets stashed there. This had started out so well, and it had looked like his stomach was going to get a little rest this time. More news like this, and he'd be living on the things.

"I suggest that we all go to the War Room and talk this thing out ourselves," Price said.

Without a word, Brognola turned and headed for the door.

PRICE HAD CALLED AHEAD and a coffee service was waiting in the War Room by the time Kurtzman arrived. The computer man stopped his wheelchair by the table and poured himself a cup before taking his place at the end of the conference table. It wasn't the high-test brew he made in the Computer Room, but it would do until he could get back to the good stuff.

"Okay," Brognola began, "considering everything that's gone down, what's our next move?"

"Before we get into that, Hal," Price said. "If you don't mind, I'd like to take a time-out."

"What do you mean? We have to get this mission back on track."

"What I mean is that we need to stop and take however long it takes to go over this entire thing and see if we can find anything that points to a leak that could have contributed to Able Team's ambush."

"Do you really think that a leak from here is likely?"

"Not a leak from this end, no," she said. "But I want to do it anyway. When Katz calls back, I want to be able to reassure him that their communications with us are safe."

She took a deep breath. "Then, as long as the teams remain in the field, I want to cut the White House out of the loop for the rest of the mission. Particularly I want to cut off information to the Russians, and the only way to do that is to shut the President out.

"Nothing against him personally, you understand," she added quickly. "But, as you well know, anything we tell him, he'll pass on to them."

"You know I can't do that, Barbara." Brognola slowly shook his head. "And you know that we only exist at the President's pleasure. I agree with the sentiment, but I'm afraid that's a no go."

"Then," she said, locking eyes with him, "I strongly recommend that we immediately go into mission closure. If we cannot insure that our people aren't being betrayed, we have no business being in the business."

"This isn't the first time that something has gone wrong with one of our missions," Brognola reminded her.

"Don't try to teach your granny to suck eggs," she snapped back.

Brognola blinked. T. J. Hawkins was starting to have a bad effect on everyone around here. Every time he turned around, someone was whipping out another snappy redneck southern comeback.

"I'm more aware of that than anyone else around this place," Price said. "If you'll remember, Hal, I've been the mission controller for some time."

Brognola instantly regrouped. "What I'm saying is—"

"I really don't want to hear what you have to say, unless you want to tell me that your first and only concern is to protect the lives of our men in the field. Anything other than that is political crap, and I'm not in the mood to listen to that right now. Two of my friends are dead, and I don't want to lose any more of them.''

Brognola couldn't meet her gaze. She was dead right, and nothing he could say would change that. They had already lost two men on a mission that didn't immediately affect the security of the United States, and he didn't want to lose any more either.

''Okay,'' he said. ''Let's stand down until we can go over the mission from the beginning and see if we can find out what went wrong.''

''And you will keep from informing the President about what we're doing until it's over?''

''I'll try.''

''You'd better try hard, Hal,'' she warned.

WHEN GADGETS SCHWARZ regained consciousness, he found himself laying facedown on a bare concrete floor with his hands and feet bound. His head was swimming, and he felt as if he were coming off of a week-long drunk. His head ached, his mouth felt as though it were stuffed with cotton and he was having trouble seeing clearly in the dim light. The last time he had felt like this, he had been drugged.

He laid where he was, breathing deeply to try to clear the toxins from his system. When his vision cleared a few minutes later, he twisted onto his side and saw that Rosario Blancanales was laying a few feet away from him.

Even in the dim light, Blancanales looked like he had been worked over with a baseball bat in the hands of an expert. His face was swollen and covered with blood. Both of his eyes were closed, and Schwarz couldn't see if he was breathing. Whatever had happened in that abandoned Prague factory, it had been a major disaster.

All he remembered was that the Czechs had opened up on them out of the blue. He remembered feeling the slugs hit, then there was a blinding flash followed by blackness. Apparently they had been hit by a concussion grenade and the fact that he had been standing a little behind Blancanales probably accounted for his waking up first. His friend had taken most of the blast, and he showed it.

Since Bolan and Carl Lyons weren't sharing the cell with them, it meant that the two men were either dead or they had escaped. Schwarz opted to believe that they had escaped and would be mounting a rescue. He had no proof for or against that conclusion, but that was how he was going to handle the situation until someone proved him wrong. And that was going to require showing him the bodies before he would believe that they had been killed.

Lyons had been standing by the door, and he should have been able to escape when it all went to hell. He had no idea what had set off the Czechs, but something had, and all he could do now was hold on and hope that Katz figured it out.

He started to inch across the floor toward Blancanales to see if there was anything he could do for him. With his hands tied behind him, that really wouldn't be much. But, regardless, he had to try to help his teammate.

As he crawled, he became aware of his own injuries. He felt like he, too, had been worked over with a baseball bat and was glad that he couldn't see his own face. He was afraid that it would look as bad as Pol's.

When he reached Blancanales's side, he saw that his teammate was breathing, but just barely.

"Pol?" he whispered in his ear. "Wake up, man, wake up! Pol?"

When there was no response, he put his ear to Blancanales's chest to see if he could detect his heartbeat. It was there, but sounded weak.

"Hey!" he yelled at the top of his lungs. "We need help in here! Guard! Guard!"

When no one came to see what all the yelling was about, he yelled again.

When he finally heard the door open, Schwarz twisted to face whomever it was. He was surprised to see a tall, well-built man who looked out of place in civilian clothes. He had expected a goon, not someone who looked like he had stepped out of a James Bond movie.

"Allow me to introduce myself," the man said in barely accented English. "I am Gregor Rostoff. And, if I am not mistaken, you are Hermann Schwarz. Your teammate with you is Rosario Blancanales. I am sorry to inform you that your other teammate, Carl Lyons, died of his wounds. You may be comforted to know that he died fighting."

"Where's his body?" was Schwarz's first response. How this Rostoff guy knew who he was wasn't important now. What had happened to Lyons was.

"It was disposed of properly," Rostoff said solemnly. "But I must say without much fanfare. His grave is without a marker."

Rostoff's matter-of-fact reporting of Lyons's death struck Schwarz as being truthful. If he couldn't produce the body, however, he wasn't buying it. But he wasn't going to let this guy know what he thought.

"And what are you going to do with Blancanales?" he asked. "He's hurt bad and needs medical attention."

"Both of you will be seen to immediately," Rostoff promised. "I do not want you to die on me."

"And then what?"

"And then we'll talk."

At Rostoff's command, four men dressed in

white lab coats walked in and removed the restraints from both Schwarz and Blancanales. As he was lifted to his feet, Schwarz saw the dark splotches covering the front of his rumpled clothing. They looked like bloodstains, but he felt no wounds.

Looking closer, he saw that the stains weren't blood. This was some kind of fake blood like they used in movie special-effects scenes. It became clear that he and Blancanales had been shot at with special-effects cartridges so that Lyons would think that they had been killed.

He turned back to the Russian. "You bastard, you faked our deaths! Why in hell did you do that?"

Rostoff smiled. "It was necessary so your comrades will not come looking for you. They think that you two are dead and that their cover, as you Americans say, has been blown. Now they will go home."

"That'll never happen," Schwarz said.

"Oh, yes, it will," Rostoff stated. "One way or the other, they will cease their operations and go back to America. When it is learned that a certain prominent minister in the Russian government invited a secret American strike force into our country to kill other Russians, I can assure you that your friends will be invited to go home. And it can't come soon enough for me. Your government has no business sticking their long noses into our affairs. The so-called American Century is over, and the sooner your people discover that, the better it will be for all of you.''

This wasn't the first time Schwarz had heard a Russian nationalist say that the U.S. needed to butt out of their affairs. But it wasn't the time, nor the place, to get into a long discussion of the role of the United States in world politics. That would take place later, preferably when he had a weapon in his hand.

CHAPTER SEVEN

Nürnberg, Germany

The trip from Prague had taken a little over three hours and it was early in the morning when the Stony Man warriors reached the small hotel outside the medieval town of Nürnberg, *Zum Wilden Bach.* Katzenelenbogen knew the place from numerous visits and had recommended it for its remote location. Until they decided what their next move was going to be, they needed to keep a low profile.

After grabbing quick showers in their rooms and breakfast in the hotel's dining room, the commandos went back to the parking lot and crowded into the back of Katzenelenbogen's CP van. It was a tight fit, but Katz's electronics scrubbers could make sure that their meeting wouldn't be overheard by eavesdroppers. The ambush had driven home the nasty fact that their cover had been blown. Even though they had left Prague, someone knew who they were, so they could take no chances.

Chairing the meeting fell on Katzenelenbogen's shoulders after Bolan declined the honor. Even though the Executioner worked closely with the Stony Man teams on almost every one of their missions, he was and always would be, completely independent from them. No matter what Lyons, Katz and Phoenix Force finally decided to do about this, he would take his own path as he always did.

And that path would be the same one it had been since he started his life as the Executioner, retribution sure and swift.

A crime had been committed, two good men had died and he would see that their killers paid the price. In the world Mack Bolan had created for himself, death was the only price that was appropriate for such a crime.

"Okay, guys," Katz said as soon as everyone had found a place to sit. "We all know what went down, so I won't go over it. The question is what are we going to do about it?"

"I don't know about the rest of you guys," Lyons said quietly, "but I know what I'm going to do. No matter what comes out of the Farm over this, I'm not going to stand down. Nor am I going to let Hal tell me who or what to target. I'm going after the bastards who killed Gadgets and Pol, and when I catch up with them, I'm going to waste them."

Katz didn't reply to Lyons's words; he had expected no less from the Ironman. Lyons hadn't picked up his nickname by being indecisive. He also was certain that the rest of the men felt that way as well, and for the same reasons. "Anybody have anything else?"

"I agree completely with Carl," David McCarter said. "And I would like to suggest that we take a serious look at completely cutting ourselves off from the Farm until this operation is concluded. From the way that ambush went down, it is readily apparent that Able Team was bloody well set up.

"Now," he cautioned, "I'm not saying that anyone at the Farm let something slip. We all know that didn't happen. The problem is that we are, in effect, working for the Russians this time, and I don't trust them."

"You're saying that you think the Russians leaked the information about the Prague operation?" Katz asked.

"Who else?" McCarter replied. "Carl and his people were working on a tip we received through the bloody Russians. They went to the meet that had been set up, and it exploded on them. That wasn't happenstance, and it wasn't simply bad luck. Hal gave our plan to the Russians and they bloody well shopped us."

"Are we all agreed that the Russians leaked us and we need to shut them out?" Katz looked at every face in turn.

When everyone nodded, he continued. "Okay then, what do we tell Hal?"

McCarter didn't hesitate. "How about having him tell the Russians to stuff it in their bloody kit bags? This isn't our fight, Katz, and we never should have been called in on it. There are more than enough problems in the world that directly affect the States. Let the bastards take care of their own damned problems."

"Even if it means that the Russian army puts itself back in power to impose order?"

The ex-SAS commando shrugged. "If they give us any trouble, we can nuke the bastards and finally be done with them."

"I don't particularly care what you tell Brognola," Lyons spoke up. "All I can tell you is that I'm not going to cooperate in any way with the Farm until I'm done here. If you like, in effect, I have just tendered my resignation from the Sensitive Operations Group."

He shrugged. "What happens after I track the bastards down, I really don't care."

Lyons looked around at the faces of his remaining friends. "And, no offense, but I don't think I'm going to be playing this Stony Man game with you guys anymore."

"Keeping the Russians out of this and talking to the Farm are two very different things, guys," Gary Manning pointed out. "I agree that we need to cut the Russians out of the loop. But, if we're going to go after these guys for some serious payback, we're still going to need the Farm. We need the Bear and his people to do our background work for us. If we try to go this on our own, it'll take us months, if not years, to track those guys down."

"We can do it on our own," Lyons growled. "I did my own legwork for years before the Farm was even invented."

"We're good," Manning replied, "but we're not as fast as the Bear's electronics. We need his cyberspace connection, the satellite overwatch and all the rest of the input that we've come to depend on for so long now. This isn't like the days of the Mafia Wars when Striker was out there banging heads all by himself with a Texaco road map in one hand and an AT&T phone book in the other."

"I had help even back then," Bolan spoke up to correct the record. "And some of my best information came from a Justice Department guy named Hal Brognola."

"But that was before Hal became joined at the hip with the White House," Rafael Encizo stated. "Don't forget that, Striker. He has a new boss now, and, as has happened all too many times in the past, the man in the Oval Office isn't necessarily on our side."

"But," Calvin James joined in, "while I also agree that we need to cut the Russians out, and that means breaking contact with the White House and Hal, how do we do that and still keep getting the information we need from the Farm? Gary is right about that and our resident Southerner has a well-worn but pertinent phrase about not throwing the baby out with the bathwater.''

Hawkins grinned. ''I also have one about not pissing into the wind 'cause it gets all over you. If we're going to get some payback for Gadgets and Rosario, we're going to need the Farm, big-time, Carl. Without it, we'll be stumbling around in the dark not able to find our asses with both hands and a strong flashlight.''

Katzenelenbogen looked over to Jack Grimaldi who had been silent so far. ''Jack, do you want to get in on this?''

The pilot shook his head. ''Not really. Whatever you guys decide to do is okay with me. Since we don't have anything to fly this time, I don't care.''

''Anything else?'' Katz asked and looked around the room at determined faces.

Everything had been said, so he tried to wrap it up. ''Okay then, what if I have a talk with Barbara and Aaron?'' he suggested. ''I'll explain our concerns and see what they might be able to do to secure this operation and keep feeding us information.''

''Do what you want,'' Lyons said. ''But while you're talking, I'm going to hit the bricks and see what I can come up with on my own. I solved crimes for years without the help of any damned computers.''

"I'll come with you, Carl," Bolan said. "The two of us will be able to cover more ground than if you try to do it on your own."

The ex-LAPD cop got to his feet. "Let's do it, Striker."

"First," Bolan replied. "I want to move our focus away from the Czech Republic. We got burned badly there, and, since we really don't know who our opposition is, I don't want to go back there right yet. I'd like to go to another major city here in the West where we might be able to keep out of sight a little better and we can start all over again at square one."

"How about trying Dresden?" Katz suggested. "It's in Germany now, but the Russian connection is still pretty strong there."

"How far away is it?" Lyons asked.

"You can be there and ready to go by tomorrow morning."

"That'll do. How soon can we be on the road?"

"As soon as I pay the bill here. I don't want the German cops after us for dining and dashing."

Stony Man Farm, Virginia

AARON KURTZMAN WAS DEEP in thought as he wheeled himself down the hall to the Computer

Room. He still couldn't believe that Schwarz and Blancanales were dead. A world without Gadgets and the Pol was going to be a poorer place. He would be willing to trade ten years of what was left of his life if he could somehow get out of his damned wheelchair and stand beside Carl Lyons when he extracted his vengeance for their deaths.

It was a nice thought, but it wasn't going to happen, not in this lifetime. The only thing he could do to help see that the man, or men, who were responsible for this were brought to justice was to do what he did so well.

He was the monarch of a cyberspace kingdom that knew no boundaries, and everything that he ever needed to know was somewhere within that kingdom. With Huntington Wethers, Akira Tokaido and Carmen Delahunt as his assistant wizards, everything would be known before they were through. And that knowledge would put Lyons and his friends in place to extract the price for his partners' deaths.

After stopping to fill his coffee cup from his ever-brewing pot, he wheeled himself over to his workstation and parked his chair in front of his keyboard. Emptying his mind of everything except the problem at hand, he started trying to find out how Able Team had been betrayed. He would start from the beginning.

AS EVERYONE in the Computer Room had expected, the in-depth review of the Prague mission buildup didn't reveal anything on their end that might have contributed to Able Team's ambush. Every line of every message and briefing paper had been assessed, and the secure communications equipment had all been tested. Everything had checked out to the last decimal place. The error hadn't occurred at the Farm.

Unless they were ready to accept that an act of God had taken down Able Team, the only answer could be that the leak had originated with either the White House or with the Russians who had asked for the President's help. While the inhabitants of the halls of power in Washington, D.C., weren't the favorite people of anyone who worked at Stony Man Farm, no one was ready to put the blame on them without positive proof of betrayal.

The Russians, however, were entirely another matter. After all, it was the Russians who had passed on the information about the Czech drug dealers that had sent Able Team to Prague in the first place. Vallinsikov himself had warned the President about the level of infiltration the Mafia had made into the government, so it had to be the Russians.

Kurtzman was reaching out to punch the intercom button to Price's office when he saw that he had an incoming message from Katzenelenbogen.

Flashing it up onto the screen, he saw that it had a "read me" prologue. After reading it, his finger flashed for the intercom button.

A few minutes later, Kurtzman and Price sat side by side at his workstation reading Katzenelenbogen's "read once" message as it slowly scrolled down the monitor. When it reached the end of the text, the message would disappear into cyberspace where all erased messages went, never to be retrieved. It also had a tag in the code that prevented them from printing a hard copy of the message. They had to read it and get it the first time.

In short, concise terms, Katz outlined what Carl Lyons and Mack Bolan had decided to do, adding that Phoenix Force had signed up with them as well. In effect, he was delivering their mass resignation from Stony Man Farm. He did, however, say that if Kurtzman and Price wanted to help them, they would accept their assistance. He gave them a radio frequency he would be monitoring if they wanted to discuss the matter.

"I'd say that we have a problem." Kurtzman understated the situation when the text blinked out of existence.

"That's putting it mildly," Price replied.

"What are we going to do about it?"

She turned to face him squarely. "I'll be damned if I know, Aaron. I really don't. Do we talk to Hal about this?" The message had been addressed ''eyes only'' to the pair of them and, so far, they had respected Katz's wishes.

It was rare that she asked Kurtzman for advice that wasn't connected to his gathering information from cyberspace, but he didn't hesitate in his answer. ''No,'' he stated bluntly. ''If we do that, there's a risk that he'll tell the President and the Man will declare them rogues.''

One of the few ways that a nation, any nation, could control the activities of their field agents was to hang the threat of their being declared rogues over their head. Such a declaration would have every police officer and intelligence agent in the world after them with orders to kill on sight. It was rarely invoked, but when it was, the rogue agent didn't last very long.

''What do we do then?''

''We take care of it ourselves. But I don't know how.''

''It's going to be hard to hide what they're doing from Hal.''

''I guess that they're going to have to go off the air then.''

''Isn't that a little too obvious?'' she asked. ''I mean, every team in the field that wants to cut out the bullshit from headquarters goes off the air?''

''I think they can do it in such a way that it will make the news on CNN.'' He risked a small smile.

"And, as everyone knows, if it's on TV it has to be true. Particularly if it's on CNN."

"What do you have in mind?"

"Well , I think we can do two things. First, I want to talk to Katz about putting together some razzle-dazzle moves. Then, we need to go into a serious deception mode around here. We're going to have to hide everything we do from Hal because you know damned good and well that he's not going to see this thing our way."

Kurtzman saw the faint trace of a smile form on Price's face. "That's an understatement if I ever heard one. Get on it."

"And remember, Barbara, don't believe everything you see on the six-o'clock news."

"I know better than that. I've worked with the Lords of Illusion for years now."

CHAPTER EIGHT

Russia

Boris Detlov was chagrined to learn that the American covert action team had pulled out of Prague, particularly when he didn't know where they had gone. His Czech operatives had been caught off guard and had let them get away unseen, presumably to the West. He now realized that he should have put some of his ex-KGB people on them, but he'd been caught off guard himself. The Americans had stumbled into his ambush at the factory so easily that he had discounted them, but he wouldn't make that mistake again. If they hadn't left Europe yet, he had no fear that he'd be able to get a lead on them before too long. The Rostoff organization had hundreds of eyes in Western Europe.

He also had no answer to Rostoff's question about the Americans being recalled. His informant in Vallinsikov's office indicated that the minister had had no new information from the White House since before the ambush in Prague. In fact he hadn't even been informed that the mission he had set in motion had been a disaster. It was obvious that the American government was trying to hide their failure from him. The question was why?

Since he couldn't afford to wait to find out what was happening, Detlov decided to talk to his boss about trying to get the information directly from their American captives. He knew that they wouldn't freely volunteer the information, but there was more than one way to make a man tell you what you wanted to know. The Russians were masters when it came to the fine art of interrogation.

There was always danger of a drug reaction from the chemical interrogation, but Rostoff had an experienced ex-KGB doctor on his staff so the risk to the valuable prisoners would be minimized. Rostoff needed those two men alive, but he also needed access to the information in their heads.

Germany

"DO YOU REALLY THINK this is going to work, Katz?" Hawkins looked around the busy early-evening streets of Nürnberg. "This is a little too much like something out of a made-for-TV movie for my tastes."

"It should work," Katzenelenbogen replied as he parked the van they were driving directly across the street from the biggest TV studio in the city. "If we're being tracked by the van, this should put them off our trail for a while at least."

After receiving Aaron Kurtzman's call about losing Hal Brognola, he and Katzenelenbogen had remained in Nürnberg while Bolan, Lyons and the rest of Stony Man went on to Dresden to start their new mission of retribution.

Their first move in implementing Kurtzman's deception plan had been to steal a white Mercedes van they spotted in the back lot of a furniture factory. It was the same model as the one the team had been using as their mobile CP, and, with the CNN logos applied to the side and one of the spare antennas fixed to the roof, it was difficult to tell the two trucks apart. Particularly since they had removed all of the new van's vehicle ID number tags, including grinding the one off the engine block.

Knowing that the police would examine anything they left behind, the commandos had purchased several used televisions and computers from secondhand stores and had installed them in the back.

When that was done, Katz's original CP van was suitably disguised with a quick partial paint job. The vehicle's front fenders and doors were now blue and the side carried the logo of a well-known publishing house.

"Are you ready?" Katz asked as Hawkins turned to check the connections for the detonators to the incendiary devices he had planted in the cab and the cargo area.

"I'm go when you are."

"Give me time to get to that phone booth on the corner of the square, and then do it," Katz answered. "I'll meet you there."

As soon as Katz reached the phone, Hawkins hit the timer and exited the cab. He had only sixty seconds, but he forced himself not to hurry. This was no time to attract attention. He was still a few yards from the corner when the truck exploded with a crump and a whoosh as the diesel fuel he had splashed all over it ignited.

Katz had dialed all but the last number of the TV station and hit the last button when the truck exploded.

"Sender Sud," the voice said, giving the name of the TV station. "Can I help you?"

"Look out your front windows," Katz said. He spoke excellent German, and his accent could pass for someone living on the French border. "There is a Yankee TV van burning in front of your building. We do not need imperialist propaganda in the new Europe."

"Who is this?"

Katz hung up the phone.

As he had expected, it took less than a minute for a small group of people to come running out of the TV station, several with video cameras in their hands. As the blaze burned the truck down to the frame, it was all caught on camera. One of the spectators, obviously a reporter, even started doing the voice-over to be used with the broadcast later.

Katz and Hawkins watched from the darkness until the fire department showed. "That should do it," Katz said.

"I should have set that timer for a couple more seconds," Hawkins said as he brushed the seat of his blue jeans. "I damned near got my buns toasted real good that time."

The two faded into the night and headed for the truck they had parked two blocks away. By morning, they would be in Dresden and would link up with the rest of the team.

THE EXPLOSION of the van in Nürnberg made it onto CNN *Headline News* that evening as part of a story on the new wave of terrorism that was sweeping Europe. The vehicle's destruction was blamed on drug-gang violence and was linked with the earlier raid on the flak tower in Berlin and half a dozen other recent terrorist acts in Western Europe.

CNN had put one of the overseas big guns on the story and the network's characteristic "the-sky-is-falling" spin was put on the story. The fact that CNN's European bureau wasn't missing a mobile van was either not known or covered up. Every network liked to be a target, particularly during sweeps month.

Stony Man Farm, Virginia

"WAS THAT THE TEAM'S VAN?" Hal Brognola asked, his eyes glued to the big monitor. Aaron Kurtzman and Barbara Price had called him down to the Computer Room to watch the tape.

"It sure as hell looks like their van," Price replied honestly.

"Were any bodies recovered?"

"We don't know yet," Kurtzman said.

Brognola watched until the end of the tape, then turned and started for the door. "Keep me informed," he said. "I need to know the instant they get back in contact."

"Will do," Price replied.

"That's that," Kurtzman said when he heard his footsteps vanish down the hall.

"Do you really think this is going to work very long, Aaron?" she asked. "It seems a little too much like something out of a movie."

"I'll be damned if I know," he replied. "But I don't see that we have much choice. For the guys to be able to do anything useful over there, they have to be cut loose from the White House and that means cutting Hal out of the loop. It was either try something like this or call it quits and accept everyone's resignation. So, if this doesn't do it, we can always try our hand at chicken farming in Arkansas.''

Germany

FOR TWO GUYS who didn't speak the language very well, Mack Bolan and Carl Lyons were making good progress on their first day on the streets of Dresden. The town was booming with the new construction brought about by reunification. That meant that a lot of money was changing hands, and the drug trade always followed money. They figured that all it would take in a place like this was a little old-fashioned ''bull 'em and bust 'em'' street-cop work to start getting results.

It was a routine they were both well practiced at.

They started out as if they were operating in any large American city—they went to the center of town and looked around. The initial step was taken with the first street dealer they ran across, a guy in punk-rock clothing dealing single hash joints to support his habit.

''Mister,'' the dealer called out in German as they walked past the alley he was standing in, ''you want hashish?''

Bolan and Lyons exchanged glances and went into their routine. With Bolan blocking the line of sight from the other passersby, Lyons simply stepped up to the guy, spun him and snapped his right arm into a ''come along'' hold. The kid tried to struggle against Lyons's grip, but the big ex-cop hissed in his ear to keep quiet or die. The words were strange, but the kid knew the tune and didn't want his arm dislocated, so he went along with the program.

The two men marched him down the alley far enough to have a quiet little chat without attracting attention. As they had hoped, their mark spoke a little English. Not enough to hold a long conversation, but enough to tell them who he bought his goods from. Armed with that information, they made the kid dump his pockets and grind the joints into the cobblestones before sending him on his way.

Snatching the second line supplier went much the same way, except that this guy didn't have much English and it took a little longer for the two men to get their point across. But threatening to break one of his hands did a lot to brush up his few words of English. Suddenly he spoke the language a lot better than either Bolan or Lyons did German.

According to his story, his wholesaler wasn't a German, he was a Serb who had immigrated during the Bosnian war and had taken up the drug trade. He conducted his business out of a small tobacco shop in a part of town that wasn't being rebuilt yet.

After getting a street address, Bolan turned the punk loose and the guy disappeared fast.

AFTER CALLING in their intentions to David Mc-Carter, Bolan and Lyons drove their rented silver BMW to the outskirts of town. As their informant had said, there was a tobacco shop at the location he had given up. Parking their car at the curb in front, they stepped out ready for business. The man behind the counter took one look at Bolan and Lyons as they walked through the door and tried to make a break for it. Lyons caught him halfway out the back door and dragged him back inside.

The two street dealers had been more than ready to tell Bolan and Lyons everything they knew. The Serb, however, had his business to protect, as well as a healthy fear of retribution from the Russians if he talked. With him, they had to point out that his life depended on their finding out what they wanted to know.

"If I talk to you," the supplier said in passable English, "I know that the Russians will kill me." He shrugged. "You say that you will kill me if I don't talk, so it doesn't matter. Either way I am dead."

"That could be," Lyons agreed. "But there is the matter of what happens to you before you die. If I kill you, it'll only be after I am convinced that you really don't know what I want to know. And,

I promise that it will take a lot of convincing before I'm satisfied. It will be painful. But I'm not going to do anything time-consuming like beating you. That's a complete waste of time. I'm simply going to start cutting things off, starting with your balls. And if that doesn't convince you to tell me what I want to know, I'll start on your eyes next.''

He shrugged. ''When I'm finally done with you, I think you'll be ready to die. So, if you like, I'll put a tag on you so the authorities will know which particular piece of street shit you are, because no one will ever be able to recognize you.''

''You Americans don't do things like that,'' the dealer said, gathering his courage for one last try. ''I know all about how your DEA and your FBI works.''

''Well,'' Bolan replied, leaning closer to him, ''let me explain something to you. Your luck isn't good this time. We're not from the DEA or the FBI. We're not even from the CIA. We're just two Americans on a buying trip to Europe who have decided to get into business here and we want to buy from the top man, not some scumbag like you.''

The light came on in the Serb's eyes. ''You are from the Mafia!''

Bolan's wolfish smile served as an unspoken answer, and their captive immediately decided to play ball with the American gangsters. The Russians he dealt with might be brutal, but the American Mafia was a real force to be reckoned with.

"I get my supplies from the Russians," the Serb said quickly.

"And where can we find these Russian friends of yours?"

"There is a Russian-owned restaurant on Muller Street off the Cathedral Plaza called the Moscow. The Russians use it to make their deals. The man you want to see there is called Boris."

"They're all called Boris," Lyons growled. "Does he have a last name?"

The Serb shrugged. "I only know him as Boris. You can't miss him. He's a big bastard."

"Tell me about this Moscow restaurant," Bolan said. "I want to know how big it is, how late it's open and where the doors are."

"Do you have a piece of paper?" the dealer asked. "I will make a drawing for you."

"That's a very good drawing," Lyons said as the Serb carefully penciled in the windows, doors and even the tables, bar and kitchen area, giving dimensions in meters.

"I was an architect in Sarajevo," he replied, shrugging.

"You might want to go back to that profession," Bolan cautioned him. "Drug dealers are going to become unpopular around here real soon."

The Serb thought fast. "I have a cousin in the

building trade in Berlin. I can always go to work for him.''

"That's a good plan." Lyons leaned closer to him, his eyes glittering. "Because if I ever see your face again, I'm going to put a bullet in it."

The Serb shuddered as he looked into the big blond man's face and saw death personified. "You will never seen me again, sir. I promise that."

"Get out of here," Bolan growled, pointing to the door.

The Serb didn't even bother to take his coat from the back of the chair. What was an inexpensive jacket when he had been given his life?

"What are we going to do with this shit?" Lyons asked as his eyes took in the Serb's goods. Most of it was hashish, but there were a few blocks of tar heroin as well.

"Burn it," Bolan said. "We don't have time to waste calling the police about it. What doesn't burn, the fire department will take care of."

CHAPTER NINE

Stony Man Farm, Virginia

Until all of the reports were in from the firebombing of Phoenix Force's van in Nürnberg, Hal Brognola was hanging around the Farm. Once he knew the full extent of the damage to the teams, he would have to work up a proposal to present to the President on where they would go from here. The way it was looking so far, he half expected the Man to want to shut down Stony Man Farm. He hated to see it happen, but maybe the time had come for it to be closed out.

The Sensitive Operations Group, as the Farm was known to those very few outsiders who had a "need to know," had been an overwhelming success. Phoenix Force and Able Team were without a doubt the two best covert action groups that had ever taken to the field. And, with Aaron Kurtzman's cybercrew backing them up, they had provided America with muscle that could be applied without having to go through the labyrinth of petty politics that had doomed so many U.S. covert operations in the past.

Had the Farm been in existence during the Cuban Missile Crisis or the Bay of Pigs, American history would look a lot different than it did today. But things had been different back then before the computer revolution.

Stony Man Farm had been born out of the cyberrevolution and relied almost completely on the Computer Room staff's ability to pull rabbits out of cyberspace hats time and time again. Without the work of Aaron Kurtzman's computer people, the action teams wouldn't have been half as effective as they had been. Having the world's best fighting men ready to unleash on the target wasn't enough. They had to know exactly who and where the target was, as well as everything there was to know about it.

Now that he was thinking about the cyberinput, he started to wonder why Kurtzman's crew hadn't been able to come up with more information about the Prague and Nürnberg incidents that had befallen the teams. Almost everything Kurtzman had reported to him so far were things that had originated from the TV news broadcasts and print-media reports. So far, he had not come up with any hard facts from his computers.

Brognola knew that some of that could be put

down to the shock that everyone was feeling about the loss of Blancanales and Schwarz, as well as the uncertainty about the fate of Striker, Katz and Phoenix Force. The overt grieving for their dead comrades had passed, but the shock was still felt. A milestone had been passed, a fork in the road had been taken and things would never be the same again. Now, there were the rest of the men to worry about too.

Everyone was feeling the strain, even him, but he'd thought that Kurtzman was tougher than that. He always had been before. Wanting to think this through before he said anything to Kurtzman or Price, he stepped outside the farmhouse to take a short walk around the grounds.

As always, the view of the Shenandoah Valley and Stony Man Mountain was magnificent. The peach orchard was blossoming, and a couple of the "farm hands" were doing a little pruning. Another group was working on the tractor and machinery they'd use in a few days to start the spring plowing. The Farm was really a working farm, and the agricultural work always had to be done to keep it operational.

Walking behind the main house, he recognized two men from the blacksuit security force who were talking to John "Cowboy" Kissinger as they loaded crates into the back of one of the Farm's unmarked vans. That wasn't unusual. What started him thinking about what they were doing was the startled look on Kissinger's face when he was spotted. Even stranger was the weaponsmith walking over to meet him.

Deciding to meet him halfway, Brognola got close enough to read the markings on the crates. They were marked in both German and English, and, while he was no linguist, he could read the words *FedEx Air Freight Holding Facility,* Frankfurt, as well as the next man. Since he hadn't been told about any shipments going from the Farm to Europe, he had to wonder.

"Where's the shipment going?" he asked Kissinger.

The gunsmith looked a little guilty. "Oh, that's just some stuff Katz wanted sent over. And since we have the time, I thought we'd get it over there so they can pick it up when they need it."

That made sense. Once Phoenix Force and Striker surfaced again, they would need the shipment, whatever it was. But why was Kissinger so jumpy?

"Is there any news?" Kissinger asked to change the subject.

"Not yet."

AARON KURTZMAN CAUGHT Brognola coming down the hallway on the interior security camera and hit a code on his keyboard. Instantly his monitor, and the monitors of everyone else in the room, changed.

"Anything new, Aaron?" Brognola asked as he stopped at the coffeepot. He usually didn't drink Kurtzman's brew, but he felt the need to jolt his brain.

Kurtzman shook his head. "Not really. The Frankfurt police are still doing their forensic examination of the van, but they haven't released much yet."

"Anything on the bodies?"

"Not yet."

According to the media reports, burned bone fragments had been found in the incinerated wreckage. Since CNN claimed no personnel missing, the identity of the dead was yet unknown. They had also claimed not to have a missing van at all, but little notice had been taken of that inconvenient fact.

"I guess they're still trying to get DNA readings on the bone fragments," Kurtzman suggested.

"Keep on it."

As Brognola turned to leave, it suddenly hit him that while Schwarz and Blancanales were still being mourned, there was a decided lack of similar concern for the fate of Katz, Striker and Phoenix Force. To be sure, concerned questions were being asked about them, but the same sense of impending doom wasn't in the voices. It was true that no one had reported them dead yet, but, considering the spectacular destruction of the CP van and the fact that they still were not back in contact, people should be frantic and they simply were not.

Brognola was beginning to think that someone was putting the shuck on him, as Hawkins would say. Knowing that he would get nothing but innocent looks from Kurtzman, he went looking for Barbara Price.

BROGNOLA CAUGHT UP with Price in the hallway leading to the War Room. "Look, Barbara," he said, "I just figured out what's been going on around here and I think we need to talk about it."

"What's that?" she asked, her eyes level with his.

"You've set me up with the perfect alibi to give the Man, haven't you?"

"I don't know what you're talking about, Hal."

"Dammit, Barbara, the van. You had Katz blow up the damned van to cut Phoenix loose."

"We didn't blow up the van, Hal," she replied calmly. "And, as far as Phoenix is concerned, you know as much about where they are and what they're doing as I do. You get every report that comes into this place."

"It's what's not being reported that bothers me," he said. "I don't want to see on CNN that half of

Europe has been destroyed in some sort of rampage.''

While the average Stony Man operation went well beyond the normal level of hard-core, covert operations, there was a limit to what even they could be authorized to do. Even on one of their scorched earth missions, there was a limit on who or what could be a target. The fine line between acting in the national interest and terrorism was razor thin, and it was all too easy to cross.

If his hunch was right, what was going on behind his back this time was more like what Mack Bolan had done back in his Mafia wars days, a no-holds-barred assault and damned be the consequences. ''The President isn't going to be very happy about this when it's over,'' he predicted.

Price looked him straight in the eye. ''We serve at the President's pleasure, Hal, and he can ask for our resignations anytime he wants. Just give us the word, and we can be out of here in a couple of hours.''

Brognola took a deep breath. Why did he always get cast in the role of the heavy? He wasn't the enemy, and neither was the President. Why did she refuse to see that he had to know what was going on? If, for no other reason, so he could help her keep the President off them.

''I'm not threatening anyone. I just want to be let in on what's going down over there so I can help all of you cover your collective asses. If a war's about to break out in Eastern Europe, someone is sure to put two and two together and come up with Stony Man Farm before too long. There's only so many people who can pull something like that off.''

''I guess we'll just have to worry about that when it happens then, won't we?''

''Have it your way,'' he replied, a note of defeat in his voice. ''But don't ask me to bail your butts out when it all goes to hell.''

''Don't worry. We can always ask Minister Vallinsikov to vouch for any activities that might take place over there. After all, we are supposed to be working for the Russians this time, aren't we?''

Suddenly it clicked. Katz had decided that the Russians had leaked the Prague operation, and he and Barbara had decided to break contact so they wouldn't get burned again. It made sense and in the same situation, he probably would have done the same.

''I just hope you know what you're doing,'' he said, '''cause I sure as hell don't.''

She smiled. That was exactly the way she wanted it.

Russia

''THAT IS QUITE an organization you belong to,'' Gregor Rostoff told Gadgets Schwarz and Rosario

Blancanales. The two Able Team commandos had been brought into the conference room and had been shown to chairs across a table from their captor. Four of the Russian's gunmen were standing behind them to insure that they didn't try to get physical.

"And it has such an interesting name—Stony Man Farm."

That was the first time the teammates had been in the same room together since waking up in the cell. Neither one of them was sure how much time had passed since they had been captured. All they knew was that they had slept several times since they had arrived wherever they were.

"How do you know about Stony Man Farm?" Blancanales asked. "You didn't get that information from us."

"Oh, but I did." Rostoff smiled.

"Bullshit," Schwarz said. "You haven't even brought out the rubber hoses yet."

"You really did not think that I would waste my time trying to beat the information out of you or anything primitive like that, did you? I am shocked."

When neither one of the Americans answered, he continued. "Russians understand interrogation techniques and we know how to get the information we want. I know that the old KGB had a reputation for brutality. A well-deserved reputation, I might add. But they were brutal for fun. They did it because they enjoyed it. When they really wanted to get information from a man, or a woman for that matter, quickly, they simply used chemicals. They used a mixture that translates into, I think you would say it, 'babble juice.' It is extraordinarily effective.''

Now the two Able Team members knew why they had awakened feeling groggy. They had been drugged. Whatever was used, it could have been put in their food, or they simply could have been gassed while they slept.

Rostoff glanced down at the printouts on the table in front of him. ''Even though I have some information on your operation, I still have questions.''

''If your methods are so good,'' Schwarz said, ''why do you need to talk to us? What do you think we're going to tell you that you don't already know?''

''The chemical interrogation works strangely,'' Rostoff explained. ''And it provided only some of the information I need to know. For instance, I know the eye color of the lovely woman who seems to be your operations officer. But I still do not know much about the way she thinks.

''The same goes for what I learned about your leader, Mr. Hal Brognola. I find it a bit odd that he is from your Justice Department instead of one of your intelligence agencies as one would have expected.''

When that got no response, he continued. ''Now, I know a little about Brognola's background, but, I do not know what he is likely to do now that his mission has been disrupted. Will he think, and rightfully so, that you were sold-out by the Moscow government, or will he just chalk it up, as I think you say, to bad luck?''

Once more there was only silence.

''More importantly, though,'' Rostoff tried again, ''I do not know how your Phoenix Force comrades are going to deal with your assumed deaths. Are they going to follow their orders, whatever they may be, like good soldiers or are they going to try to avenge your deaths?''

Schwarz smiled slowly. ''What do you think?''

Rostoff studied him for a time. ''That is the only question, isn't it? I daresay that I will learn the answer before too much longer.''

''What happens to us?'' Schwarz asked.

''You will remain here as my guests until this has been played out.''

''Then what?''

''Then you may be freed.'' He paused for a long moment. ''Or you may be killed. It all depends.''

Schwarz knew that the Russian was playing with him, and didn't let it get to him. Rostoff wanted him to cling to the faint promise of life and not do anything to risk that chance. He knew full well, however, that it was pure crap. There was no way that the Russian was going to let him and Blancanales live. Not with what they now knew about him and his organization. To release them would be to invite retaliation.

His only realistic option would be to kill them when they were no longer useful to him.

Schwarz did, however, plan to take someone with him when it came time for him to go down. He still had confidence in Bolan, Lyons and Phoenix Force. But, if they didn't make it in time, he'd still get his. There was no way that he was going to go out without taking someone with him. And, this Rostoff guy would be a good one to take to hell with him. After he got the bastard down there, he'd tear his throat out with his teeth.

Schwarz smiled broadly. "Why don't you just kill us now and get it over with? The accommodations around here suck, and I might as well try my luck in hell. It can't be any worse than this place."

Rostoff didn't rise to the bait. "Like I said, Mr. Schwarz, no decisions will be made until the conclusion of this operation."

CHAPTER TEN

Stony Man Farm, Virginia

Now that Stony Man's covert European operation had gone ultracovert, if there was such a word, Aaron Kurtzman finally had time to do something that he should have done before this mess had been allowed to get started. Namely, he was going to do an in-depth, background workup on the topic of the Russian Mafia.

All of the information they had used on the pre-mission workup had come from the Russians. And, even though Kurtzman didn't trust them any farther than he could walk unassisted, he had to admit that the Berlin mission had gone off without a hitch. The information they had provided for that raid had been spot on. Because of that success, he had accepted the Prague information without hesitation.

His main question now was, since the Prague mission had been a Russian Mafia setup, and he had no doubts that it had been, why had they allowed the Stony Man team to take out their Berlin operation? It made no sense that they would willingly give up an asset that valuable. That told him that they hadn't been in the loop when the Berlin raid went down. Even though they had their moles and operatives inside the Russian government, they had been asleep at the switch when the team took out the flak tower.

The speed of their reaction, however, told him a lot about this shadowy organization. They had heard the wake-up call and had taken immediate steps to eliminate the threat. The fact that they had limited their reaction to taking out Able Team instead of targeting the entire Stony Man force could be because of a lack of intelligence on their part. It could also be that their response had been measured for some reason. That was only one of the more critical questions that needed to be answered.

Shifting into the zone that he used to channel half-thoughts and random hunches directly from the deepest recesses of the right half of his brain through his fingertips to the computer, he started drawing in everything he could find about the activities of the Russian Mafia. He purposefully limited his search to the past thirty-six months for this phase. It was only in the past three years that Russia's criminals had grown beyond being a problem in just a few large Russian cities. If he didn't find what he wanted in that time period, however, he would expand the search.

He didn't know exactly what he was looking for, but he knew that he would recognize it when he saw it. In general, he was looking for a guiding mind behind these operations. He was looking for the traces of a personality, those traits and quirks of an individual mind that couldn't be hidden. Right now it wasn't as important to be able to put a name to this figure; that would come later. If he could find those keys, he could use them to project the moves this person might make in the near future. And right now, that's what he needed to know most.

Since Katz and the team had gone freelance, they had lost the information stream the Russians were supposed to provide them to plan their missions. Without that input, however devious or misleading it had been in Prague, the team needed every bit of intelligence he could come up with so they wouldn't get sandbagged again. As Kurtzman ran through everything in his cyberfiles about the Russian Mafia, a picture started to form deep in his mind.

Unlike with the American crime families, the Russian Mafia hadn't developed along ethnic or family lines. White Russians, Ukrainians, and almost every other ethnic group that made up the greater mix of peoples that most Americans called

Russians, were involved. And, with very few exceptions, this didn't appear to be a family business. But it was true that the crime wave hadn't lasted long enough to be passed on to the next generation. Left unchecked, though, it could turn into the family business it was in the States.

From everything he was seeing so far, the Russian Mafia had been born in the late-eighties when Mikhail Gorbachev had tried to put curbs on the state-run vodka industry in a vain attempt to limit drunkenness. If the man had bothered to take a good look at the American experience with prohibition, he might have had second thoughts about trying to dry out the Russians. But he hadn't, and all his good intentions got him was the same organized evil that prohibition had given America.

It was but one more proof of the old adage that the road to hell was paved with good intentions. It was also proof of the adage that those who didn't know history were doomed to repeat it.

Now the Russian Mafia was almost a shadow government in the mother country. Like the legendary Hydra of a thousand heads, their hands could be found in almost every aspect of Russian life from making vodka to issuing the permits needed to open a small shop. There was hardly any area of life that they didn't influence to some degree or other. It was easy to see why Vallinsikov had been so eager to get American help to deal with this problem.

Kurtzman quickly saw the genesis of the problem as well. How the gangsters had gone from being bootleggers to power brokers. At first there had been hundreds of small gangs and they had fought one another in the traditional manner, the strong eating the weak. For the past year and a half, however, it looked like the internal gang wars had ceased. In the same time frame, reports of gang warfare outside Mother Russia herself had increased. Particularly, reports grew of attacks against elements of the established Western European crime organizations who had also tried to move into the new Eastern democracies.

It was apparent to Kurtzman that the Russian Mafia had fallen under the control of one man, a man who he was willing to bet his pension was ex-military. And it was also apparent that this man was looking to expand his empire by traditional military means—attack, attack, attack.

So far, this all fit with the background information they had from the Russians via the White House. It was good to have that confirmed, but he still had to look deeper into his cybercrystal ball until the face of this mystery man appeared.

Germany

JACK GRIMALDI WAS at the wheel of the silver four-door BMW Five Series sports sedan as he drove

Mack Bolan and Carl Lyons through the late-night streets of Dresden. Unlike the version of the same car that was sold in the States, this vehicle could crack off 165 miles per hour on the Autobahn.

Not that he would be able to open up the machine in downtown Dresden. As with most of the major German cities, the World War II urban renewal, courtesy of the United States Air Force, had left the city planners with lots of open ground to build modern roads. Broad boulevards crisscrossed the town, but even at that time of night there was too much traffic for that kind of driving. But it was nice to have the power and the handling available if they had to make a speedy getaway.

"Pull over at the corner," Bolan told him when they were in the heart of the city. "We're a block away from the Moscow restaurant."

Grimaldi complied.

Stepping out of the car, Lyons carefully smoothed the thin black leather gloves over his fingers. For the kind of work he had ahead of him tonight, he didn't want his hands to slip.

Opening the BMW's trunk, he pulled out a SPAS 12 shotgun. The extended magazine was filled with the special Magnum buckshot rounds Cowboy Kissinger whipped up for them at the Farm. Instead of packing nine .36-caliber lead balls, his home-brewed rounds were loaded with a dozen .25-caliber frangible steel balls. When they hit their target, they broke apart into four orange-slice-shaped segments that tore much bigger holes than did the lead balls. A bag of detachable tubular magazines for the SPAS and half a dozen speed loaders for his Colt Python completed his hit kit.

Bolan already had his .44 Magnum Desert Eagle on his hip, and his Beretta 93-R hung in shoulder leather. From the trunk, he brought out an M-249 SAW with a sawed-off barrel. The lightweight, 5.56 mm machine gun was loaded with a 600-round plastic assault magazine. At the weapon's cyclic rate of 725 rounds per minute, that was less than fifty seconds' worth of firepower. But a man could do a lot of damage with a SAW in those brief fifty seconds.

A bag with two extra assault magazines for the machine gun and a second, larger bag with prepared demo charges went over his shoulder, and he was ready.

The sound of the party in the restaurant could be heard clearly as they approached the building. After checking to see that the street was clear, Bolan handed Lyons the SAW and took out a tapered steel wedge from a side pants pocket. Crouching down to clear the windows, he duckwalked over to the front door while Lyons kept guard.

After pulling the covering strip off of the bottom

of the wedge, Bolan slid the tapered end under the lock side of the door as far as it would go, then pressed it down against the doorframe to set the adhesive. For the surprise they had planned, they didn't want anyone to leave by the front door and miss the party.

Bolan rejoined Lyons and the two men slipped down the side of the restaurant to the alley behind. Finding it clear as well, they went to the rear door that their Serb informant reported opened into the kitchen.

According to the Serb, this door was always kept locked. That wasn't a problem. The thin titanium pry bar in Lyons's hands made short work of the antique lock.

Slipping through the door, they found the kitchen was deserted. Apparently the staff had been allowed to go home early. Several trays of prepared cold cuts were waiting, however, if the Russians got hungry and wanted something to soak up the vodka they were guzzling. From the empty bottles littering the counter, it was evident that the party had been going on for quite some time.

As the Serb had marked on his diagram, the door at the far end of the kitchen opened into a storage area. The strong smell of hash that hit them when they opened it told them that they had found the right place. Opening his demolitions bag, Bolan quickly set the charges around the room and flicked the detonators to remote fire.

"Okay," he said after placing the last charge, "let's crash the party."

Their rubber-soled combat boots made no noise as they moved into position. The kitchen opened into the raised bar area, and they took their places at the top of the low steps that led into the eating area.

A quick count revealed sixteen men and maybe half as many young women, sitting at long bench tables eating, drinking, laughing, groping and generally having a good time.

The two Stony Man commandos stood for a moment, mentally marking the locations of the targets as they waited for a go sign. One of the men, beefy-faced with white-blond hair, focused long enough to see the two black-clad figures standing at the back of the room. He was fumbling for something under his open jacket when Lyons triggered the SPAS.

The load of buckshot turned his head and upper body into a bloody ruin and slammed him out of his chair, which got everyone's immediate attention.

A young German girl panicked, jumped to her feet and dashed into the line of fire of the two fastest Russians. Her slender body jerked with the impact of shots meant for Bolan.

As she fell, the Executioner tripped the SAW's trigger for two long bursts. The two gunmen who had killed the girl were chewed up by a dozen 5.56 mm slugs apiece.

Swinging the SAW back to the left, he drilled a longer burst across the long table, making sure to miss the women. Three more gangsters collected a handful of 5.56 mm lead and collapsed facedown on the table.

Lyons stood at the top of the stairs like an avenging angel, the SPAS in his hands belching flame and death. He was yelling as he fired, but his words weren't audible over the roar of gunfire.

The Russians had been caught by surprise, and they were outgunned, but none of them tried to opt out and surrender. A steady drumbeat of 9 mm Makarov pistol fire snapped across the room, most of it aimed at Lyons. Bolan backed up his partner with the fast-firing SAW, and when Lyons paused to snap in a fresh magazine, Bolan stepped out.

Only a man as experienced with firearms as the Executioner could have made the cut-down machine gun sing the way he did. Snapping out staccato 3-round bursts like a rock band drummer, he marched his fire from one end of the room to the other. Every time he fired, a Russian went down. By the time Lyons had his SPAS reloaded, the last gangster was clawing at the front door in a futile attempt to escape the sure death that was being served in the Moscow restaurant.

Lyons lowered the smoking SPAS, drew his Python, carefully leveled a bead and put a .357 Magnum slug in the back of the Russian's head.

For a long moment, there was silence. Then, the women started to scream. They were professional party girls, but this wasn't the kind of party they had signed on for.

"Out! Out! Out!" Bolan shouted at them in German, pointing to the rear entrance.

The survivors needed no prompting and raced for the exit. After checking the woman who had got in the line of fire, and finding that she was dead, the two quickly rifled the pockets of the dead and collected their wallets and papers. Pocketing the results, they, too, headed for the rear exit.

"Let's go! Let's go!" Grimaldi called out to them when they exited the alley. In the distance, the warbling of German police and emergency-vehicle sirens could be heard.

Not bothering to hide their weapons in the trunk, the two men slid into the BMW, and Grimaldi was off before they even had the doors shut. With a squeal of rubber, the vehicle pulled away from the curb. He turned at the first block and powered away from the restaurant. In a flash, he was doing sixty down the cobblestone street.

"Watch it, hotshot," Lyons muttered as the car skittered on the slick surface.

"I've got it, Ironman," Grimaldi shot back. "We don't want to be too close when Striker goes for Phase Three."

On cue, Bolan reached into the glove box, took out the small transmitter, extended the antenna and hit the red button. Three blocks behind them, the restaurant's cellar erupted in an explosion that blew a million dollars' worth of drugs into oblivion.

"That's one," Lyons said.

"How many are you going to go for, Ironman?" Bolan asked, knowing that Lyons was counting payback.

Lyons's face was set. "However many it takes, Striker."

"THEY'RE OUT," Katz announced to the Phoenix Force warriors crowded into the CP van following the raid on the com link radios.

"All right!" Calvin James high-fived the air.

For the start of Bolan and Lyons's rat hunt, Phoenix Force was being kept on standby. Until the two found a target big enough to need their help, they would be working by themselves. That way, if they were tagged and followed, running into Phoenix Force reinforcements would be an unpleasant surprise.

"I'm starting to get some action on the police

emergency frequencies,'' Hawkins reported. With Gadgets Schwarz gone, he had stepped up to be the team's new radio and electronics man.

"Switch it over to my headset,'' Katz said.

After listening for a moment to the chatter on his headphones, Katz smiled. ''It's just the usual response to a report of gunfire and explosions. There's no mention of pursuit, so they're in the clear.''

He turned to McCarter. ''Are we ready to move on?''

''As soon as they get back.''

''Good. I'll update the Bear before we pull out.''

''How long do you think we're going to be able to get away with this?'' Hawkins asked.

Katz's eyes met his squarely. ''As long as it takes to do the job.''

The ex-Ranger smiled. ''I can live with that.''

CHAPTER ELEVEN

Stony Man Farm, Virginia

Aaron Kurtzman didn't need to have heard from Katzenelenbogen to know what had gone down in Dresden. He saw the Executioner's fingerprints all over the TV coverage of the restaurant shoot-out, and the story read like a page that had been ripped right out of a history of the old Mafia Wars. Gangsters were supposed to like to eat and party in large groups, and restaurants were always a good place to go for a little payback.

The German media was going ballistic over the incident, and CNN was giving it the top of the news, half-hourly coverage. He had to admit that even for Bolan and Lyons it had been a spectacular hit. The body count was seventeen, eleven Russians and six Germans, one of them a young woman. There had been other women there as well, but none of them had been hit. It was always bad news when a civilian got caught in the crossfire, but it could also be said that those who ran with gangsters were putting themselves in the line of fire.

In a brief call, Katz had reported that the team would be moving on to Munich next, and Kurtzman knew that he could expect more fireworks when they reached their new destination. In the meantime, he and his Computer Room staff would continue monitoring cyberspace for tracks leading to the elusive Russian Mafia leadership. He felt certain that they would have to respond to the Dresden attack in some fashion. And when they did, he'd get a hook into them.

HAL BROGNOLA HAD ALSO caught the CNN feed about the Dresden shoot-out. Since he had worked with Mack Bolan longer than anyone, he knew instantly what had happened. The Executioner had struck out of the night, leaving death and destruction behind. He had no problem with that, particularly not when most of the bodies had been identified as Russian Mafia and their German confederates.

The hit had been a stunning success and should put the Russian Mafia's plans to infiltrate the German drug markets on hold for quite some time. The downside was that since the raid had been made without official sanction, he couldn't report it to the White House.

In fact he'd had nothing to report to the President

since Katzenelenbogen had cut Phoenix Force loose from Stony Man control. To keep from having to admit to the Man that the Stony Man teams had gone rogue, he'd been playing along with the burned-van ploy. How much longer he would be able to get away with that flimsy excuse, he didn't know. But before the President caught up with him and put his butt on the grill, he had to try to talk to Price one more time.

He caught up with her in her office, apparently doing her routine work as if nothing out of the ordinary was going on.

"Barbara," he began, "can I come in for a minute? We need to talk."

She swung her booted feet up onto her desk, leaned back in her chair and grinned. Thanks to Kurtzman's in-house video surveillance system, she hadn't been caught unaware by Brognola's unexpected visit. The computer expert had warned her that he was on his way to her office.

"What's on your mind, Hal? Pull up a chair and talk to me."

"Specifically," he said, ignoring her studied pose, "we need to talk about the Dresden hit. I need to be able to tell the President something about it."

"You can tell him anything you like," she countered. "Just don't tell him that we had anything to do with it, because we didn't. Katz still hasn't got in contact, so I don't know what the situation is with him. Make sure that the Man tells that to the Russians, as well.''

''You can't keep this up too much longer, you know.'' He was trying hard to keep it together, but he knew that he wasn't going to make it much longer.

''Keep up what, Hal?''

''Dammit, Barbara. I can't help you if I don't know what's going on over there.''

She instantly dropped the smile. ''You also can't help me, as you put it, if the President blabs to the Russians again. You've got to take a stand, Hal.''

Seeing that this was going nowhere fast, he simply got up and left her office while he still could. Maybe some other time.

Germany

MUNICH DIDN'T LOOK like a place that could be the hub of the international weapons black market, but reports were indicating that it was in fact the source for many of the small arms ending up in the hands of the gangs—ex-Russian army small arms.

Though Munich was a well-known good-time town—it put the words Oktoberfest into the world's vocabulary—it was also the birthplace of the Nazi party. That was a long time ago, but even in the late-nineties, the good-time Charlies and the raging radicals still mixed in Munich, particularly within its large student population.

The radicals still dreamed their worn-out schemes of social engineering, and their plans all required firepower. Munich's geographical location in southern Germany made it a perfect hub giving access to eastern as well as northern and southern Europe. Guns and drugs from the East could easily move on to willing buyers in the rest of Western Europe.

Katzenelenbogen set up the Munich operation to work the same way as in Dresden, but with one difference. This time, Bolan and Lyons would have assistance from Phoenix Force. David McCarter and T. J. Hawkins also took to the streets in phase one to start working the low-level dealers. One evening's work was all they needed to get their first leads, and Lyons scored first off a street-corner pusher.

"Take a look at this, Striker," Lyons said, holding out the semiauto pistol he'd found in the coat pocket of his mark. "It's still got the Comsmoline on it."

The matte blue pistol in question was a standard military issue Russian 9 mm Makarov PM. Looking on the side of the slide, Bolan saw that it had been manufactured in 1988 in State Factory Number 64. State Factory 64 had been in the old Soviet Ukraine and when the Soviet Union came apart, the Russians had been forced to leave the factory to the newly independent Ukrainian Republic. But they weren't about to leave the arsenal it contained behind for potential enemies to use against them. They loaded all of the factory's vast stocks of weapons for rail shipment back to safety within the new boundaries of Mother Russia.

In the confusion, however, several train cars full of weapons never reached their destination. Not long after that, thousands of Kalashnikov assault rifles and Makarov pistols bearing the stamp of State Factory 64 hit the arms black market, and they were still being sold.

"Where did you get this weapon?" Bolan asked the dealer.

The man looked stricken. In Germany the ownership of all weapons, particularly handguns, was strictly controlled and being caught with one without a permit was a serious offense worth a long prison stay.

"The streets are dangerous," the dealer said without answering the question. "One of my friends was shot last week, and I wanted to protect myself."

"So you bought this from the same guy who you buy your hashish from, right?"

"No." The dealer looked surprised at that question. "He just told me where to go to get it."

"And where is that?"

WHEN THE TWO sweep teams got back to Katz's CP to compare notes, they had very similar stories to tell.

"Things are getting serious in this town, Striker," McCarter said. "Of the three guys we busted, two of them were packing."

"Makarovs, right?"

"Your guys too?"

"One of them was packing one," Lyons replied, "and he volunteered the name and address of the gun dealer."

"One of mine said that he got it from a friend, but the other one gave up his source, as well."

"A warehouse on Addler Strasse, right?"

"That's the place."

"You know," Katz said thoughtfully, "this is the same way that the war between the Bloods and Crips got started in California. This could be the first stage of that process."

"Here, though," Bolan said, "since handguns are almost impossible to buy, the drug wholesalers are providing their dealers with their weaponry as well as the product.

"Was your Makarov made in State Factory 64?" he asked McCarter.

"Yes, it was," the Briton stated. "And it doesn't look like it's ever been fired."

"Rather than just popping the drug wholesalers this time," Katz offered, "I think we should take out this gunrunner operation as well. That should make somebody sit up and take notice.''

"And we need to go for a prisoner this time if we can," Lyons said. "Taking out the low-level scum is all fine and good, but we need to talk to somebody so we can get at those Russian bastards ASAP."

Hearing Lyons ask for prisoners was something different, but McCarter saw his point. "We'll give it a try."

WHILE THE REST of the team prepared, Jack Grimaldi drove Bolan and Lyons to recon the warehouse that supposedly held the weapons. Like many of the towns in southern Germany, Munich still had much of its original street plan intact. Addler Strasse was in the heart of the old commercial district and was flanked by multistory brick buildings on both sides of the street.

The address was easy to find, and Grimaldi stopped his BMW a block past it to let the two men out. "I'll be on the horn if you need a quick extract."

"We'll be okay," Lyons replied. "It's daylight."

The two men found an empty building behind their target and took positions on the second floor looking down onto the building's loading docks. From the logos on the sides of the trucks that were parked for unloading, it was hard to tell exactly what was being stored in the building. There were furniture vans, rug suppliers and wine trucks off-loading, as well as others marked only as being from transportation companies all over Europe.

The building's back wall facing the loading dock was blank with no windows, as were the side walls. The second and third floors had windows, but they appeared to have been painted over.

"We're going to have to move in a little closer, Striker," Lyons said. "Like all the way inside, to make sure that this is the right place. The last thing we need right now is to hit the wrong warehouse."

Bolan could only agree with that. There was no point in alerting the Munich police unless it was for a good cause. "We'll move in as soon as everyone goes home for the day."

THE LAST TRUCK didn't leave the warehouse loading dock until right before dusk. And, as darkness fell, the two men saw that several lights had been left on inside the second and third floors of the old brick building.

"Just what I wanted," Lyons stated. "We'll have someone to call on. I hate raiding a place when no one's home. There's no one to talk to."

"Take it easy, Carl," Bolan said dryly. "Remember that we need to recon that place first before we start busting heads."

"I was afraid that you were going to remind me of that."

By this time, Katz had the van parked around the corner ready to move on Bolan's command. He agreed that they needed to make sure that weapons were being stored there before they destroyed the place. Figuring that the building's security system wouldn't have been activated because of the workers inside, Lyons decided to try one of the side doors.

Finding it locked, Bolan stood guard while Lyons took out his well-used lock-pick set and had it open in a few seconds. But rather than go right in, he opened the door a crack and looked around the opening for any sign of an alarm. Seeing none, he was ready to slip inside, when he spotted a guard coming down the stairs from the second floor.

The guy had to be a Russian. His broad face, buzz cut and faded blue eyes made him look like the guy in an old Red Army recruiting poster. The sound-suppressed subgun slung across his shoulder was a Czech-made Skorpion machine pistol, an old Soviet favorite.

"This has to be the place," Lyons whispered as he eyed the guard through the crack in the door.

Bolan keyed his throat mike and called McCarter. "The target is good," he said. "Come on in. There's a side door on the east that's open, and we'll be waiting outside."

"Roger," the Briton answered. "We're on the way."

IN THE FEW MINUTES that it took Phoenix Force to arrive, Bolan and Lyons watched the guard go back up the stairs to the second floor. Hopefully now, the first floor would be clear and they could make their entry unseen.

McCarter left Encizo to cover the loading dock and sent Manning around to watch the front while he, James and Hawkins joined Bolan and Lyons. Since they didn't know how many opponents they were facing, they made a stealthy entry, and, checking the first floor, came up with nothing interesting, not even crates with Russian lettering. Apparently that floor was legitimate, a front for the public.

Since this was an older building, it had no elevators, but two staircases led to the upper floors. Bolan and Lyons took one stairwell while the three Phoenix Force commandos took the other. When James caught McCarter's attention and tapped the flash-bang grenade on his harness, McCarter shook his head.

The second floor was also clean, but they could hear faint voices from the third. As they started up the stairs again, McCarter clicked his com link and pulled a flash-bang from his harness. The others followed suit, preparing to announce their arrival with a bang.

Lyons followed close behind Bolan as they slowly climbed the stairs. They were halfway up when the big, blond Russian guard started down. His head was turned to say something to his comrades, so he didn't spot the intruders until he took his second step. He yelled and tried to bring his subgun into play, but Lyons triggered his SPAS first.

The buckshot blast put the Russian down, and Lyons sidestepped his body as he raced up the rest of the steps.

In the other stairwell, McCarter and James tossed their grenades, then charged to the top.

The four hardmen had been taken by surprise and stunned by the flash-bangs, but they had no intention of giving up without a fight. The Stony Man team was greeted by a blaze of gunfire. Hugging the top step, Lyons emptied his SPAS into the enemy gunners, and the frangible buckshot cut a bloody swath.

In the other stairwell, McCarter and his men took their cue from Lyons and didn't even try to step out into the open. The floor was three-inch-thick timber, and the wood soaked up the enemy fire better than Kevlar.

The attackers' concentrated fire lasted only a few brief seconds, but it had been enough. Five bodies lay collapsed on the floor.

Lyons checked the bodies while Bolan and

McCarter scoped out the room. Much of the space was taken up with crated Russian weapons, AK-47 assault rifles and Makarov pistols. No attempt had been made to disguise the crates; they still bore their Russian military markings.

"Someone's planning on starting a war around here," James commented as he started to count the crates.

"As well as a hell of a party," Hawkins said when he spotted a table in the corner with an electronic scale and a large pile of hashish packages.

"It's time to clear out, Striker," Katz called over the com link. "I just picked up radio traffic from the fire brigade and the cops. They're both en route to your location."

"We're out of here," Bolan replied, reaching for the thermite grenades on his harness. He popped the incendiary grenades and dropped them on top of the weapons crates. They would burn through and fuse the steel into lumps of slag. No one would be killing anyone with these weapons.

Following the others to the stairs, Hawkins pulled the pins of two more thermite grenades and tossed the bombs behind him. With the fire units coming, he wanted to insure that nothing was going to save this place.

As they ran for the van, Lyons wasn't unhappy that he hadn't gotten the prisoners he'd wanted. He was content just to have the body count. The drugs and weapons that were going up in flames were an added bonus, but for him it was the blood that counted the most.

CHAPTER TWELVE

Russia

Gregor Rostoff was becoming concerned about his Western European operations. The raid on the restaurant hangout in Dresden had put a serious dent in his growing German business. Dresden's central location made it a good place for him to focus his inventory. The loss hurt, but he would be able to replace it. All it would take was time, but it would be an added expense. While cash flow wasn't a problem for him, he had to insure that something like that didn't happen again.

Allowing someone, anyone, to attack his organization wasn't good business for a man in his position. The only way he could successfully run the organization he had created was for him to be feared. But for him to be feared, he had to know who to intimidate.

The raid could have been the work of one of the Western narcogangs who were trying to send him a message. The savage execution of his associates and the destruction of the restaurant bore their stamp. But it appeared that the inventory had been left behind, as it had been in the raid on Blatz's operation in Berlin. That could have been to show him that the product was unimportant compared to his taking over someone's established turf.

Or, this could mean that Vallinsikov's Americans were still working against him. His agent in the minister's office had reported that he hadn't been informed about any more American actions since Prague. The minister also hadn't been told that they had gone back to America.

Regardless of who had raided him with such ferocity, force would be matched with force. And it wasn't a problem for him to bring force to bear. No matter how much force was directed at him, he could return it in spades. One of the things that made the Russian Mafia different from the gangs of Western Europe was the military background of most of its members, and their ready access to modern military weaponry.

With the fall of the Red Army, millions of small arms, both modern and vintage, had come up for the taking. The Soviets had maintained vast arsenals. The harsh lessons they had learned in the earliest days of World War II had taught them that if you needed weapons, you needed them immediately. To insure that the Russian people would never again be without arms to defend themselves, arsenals had been spotted all over the Red Empire. Along with his headquarters complex, Rostoff had bought the contents of several arsenals outright.

Along with this vast arsenal to call upon, Rostoff had more than enough men to use his weapons. Not only did he have many ex-Red Army veterans in his organization, he had also recruited heavily from dozens of out-of-work European terrorist groups. With the fall of the Soviet Union, the traditional European Leftist organizations had lost their paymaster and sponsor. With no money coming in, many of these terrorist groups broke up.

Rostoff stepped into the void that had been created and had recruited quite a few of these leftist terrorists. He hadn't taken them on because of their politics. He was far from being a Marxist and was well aware that communism was an ill-conceived ideology. If the Soviet Union hadn't been able to make the cumbersome system work, no one could.

The only leftists he had taken into his organization were those who could provide a service he needed. Even with the ex-military personnel he had on hand, there were some jobs that terrorists did better than soldiers. When it came to assassinations and terrorist bombings, the military didn't necessarily have the best men.

While the IRA wasn't the threat it had once been, its members were among the most experienced terrorists in all of Europe. Now that the KGB was no longer funding them and the donations from the Irish-American community had also fallen, the IRA was hurting for money. He had recruited some two-dozen ex-IRA members and had formed them into special hit teams. He would put them to work solving his problem.

The Irish hit teams were noted for getting the most out of solving a problem. There was no act too brutal that they wouldn't gladly undertake. Particularly if they could leave a broken body or two in a prominent place for someone to find. And the bloodier the body, the better.

Whoever was moving against Rostoff had to be taught a lesson they would never forget, and leaving broken bodies behind was a good teaching aid. He would find out who was behind this and when he did, they would fervently wish that they hadn't got involved with him. Every man had a weakness; even the most hardened criminal had family or friends that he cared about. Before he could send his hit teams into action, however, he needed to know who to send them against.

He had just ordered Boris Detlov to extend an invitation to the leaders of the largest European gangs to meet him in Budapest for a summit meeting. The invitation was couched in such a manner that he was confident that most of them would respond. When he had them at the table, he intended to work out a truce with them and explain why it was to their advantage not to get in his way. They could either decide to cut him in for a large piece of the Western European pie, or they could face a turf war the likes of which they had never seen before. Anyone who didn't get onboard his program would be targeted immediately.

He also intended to have another talk with his two captives to try to develop more information about the covert teams. As he had bragged to them, the chemical interrogation worked wonders, but he also knew that well-trained operatives didn't tell everything they knew on the first session. Sometimes it took several sessions before their will was completely overcome, but he wasn't willing to wait. Someone was attacking him and if it was their teammates, he needed that information quickly.

Fortunately chemicals weren't the only interrogation tools he had inherited from the old KGB. There was also the matter of the nerve induction device. While cruder, it had a good track record and wouldn't leave evidence that might prove embarrassing at the public trials he had planned for Schwarz and Blancanales.

GADGETS SCHWARZ WAS TIRED of sitting in a cell. Even with Rosario Blancanales for company, it was getting boring.

In other circumstances, the two of them would

have kept themselves busy trying to figure out a way to break out, but they had been forced into inactivity this time. The problem was that they were both very much aware of the video eyes that covered every inch of the twelve-by-sixteen-foot cell. Those electronic eyes never blinked, and they never grew tired. There was nothing they could say or do that wasn't recorded for Rostoff to go over whenever he wanted.

Schwarz hadn't earned his nickname for nothing. But there was absolutely nothing in the cell for him to work with. Whatever he thought about Rostoff personally, the Russian was a real pro when it came to running a prison.

The windowless cell contained concrete ledges extending from the walls for bunks, a one-piece, stainless-steel sink and a Euro-style hole-in-the-bare-floor toilet. Period. Even the light fixture was sunk into the ceiling and covered with a thick plate of glass. He had seen solitary confinement rooms with more lavish furnishings. This place was more like the freak-out room in a psycho ward than a prison.

Blancanales watched Schwarz's eyes sweep the room again and again and knew full well what was going through his teammate's mind.

"You might as well hang it up, old buddy," he said. "The Russians know how to build holding cells. God knows they've had enough practice at it.

Even before Lenin, the czar's secret police had hundreds of Russians in escape-proof cells.''

Before Schwarz could think up a snappy retort, he heard steps coming toward their door. When it opened, Detlov walked in flanked by four armed guards. ''Mr. Schwarz, my colonel wants to see you.''

''I THOUGHT YOU SAID that you Russians didn't need to resort to using pain to get your information,'' Schwarz said as he watched the technician insert the steel needles into the nerves of his right arm. Strapped in the heavy chair, there was little he could do but try to endure whatever was coming next.

''The chemicals work well enough with most people,'' Rostoff explained, ''but there are those cases where a little physical stimulation in conjunction with the chemicals is required.''

He shrugged. ''Unfortunately, Mr. Schwarz, you are one of those cases.''

Motioning to the technician, he ordered, ''Begin.''

The technician turned a knob, and Schwarz had to bite back a scream. His hand felt as if it were on fire. The pain seemed to last forever. When it finally subsided, he sucked in deep breaths and tried to steel himself for whatever was coming next. Out of the corners of his watering eyes, he saw the technician make an adjustment to his machine before hitting the switch again.

This time, his entire arm felt like it had been dipped in molten lead. He really intended to resist whatever Rostoff did to him, but the scream burst from his mouth before he could stop it. And, once he had started screaming, it was impossible to stop.

Screaming didn't stop the pain, however, and at some point in the procedure, he slipped into the welcoming darkness of oblivion.

An ammonia capsule snapped Schwarz awake to find that from his fingertips to his elbow, his right arm was still in unbelievable agony. When he could focus his eyes, he looked to see how badly he had been hurt. He couldn't believe that his arm looked completely normal. There was no blood, none of the bones had been broken and except for the small dots where the electrodes had been attached he was unmarked. In fact the only mark his body bore was where he had bitten through his lip in his agony.

When he was helped up to his feet, he could hardly walk. His whole body felt like he had been beaten by a team of experts. When he was led back to the cell he shared with Blancanales, he knew that it wasn't some sign of Rostoff's compassion. It was just a further interrogation tactic. With the cell wired, anything they did or said would be recorded.

As THE TWO Able Team commandos expected, Rostoff and Detlov were in the control room watching when Schwarz was returned to the lockup.

"Those two men are tough," Detlov said with grudging admiration as he watched Blancanales try to make his partner more comfortable. "I have to give them that."

"They are," his leader agreed. "But this is one time when toughness, while admirable, is not going to do them much good. The next time I put them under the chemicals, their subconscious minds will remember the nerve induction technique. And while their conscious minds are tough enough to withhold information regardless of the consequences, their subconscious wants to avoid pain at all costs. It is a survival mechanism in all humans."

He smiled. "Next time they will tell me what I want to know."

"What if they do not know?"

He shrugged. "They will still be able to tell me how to find out what I want to know."

"When do you want the other one?" Detlov asked.

"Give him a few more minutes. The wait will make the treatment more effective."

CHAPTER THIRTEEN

Stony Man Farm, Virginia

Aaron Kurtzman filled his coffee cup and settled in behind his keyboard. Tapping in a code that only he and Barbara Price knew, he activated the satellite link to Katzenelenbogen's CP van. It was daytime in Europe, and he knew Katz would be awake.

"What's next on the Ironman's program?" he asked the Israeli tactical officer.

"I've been going through the material you sent," Katzenelenbogen replied, "trying to figure out where we can get the biggest bang for our buck here and elicit a response from our Russian friends. We can't keep on doing this forever, so I want to do as much damage to them as we can before we're asked to leave town."

Kurtzman chuckled. If it ever came time for someone to ask Phoenix Force to leave town, it would be an international incident. "I have an idea that might help you smoke out the Russians," he said.

"Let's hear it," Katz replied.

"I'm getting a lot of buzz about your activities from Interpol. They're acting like someone chucked a live grenade into a church social."

"Do tell." Katz was surprised that it had taken the international police organization this long to twig to what was going on right under their noses. "What've they been doing?"

"For one thing, they've been pulling in all of their mob informants and putting them through the fifth degree trying to find out what's behind this. They're reading it as a major turf war, and they're trying to put the fire out before the civilians start getting hurt, too."

"Have they picked up on the Russian connection to any of this yet?"

"They're starting to get a glimmer of that. A couple of the bodies you left behind and the weapons in Munich couldn't be ignored. But, so far, they're sitting on that part of it because of the politics involved. No one wants to be the first one to start up the cold war again."

"That figures."

"Needless to say," Kurtzman continued, "your activities also have the old established Euro-gangs in a bit of a panic thinking that they're going to be next on whoever's hit list this is. They're so nervous, in fact, that I think you might be able to squeeze them a little and get them to turn over their Russian connections. If anyone knows who's behind this, they do.''

''What did you have in mind?''

''Well,'' Kurtzman said. ''I just happen to have a little plan I've been working on. I think you'll like it.''

''Send it.''

France

EVEN IN HIS European-styled clothes, Carl Lyons looked a little out of place in the Toulouse waterfront nightclub. It wasn't the usual seaman and workingman's bar one would have expected to find along the dock. The bar at the head of the pier had been discovered by the trendy set and was now a watering hole for the pampered adult children of Europe's wealthy classes. Glittering heiresses, playboys, rock stars and actors crowded the tables and small dance floor of the newly renamed Neptune Club. In that crowd, Lyons looked like an overgrown, rabid wolf sitting in on a peacock convention.

T. J. Hawkins fit into the crowd at the Neptune a little better than Lyons. Even though he, too, was a force to be reckoned with, he wore it a little easier than Lyons. His easy southern manner and open grin hid his intentions as well as a carnival mask. He had taken a spot at the bar and was keeping a young Italian beauty company while he nursed a tall drink of his own devising that was mostly soda and grenadine syrup.

The third inside man of the snatch team was Rafael Encizo. The Cuban was a little older than most of the partyers, but his Latin looks helped him hide in the crowd. His position at a stand-up table on the edge of the dance floor was the third point of the triangle formed by Lyons and Hawkins.

Their target in the center of their triangle was a prime example of "excess." He was in his late-twenties, wore overly flashy clothing and jewelry, talked too loudly, drank expensive whiskey and was trying very hard to give the appearance of being the man of the hour. The two thugs hovering near Napoleon Leontinis were there to make sure that none of the club's other patrons objected to their boss's ego-enhancing, drug-fueled fantasies.

The bodyguards didn't, however, try to keep the bevy of fawning women away from him. As the son of the leader of the Union Corse, Leontinis was known to be a big spender and an easy mark for a good-looking woman who didn't mind getting publicly pawed. In fact, if she proved to be the big man's pick of the evening and went home with the would-be playboy, she could expect to leave his

nearby villa the next morning with her bills paid
for the next six months.

Even the glitterati sometimes had to work to
make ends meet.

IN THE PARKING LOT in front of the club, Jack Grimaldi waited in the getaway car. This time, Katz
had scored a Citroën-Maserati SM sedan for their
use. The combination of a French chassis with a
pavement-pounding Maserati engine had created
the fastest road car France had ever produced. He
had always wanted to wring out an SM, and here
was his chance.

Two parking slots down from the SM, a big
Chevy Blazer four by four was parked nose out.
Heavy Detroit iron was the latest imported status
symbol in Europe, and it didn't look at all out of
place in front of the club. It was to be Hawkins's
ride when the snatch went down. As soon as Grimaldi hit the road, his job would be to make sure
that no one got on his tail.

Hawkins wouldn't be able to keep up with the
Citroën-Maserati, but he could sure as hell block
the narrow road until the lead car hit the Auto
Strada.

"LET'S GET THIS SHOW on the road, guys," Lyons
growled softly, but loud enough to cover the elec-

tronically amplified noise coming from the bandstand.

"We're on the way," Bolan radioed back.

Bolan and McCarter entered the club by the back door. Dressed in their blacksuits, they had both put colored windbreakers over them to hide their hardware until it came time to use it.

"We're in," Bolan reported. "Show time."

Hearing his cue, Hawkins pushed himself away from the bar. "You stay right here, sweet thing," he said as he ran his hand over the Italian woman's hip. "I'll be right back."

Lyons and Encizo had also left their places, and the three men converged on the table where Leontinis was holding court.

Leontinis's bodyguards were so intent on watching their boss fondle the breasts of a leggy redhead that they never had a chance.

Lyons had the muzzle of his Colt Python screwed into the ear of his man in a flash. "Freeze, scumbag."

When the thug tried to go for his piece anyway, Lyons whipped the butt of the heavy revolver against the side of his head. He fell as if he had been poleaxed, his head bleeding profusely.

Hawkins had the razor-sharp blade of his Ka-bar fighting knife against the throat of his man, who was smart enough not to move and risk having his throat slashed.

Napoleon Leontinis came out of his fog when the
guard Lyons had pistol-whipped fell at his feet.
When he saw Hawkins's grinning face behind the
Ka-bar, his shout couldn't be heard over the noise
from the bandstand. While he was trying to decide
what he was going to do next, Bolan, McCarter and
Encizo were on him.

McCarter jerked his right arm into a come-along
hold while Bolan let him feel the muzzle of his
Beretta against his side. "Not a sound," he ordered,
"or you die here."

When Hawkins felt his bodyguard tense as if he
were going to try something, he reversed the Ka-
bar and slammed the butt sharply behind his ear.
The thug joined his pal on the floor.

The redhead blinked in a drug-induced fog, then
collapsed to the floor in a faint.

With McCarter on one side and Bolan on the
other, Leontinis was half carried through the room
with Encizo trailing and Hawkins and Lyons covering him. As they crossed the crowded floor, a few
people noticed what was going on, but they didn't
choose to get involved.

The oversized bouncer at the door took one look
at the entourage and wisely decided that he didn't
want any of it either. He knew who Leontinis was,
and if someone had dared to take him out, it was a
little more than he wanted to get involved with. He

would, however, wait a while and make a discreet phone call or two.

In the parking lot, Hawkins and McCarter peeled away from the group and headed for the Blazer. At the waiting Citroën, Encizo jumped into the front passenger seat while Bolan and Lyons threw their captive into the back. Grimaldi was on the gas as soon as they had the doors shut.

With McCarter riding shotgun, Hawkins did his best to keep up with Grimaldi's speeding SM.

"MR. LEONTINIS?" Katz said in French when a sleepy voice answered the phone. "You need to listen carefully. If you call the Neptune Club, you will learn that your son left there tonight in the company of five men. His two bodyguards were left behind, but they can be retrieved from the local hospital."

The elder Leontinis quickly became all business. "Is my son hurt?"

"No, he is fine." Katz paused. "For now."

"What do you want from me?"

Katz quickly made his demands and gave the elder Leontinis the address of the villa they had rented outside Toulouse and a time that he would be expected.

"I do not need to tell you what will happen to you, whoever you are, if my son is harmed." The man's voice was razor-edged.

"And I do not need to tell you that your son will die instantly if you do not do exactly what I tell you to."

"I will make no mistakes."

"Neither will I."

"That went well," Bolan said when Katz broke the connection.

"The old man is a seasoned pro," the Israeli replied. "He knows how the game is played. Now as soon as Calvin and Gary check in, I can make the second call and we'll be ready to go."

WHILE BOLAN and Lyons had been putting the arm on Leontinis Junior, Calvin James and Gary Manning had been making their own move in the dockside area of Marseilles. Their target was a warehouse on the quay with a brightly lit sign out front proudly proclaiming that it was operated by Bianca Ltd., an Italian corporation with business interests all over Europe.

The company that owned the warehouse was Italian, very true, but Italian Mafia, and not all of their European interests were as innocent as the Bianca brochures would like one to believe. They were, however, profitable.

A firm as large as Bianca Ltd. could afford to keep its operation going twenty-four hours a day, and there was a six-man crew working the night shift. Even so, none of the six wanted to argue with two heavily armed men dressed in night combat suits. After herding them against the wall, James guarded them while Manning did the honors.

Reaching into the side pocket of his blacksuit, he pulled out plastic riot restraints and started binding everyone's wrists and ankles. He then pulled out a roll of two-inch-wide surgical tape and slapped a piece over each of their mouths. "You just stay there," he said in French, "and you won't be hurt."

When he turned, he saw that James was trying to drag a heavy crate, and stopped him. "You're going to give yourself a hernia. They've got a fork-lift over there."

"Can you drive it?"

"If I can't—" he jerked a thumb over to their collection of warehousemen "—I know one of these guys can."

"Give it a shot."

Climbing into the seat of the yellow machine, Manning turned the key and saw a gauge on the instrument panel come to life. "Hey," he called out, "this thing's electric. Piece of cake."

Motoring over to the stack of crates, he slid the lift forks under and hoisted them. "Where do you want these things?"

"Right in the middle of the floor, away from everything else."

As soon as Manning put the crates down, James opened one and pulled out an RPG-7 rocket launcher. "This is it," he said. "The Bear had it right on. You keep an eye on them, and I'll get this lot ready to go."

James went to work rigging the crates with thermite grenades.

As James was setting the charges, Manning saw that his prisoners weren't unaware of what explosives looked like and were visibly panicked. "Why don't I take those lads outside and park them somewhere safe?"

"I don't want us to get split up," James replied. "We don't have backup if something goes wrong."

"I'll tell you what. While you're finishing up here, I'll go put a pallet on the forklift, load those guys onto it and we'll take them out when we leave."

"Go ahead."

Finding a large pallet, he slipped the lift forks into it, raised it and drove over to where the night crew was sitting against the wall. "All aboard," he said, lowering the pallet and motioning for the men to get on.

With their wrists and ankles bound, the workmen had to struggle to get up onto the pallet. But as soon as they were all safely on board, Manning gently lifted the forks until the pallet was six feet off the ground and drove over to where James was fixing the last of the thermite grenades to the crates.

"Let's roll," he told Manning as he set the last time detonator.

The Canadian drove his forklift load out the rear door of the warehouse and into the almost empty lot in back. A safe distance away, he lowered the pallet and shut off the forklift. "Tell your boss that we'll be in touch with him later."

The foreman glared, but the tape over his mouth kept his thoughts safely to himself. Of all the warehouse's night crew, he was the only one who knew the company that signed his paycheck was "connected" as the phrase went. But, since the warehouse was posing as a legitimate operation, he hadn't been allowed to have any weapons on the premises. Except, of course, for those that were passing through, buried in the crates of machinery.

The two commandos were fading into the dark when the first of the thermite grenades went off.

CHAPTER FOURTEEN

Toulouse, France

David McCarter and Carl Lyons were standing at the top of the villa steps with Gary Manning and Calvin James when the Citroën D-19 sedan pulled into the driveway. The old man who got out of the back seat looked as if he were going to an execution—his own. Carlos Leontinis was in his sixties and wore an expensive, but slightly old-fashioned suit and didn't look anything like a powerful leader of the Union Corse, the Corsican Mafia. If anything, he looked like a middle-class, lower-level public official, a records clerk or maybe a small-town postmaster.

The two men who got out after him had to be his bodyguards. They were young, hard and their faces showed barely controlled rage. They stood stock-still as James and Manning stepped up to them and patted them down for hardware. As they had been instructed, they weren't packing as much as a fingernail file.

"They're clean," Manning said into his com link.

"Bring them on up," McCarter replied.

Bolan and Katzenelenbogen met Leontinis at the door to the villa and escorted him into the main sitting room. When the older man seated himself, his bodyguards automatically moved in to stand behind him. Unarmed as they were, they couldn't do a thing to protect their boss except maybe throw their bodies into the line of fire, but they looked ready to do even that.

Bolan purposefully didn't offer the Corsican refreshments. He knew that the old man would have to refuse to eat or drink with his son's kidnappers, and that would set a bad tone for the meeting.

"Let me see my son," the man said.

At Bolan's nod, James and Hawkins escorted the young man into the room. For having been an unwilling guest for the night, he didn't look any worse for the experience.

"I am sorry for the inconvenience this has caused you," Bolan told him, "but it was necessary."

"You will pay for that 'inconvenience,' asshole," the young Leontinis said hotly.

"Shut up, Napoleon," the old man said in English so he wouldn't be misunderstood.

Turning back to Bolan, the old man asked, "What must I do to free him?"

"I need a favor..." Bolan started.

"What are you talking about, a 'favor'?" the young man shouted. "All you're going to get from me is a bullet in your head, you Yankee bastard!"

Bolan signaled to James, and the Phoenix Force commando stepped up to the young man, his Beretta in his hand. Without a word, the ex-SEAL thumbed back the hammer and placed the muzzle against the side of the young man's head. Napoleon shut his mouth and froze.

Bolan looked back at the old man. "You might want to tell your son that if he says another word, I will have my man kill him. I came here to talk to you, not to a punk kid who is too stupid to know when to shut his mouth. And that is to say nothing about how easily he allowed himself to come into my hands."

This time, the old man spoke in the Corsican dialect, and the captive blanched.

"He will not speak again." The old man switched back to English. "Now, what is this favor you need done?"

"You have heard about the Dresden hit on the Russian Mafia and the other operations of theirs that have been taken down lately?"

The man nodded.

"I am responsible for that."

"Who are you?"

"It isn't necessary that you know that," Bolan replied. "It's only necessary for you to know that I have a printout of your major holdings in several countries, as well as a list of your major operatives. I think you'll find that it makes interesting reading."

Bolan nodded to Katz, and the Israeli handed over a computer printout in French—the information that had been forwarded from Stony Man Farm.

The man read through it and looked up, a stricken look on his face.

"I know that isn't the full extent of your operations," Bolan said. "But I also know that what is listed is accurate and represents the majority of your holdings. If that list was given to Interpol, you—" he glanced over at the young man "—and your family, would be out of business as well as in prison. Do we understand each other?"

The man nodded. "What is the price you are asking to keep this information to yourself?"

"Normally there would be no price on earth that would keep me from putting a man like you out of business. But this time I need information about one of your competitors."

"Could I have a drink?" the old man asked, signaling his acceptance of the terms.

"Certainly."

"And please have my son escorted outside."

When Bolan nodded, James and Hawkins took Napoleon's arms and led him out of the room.

Bolan left the Corsican to drink his wine for a moment. Regardless of the business he was in, the old man lived by a strict code of conduct, and informing on anyone was forbidden no matter what the price. Even to save the life of his worthless, but only son, it was hard for him to break the code he had lived by for so long.

"Who is it that you need this information on?" the old man finally asked.

"The Russian Mafia leader who has been trying to move into Eastern Europe."

The Corsican almost smiled. "You could have had that information without going to these lengths and I would have given it to you for free. The name of the man you want is Rostoff, Gregor Rostoff, and he is a man completely without honor. He has grand ideas, though, for such a man. He sent me, Carlos Leontinis, a letter ordering me to attend a meeting he is holding in Budapest."

"When is the meeting being held?"

The old man didn't even have to check his notes, but rattled off a date and the name of one of the best-known hotels in Europe. Bolan took no notes himself, but Katz was recording everything that was said.

"Beyond that," Leontinis said, "I know nothing

about him except that he is dangerous. I hope you catch up with him. He makes trouble for all of us.''

"Thank you." Bolan stood.

"That is all?" the old man asked.

"That's all. You may go."

On the way to the front door, Bolan said, "One last word of friendly advice, if I may. My agreement is with you and you alone. Apparently your son isn't the man his father is, so I caution you to keep him under strict control. Should he become a problem for me, any kind of a problem, I will have to kill him. I'm sure you understand."

Leontinis understood completely. "It is his mother's fault." The old man sighed. "She has indulged him too much. He thinks that the old ways are no longer valid. He is not, as you and I understand it, a man of honor."

"You had better find some way to convince him that I'm serious, then," Bolan warned. "One word out of him about this, or one action against me, no matter how trivial, and your wife will be without a son."

"I understand."

"I knew you would."

"THAT WENT OFF BETTER than I thought it would," McCarter said as the Citroën drove away. "I thought the Corsicans were tougher than that."

"The Corsicans understand business," Katz said.

"And the old man doesn't like the Russians because they don't follow the old code. It's no skin off his nose if they're forced out of the Western European markets. In fact it will boost his share of the pie."

"Plus," Bolan added, "he was worried about what we were going to do to his son."

"I thought we were going to have to kill that asshole kid to make your point."

"We probably should have," Bolan said. "I'm afraid that we'll be hearing from him later. He's not the kind who learns quickly."

"If we have to zero him," McCarter said, "it'll cause us trouble with the old man's Corsicans."

"I'll worry about them when it happens."

"When is the Italian due to show up?" McCarter asked.

Katz glanced at his watch. "Two hours."

"Good. I can get a nap before I have to go back to work."

"Take your time," Bolan said. "I don't think that we're going to have any trouble with the next guy either."

"That's too bad."

THE ITALIAN FLEW his own helicopter into the flat behind the villa. As one of the new breed of European criminals, he saw himself as the CEO of a large multinational corporation rather than a Mafia chieftain. That was why the e-mail invitation had worked with him and why he came alone except for his copilot. Businessmen didn't make war on each other.

When he was brought into the villa's sitting room, Katz had a coffee service ready for him and a plate of biscotti as if they were in Rome and he was making a social call.

"I am glad you could make this meeting," Bolan said.

"You did arouse my curiosity," the Italian replied as he sipped his coffee. "It is obvious that you want me to do something for you."

"You could put it that way."

The Italian dropped the facade. "And why is it that you think I will do anything *for* you instead of *to* you?"

"Let me put it to you this way," Bolan said. "I'm in the process of taking out the garbage in Eastern Europe. I know that it's a big job, but I'm not hampered by the usual legal niceties. As you have seen, I can take out anyone or anything that I want to and can get away with it."

The Italian nodded. He had to admit that the surgical strike against his Marseilles warehouse had been very well done. The shipment of Russian army surplus small arms that had been destined for the latest round of African civil wars was the only thing that had been touched. They could as easily have torched the entire warehouse and set him back hundreds of millions of lira. As it was, though, the cost had been fairly nominal. And none of his employees had been killed or even harmed, for that matter. Whoever these men were, they were professionals in the truest sense of the word.

Bolan smiled tightly. "I thought that you might want to help me in my endeavor to insure that you don't have any more problems."

The Italian laughed. "You are trying to extort something from me by blowing up one of my warehouses? That takes balls."

Bolan shrugged. "You can call it that if you like. But I like to think that I am offering you protection from any more interruptions to your shipping schedule."

"For how long?" the Italian asked to open the negotiations. Every businessman, no matter how well-connected, needed insurance now and then.

"One year."

While the Italian digested that with his coffee, Katz spoke up. "Look at it this way. The price of the protection we're offering will be cheap. So far, it has cost you the inventory you lost in our demonstration raid and the fuel it took to fly you here. If we make a deal, those will be your only expenses."

He shrugged. "If, however, we can't come to an agreement, your bottom line isn't going to look too good this year, particularly if we share our intelligence on your operation with Interpol. And you may even have to take up new quarters in an Italian prison. Neither your wife nor your mistress will like that very much.''

As one of the new breed, the Italian could project his bottom line as well as any other CEO. This had been presented to him as a straightforward business deal, and he understood business well. His MBA was from Harvard, and he had more of his money invested in legitimate business throughout Europe than he did in the more traditional Mafia enterprises.

He also understood the problems he would face if he decided to go up against these Americans. Looking out for the normal law-enforcement agencies was worrisome enough without having to deal with people who worked outside the law. There was nothing more dangerous to a criminal than another criminal. If they had been able to break his security to learn about that one arms shipment, there was no telling what else they knew about his operations.

''And what do I have to do to 'pay' for this insurance?''

''Just give me everything you know about the mastermind behind the Russian Mafia's move into Europe.''

The Italian quickly made up his mind. ''The man you are looking for is Gregor Rostoff. He is an ex-colonel in the Soviet army who was imprisoned for drug smuggling during the Afghan War. He recently approached me with a business deal too, but—'' the Italian smiled ''—his offer was not as good as yours.

"In fact," the Italian continued, "you might be interested in knowing that he has called a meeting of prospective business partners in Budapest next week. He wants to hammer out the details of the conglomerate he is putting together. I, of course, will not be attending."

"Wise move," Bolan said. "What else do you know about him?"

"Not much. He has not affected my operations yet, so I have paid little attention to him."

"But you will inform me when and if he does?"

"But of course." The Italian looked from Bolan to Katz. "I get one year's protection, and I will pass on anything I hear about the Russian's operations."

"That is the agreement," Katz said.

"And after that?"

"As long as you don't pose a problem for the United States," Bolan said, "we don't consider it our business what you do here."

"But you are DEA or FBI, are you not?"

"No," Katz said, knowing that no matter what he said, the Mafia capo would think whatever he wanted. "We are just concerned American citizens."

"Right. And I am just an Italian businessman. And—" he glanced down at his gold Rolex watch "—if we are done here, I really should be getting along."

"Just one more thing," Bolan said.

The Italian tensed, waiting for the other shoe to drop. "Yes?"

"Should you get the idea that you might want to betray us to Rostoff, I recommend that you forget it. All that will net you is a bullet in the back of the head."

After all of the civilized talk wrapped in business terminology, the Executioner's blunt threat hit as hard as a .44 slug from his Desert Eagle. The Italian blinked. "I never reveal my business partners."

"That's a very good policy."

Not quite so confident now, the Italian said his goodbyes and was escorted to where he had left his helicopter on the back lawn.

"TWO FOR TWO isn't bad," Katz said to Bolan as the Bianca Ltd. chopper took to the air and turned east for the flight back to Italy. "And this time they both told the same story. Not only did we get Rostoff's name, we got a place where the bastard's going to be."

"At least for those few days. But that should be enough. And since he's planning a Mafia summit, we should be able to cut quite a swath through the ranks of Europe's criminal element.''

''I want to pass this on to Aaron right away and see what he thinks. This may be our chance to break this thing up quickly.''

CHAPTER FIFTEEN

Stony Man Farm, Virginia

Gregor Rostoff's name wasn't entirely new to Aaron Kurtzman; he had come across it before. His files contained a reference to the Russian in a report about Red Army drug smuggling during the war in Afghanistan. Back then, Rostoff had been a highly decorated colonel of a guards regiment specializing in counterguerrilla tactics. He fell from grace when he masterminded a gruesome scheme to ship heroin to Russia packed in coffins with the bodies of Red Army casualties. When one of the coffins went astray and was opened, Rostoff had been court-martialed and sent to prison for his crimes. Obviously he had been freed and was now back in business.

Kurtzman wasn't surprised to find a man like him as the guiding hand behind the Russian Mafia. For one thing, it keyed in with other references he had picked up about ex-military personnel being heavily involved in the Russian criminal underground. It took a special kind of man to control an organization of trained soldiers, presumably combat veterans from Afghanistan, and Rostoff's rank and personal combat record would give him that caveat. Secondly a man who would ship drugs back with his own combat-dead was cold enough to do almost anything.

That also keyed into bits and pieces he had been picking up about the renewed activity among certain European terrorist groups like the Italian Red Brigades and the IRA. Now that the Soviet Union was no more, the European terrorist groups had lost their traditional paymaster and had been forced to turn to nonpolitical crime to support themselves. They, too, would feel right at home joining what was, in effect, a paramilitary criminal organization. This was something that needed to be tracked.

The best piece of information Katz had picked up, however, was the tip about the criminal summit meeting in Budapest. That had great possibilities. If Rostoff was calling all of those dogs together in the same kennel, it could only mean that he was confident that he would come out of it the top dog. Considering who he was trying to put the arm on, it was a gutsy move.

This meeting could be a great chance for Stony Man to make a sweep of the heads of the European underground. They could go for a mass killing or a selective culling of the group. On the surface, it was a very attractive idea. Maybe, though, it was too attractive. He was glad that Hal Brognola wasn't in on this one because he knew the big Fed would want to go for it without considering the alternatives. After thinking it through completely, however, Kurtzman decided that he would recommend that Katz's team not take that obvious route and avoid going for the kill.

For one thing, they would be going up against a small army. And, unlike the Dresden and Munich hits, there would be almost no chance of achieving surprise. The heads of the various organizations would be paranoid, and being in the same hotel with so many competitors would set off all of their alarm bells. They would be on the lookout for betrayal. Short of blowing up the hotel with everyone in it, it would be almost impossible to take them out.

That wasn't to say, however, that the summit couldn't be exploited to their advantage. As inviting a target as it was, there was another tack they could take that might be even more productive in the long run.

Killing the heads of the Western gangs in Budapest wouldn't defuse the threat posed by the Russian Mafia. At best, it would simply put things off for a few months until the gangs could pick new leaders. It might also create a power vacuum in

Western Europe that Rostoff would rush to fill. And, even without having a good profile on Rostoff, from what little was known about his recent activities, he wouldn't pass up an opportunity like that.

Moreover, even killing Rostoff himself might not solve the Russian situation. Since he had so little information on the details of Rostoff's organization, he couldn't make that assessment. For instance, he didn't know if his second-in-command was more of a threat than he was and if killing Rostoff would only make matters worse.

To make an impact on the activities of the Russian Mafia, as well as get payback for Schwarz and Blancanales, they needed to take the long-term view this time. They needed to burrow deeper and gather more information until they could strike at the heart, not only the head, of the organization. And the Budapest summit was a perfect place to do exactly that. There were few places that were as easy to gather information than in a hotel.

Knowing Mafia chieftains the way he did, Kurtzman figured that to insure their security, they would want to take over one complete floor of the hotel for their own use and damn the cost. That's what American capos would do, and he didn't think that the mental processes of their European counterparts were that much different. That would limit the area that would have to be covered.

Then, since this was the late-nineties, these modern gangsters would be using the latest electronic gadgets to talk to one another and their home bases. And nothing that was said over an unscrambled electronic communication device was private. He would call up an NSA electronic intercept bird and park it over Budapest for those few days and see what he could filter out of the electronic background babble of an entire city.

The best eavesdropping, however, would be from inside the hotel itself. Not having the services of Gadgets Schwarz would make that task a little more difficult. But he could see that the team received enough devices to adequately cover the event.

Quickly drawing up an equipment list, he e-mailed it to John Kissinger with instructions to start packing and shipping ASAP. He didn't need to caution him about security this time. Allowing Brognola to stumble onto that one shipment had been lesson enough. He hated seeing the Farm operating with this level of internal security, but until Hal decided to join the revolt, they had no choice but to continue locking him out.

After blocking out a tentative plan for the Budapest operation, he uplinked it to Katzenelenbogen for comment and refinement.

France

"THIS IS a bunch of bullshit, Katz." Carl Lyons was the first Stony Man commando to respond to

Kurtzman's proposed plan. "I don't believe the Bear came up with something like this. If I get that Russian bastard in my sights, I'm going to waste his sorry ass."

The Stony Man team was still in southern France while they worked on leads and planned where to hit next.

"Carl," Bolan said, "Aaron's right this time. We'll get Rostoff, you can take that one to the bank. But I want to take down his entire organization when we do it. We may have cut Hal out of the loop on this, but if we can carry out the original mission, I still want to do it."

"Okay, okay." Lyons slowly shook his head. "I'll buy a sneak-and-peek this time. But—" his eyes locked on Bolan "—if I happen to come across Rostoff, he's going down."

With that settled, the three of them got back to working out the details.

"It's been awhile since any of us have been to Budapest," Bolan pointed out to Katz, "so you might want to have Kurtzman fax us a briefing packet and current maps."

"I've got that coming," the Israeli replied. "Plus our hotel reservations."

Stony Man Farm, Virginia

HAL BROGNOLA KNEW that something big was going down. Even with everyone giving him the silent treatment on everything except the most trivial happenings, he could feel it. He had headed this group since its inception, and he could read faces as well as the next guy. Something major was being planned, and he wanted to be in it.

He had been keeping track of Stony Man's European exploits as best he could by reading the press reports and watching CNN with a critical eye. The bloody restaurant raid in Dresden had been followed by another Executioner-style shoot-out at a warehouse full of Russian military small arms in Munich. Again, the body count had been impressive. There had also been a minor exercise at a dockside warehouse in Marseilles, an unexplained fire that had destroyed a shipment of machinery destined for Africa, or so the firm controlling the warehouse reported. The problem with that explanation was that he knew the company was a front for one of the major Italian Mafia operations.

There had been no body count that time, so he wasn't sure if that incident could be properly chalked up to Bolan and the others. But he had a hunch that it could. It had been too surgical, and the use of thermite to destroy the "machinery" bore their stamp. The only thing he couldn't figure was why they had hit that target so gently. It was almost as if it had been a demonstration or a warning to show someone what they could do if they really wanted to.

Curiously enough, even with all this going down, the President hadn't asked him for an update. The Man had accepted his lame explanation that the loss of the van had put the team temporarily out of communication and that their equipment would have to be replaced before they could continue the operation. Since then, fortunately for Price and the rest of the insurrectionists, the President had been occupied putting out political fires with Mexico and visiting natural disasters in California. Hopefully his schedule would stay that full for at least another week.

By that time, Brognola hoped that he would be able to break through the code of silence that had shut him out. He knew, though, that his only chance to do that was to get through to Kurtzman. Price had made up her mind about him, and he knew that she wasn't going to change it anytime in the near future. Not until the Russians were completely out of the picture. Betrayal was one of her least-favorite things, and, though she hadn't come right out and said it, he knew that she held the President accountable for the tragedy in Prague.

He hoped, though, that he would be able to get through to Kurtzman and make him understand that he could be trusted to help with whatever they had going down.

BROGNOLA FOUND Kurtzman working late again. But then Kurtzman always worked late. In fact, except for meals, which he often ate while working, or when he was sleeping, the Bear was almost always in his den.

Glancing at Kurtzman's monitor as he approached, he saw that the screen was covered with what looked like a sea chart of the Atlantic Ocean. He had no idea of what that had to do with anything, and he suspected that Kurtzman was probably just using it as a screen saver to keep him from seeing what he was really working on.

"Aaron," he said, "we need to talk."

"Pull up a chair," Kurtzman said as he wheeled his chair away from the keyboard and turned. "What's on your mind, Hal?"

"The same thing that's on everyone else's mind around here."

"Well, as you can see, I'm working on one of my pet projects, but I don't think that anyone else around here is really interested in Type 21 U-boat movements during the last three days of the Third Reich. I'm still trying to find the one that carried all that gold away."

"Cut the crap, Aaron." Brognola was really tired of being sandbagged every time he tried to talk to anyone. "I want you to pass on a message to Barbara because I can't seem to talk to her."

"So what's the message, Hal?"

Brognola took a deep breath. "I've decided to hang it up when this thing is over, Aaron. Win, lose or draw, I think I've about outlived my usefulness around here. Believe it or not, I still have a wife and family, and I'd like to spend some time with them."

Hearing that shocked Kurtzman almost speechless. More than anyone else, the big Fed had been the driving force behind the Sensitive Operations Group from the very beginning. He had used his extensive experience with both the FBI and Justice Department to create the situation that allowed Stony Man Farm to exist in plain sight without so much as showing up as a blip on anyone's radar. He had also used his stature as an experienced crime fighter to draw in the men who made up both Able Team and Phoenix Force.

Nonetheless, he had a point. None of them were growing younger, and maybe it was time that all of them moved on. After the mission was finished, though. The mission always came first.

"It won't be the same around here without you, Hal," Kurtzman said sincerely. "But I don't think that we'll be together all that much longer anyway. I don't know how much longer we can keep this up without the Man going ballistic and shutting us down."

"But that's what I'm trying to prevent, Aaron,"

Brognola said. "I don't want to see us shut down. The President needs us, and so does the nation."

"You said 'us,' Hal. And there is no 'us' right now as far as you're concerned. We came up against a problem, we lost two of our people and you couldn't see your way clear to do what had to be done to keep it from happening again. You can't serve two masters, Hal, no one can. I realize that you work for the President, we all do, and you should have resigned rather than risk sending the teams into something like this."

Kurtzman leaned forward in his chair. "And don't try to tell me that the teams get paid to put their lives on the line. You give me that line, and I'm going to retire your ass right here and now."

When Brognola didn't respond, Kurtzman continued. "The difference this time is that you let the President loan our people out to deal with something that the Russians should have been taking care of themselves. Then, the worst thing is that this mission ties us to an intelligence source that gives us bad information and we lose Gadgets and Rosario."

"I think that's a little harsh to say that I 'let' any of this happen, Aaron."

Kurtzman knew he had his old friend on the ropes, but he didn't back off. This had to be faced. "Did you do anything to keep it from happening?"

"No," Brognola admitted, "I didn't. But I want to keep it from happening again."

"And just how do you think that you're going to do that?"

"By joining the revolt," Brognola said seriously. "I'm ready to put on a red armband, paint my ass blue or whatever I have to do to mark me as being one of the good guys around here."

Kurtzman had to laugh. "Try the ass paint. That should go over big-time in the Oval Office."

"I won't be seeing the inside of the Oval Office until this is over and I hand in my resignation."

Kurtzman locked eyes with his old friend. "You're serious about that, aren't you?"

Brognola met his gaze. "I am."

Kurtzman smiled. "Welcome aboard. I'll get you a red armband as soon as the quartermaster shows up. I think that we're temporarily out of blue ass paint."

"And—" he switched screens on his monitor "—while you're waiting to be sworn in, I might as well fill you in on what we've come up with so far."

"That would be a good place to start." Brognola grinned. "But, first, I think I need a cup of your coffee. You want me to top yours?"

"Since you're up."

CHAPTER SIXTEEN

Budapest, Hungary

The Hungarian capital city of Budapest was split by the broad, curving sweep of the Danube river. In past centuries, the city had, in fact, been two separate entities, Buda and Pest, and even now, the locals still regarded them as such. Buda was on the west bank of the river, nestled in low hills. Pest to the east marked the start of the plains that were home to the famous horsemen of the Magyar peoples.

Near the famous castle on the west side of the river stood the Gellert Hotel. This grand edifice was a survivor from Budapest's glory days of the thirties when it had been a favorite haunt of Europe's aristocracy and royalty. It had suffered during the years of Soviet occupation, but now that it had been completely refurbished, it was once again *the* place to stay in the city. This time around, however, it catered to the nouveau aristocracy of the Eastern

Republics who has access to hard currencies instead of long, but poverty-stricken, noble pedigrees.

This meant that up-and-coming politicians rubbed elbows with budding young capitalists, wealthy businessmen, TV personalities and, most of all, gangsters in the hotel's posh lounges and dining rooms. With this kind of monied clientele, the Gellert also drew the young beauties of a city long known for the beauty of its women, and the grand hotel was once more the place to be seen in the city.

It was to this renewed center of Budapest that dozens of Europe's gang leaders came for Gregor Rostoff's conference. None of them particularly were looking forward to it, but they all had their reasons not to have declined the invitation. Some of them were coming because they didn't want any more trouble from the Russians, some because they wanted a chance to personally assess their opposition and still others wanted to see what they might be able to gain from an alliance with the new players.

Rostoff also had several goals in mind for his summit. For one, he wanted to try to deal with the predation that had been eating away at his operations in both Western and Eastern Europe. If the Americans were responsible as Detlov thought, that was one thing. But if it was the competition, he wanted to put an end to it by agreement. Lastly he, too, wanted to make a personal evaluation of the men he would one day either control or destroy.

One way or the other, by the end of the conference, he fully intended to be the top crime boss in Europe. How many people he would have to kill to get that job would depend on what happened over the next two or three days. Hopefully, though, his plans would meet with approval. It would be far easier on everyone if they decided to follow his lead on their own.

THE STONY MAN TEAM was on hand for the opening day of Rostoff's venture, and they had no problem picking out the invited players from the rest of the guests at the Gellert Hotel. While the gangsters were less flashy than their American Mafia counterparts, there was still a look, an attitude that went with their line of work. In a town where success called for high fashion, the gangsters always took the look to extremes. Nonetheless, they looked nice in the pictures the watchers were taking so Kurtzman could try to ID them from his mug-shot file.

It was also easy to tell that most of the lower-level gunmen who accompanied their bosses weren't very happy about being where they were. In a place like the Gellert Hotel, it was almost impossible for them to guard their principals when there were so many people coming and going all the time. But, with the top floor reserved it would be somewhat easier.

"Why don't you let Calvin and I take a crack at being the main inside team?" Hawkins asked Katz.

"There's no way that you and Calvin are ever going to blend in with the locals," David McCarter said with a laugh. "In case you lads haven't noticed yet, there aren't all that many blacks in Hungary."

"But we won't need to blend in," Hawkins pointed out. "We can go as who we are, two Americans touring Europe."

"Some tour," James replied. "Visit the Old World, kill a few people and blow things up. It sounds like a Marine Corps recruitment poster motto."

Hawkins ignored his teammate's accurate assessment of their operation so far. "But that way we'll get tagged as Americans early on and we can draw the opposition's attention while the rest of you guys do your thing."

"What do you think, Mack?" Katz asked Bolan.

The Executioner shrugged. "That approach has worked before, but we need to send in some of the others, as well. David can go in as a British freelancer. He always looks like he's in mufti, and he can be looking for work in the open markets of the East. You do your Israeli businessman routine and Gary can be the academic from Montreal, maybe a historian. That'll leave Rafe, Jack, Carl and me to man the van and provide backup."

"Let's do it," Hawkins said. "I'm ready for a little better class of accommodation for a change."

"Cheap rooms only for you and Calvin," Katz said sternly. "Remember, you're supposed to be Americans."

TWO HOURS LATER Hawkins was ready to make his initial recon. With a fresh shave and needing a haircut, he almost looked young enough to pass for a college student in his Texas A and M football jersey and worn blue jeans. A day pack with bottled water, a couple of guide books, a pack of smokes and the other day-trip essentials helped complete the disguise. What he didn't have was any kind of weapon or communications device. Until he tested Rostoff's security, they were playing it very close to the vest.

With James and Katz in the lobby as backup, Hawkins headed for the main elevator for the trip to the top floor Rostoff had reserved for his summit meeting. Though the elevator's button for that floor had been taped over and listed as out of order, he punched it anyway and leaned back to enjoy the ride.

When the elevator doors opened at his destination, he stepped out and was immediately blocked by two large guards. "This floor had been reserved," one of the guards said in English. "No one is allowed up here."

Hawkins managed to looked surprised. "But this girl told me that there was a party going on up here and she invited me to come up."

"There is no party here," the second man growled.

Just then one of the doors opened, a girl walked out and turned to go down the hall.

"Can I ask her about the party?" Hawkins started to follow the woman.

The first guard blocked his path and slipped his hand under his unbuttoned jacket. "She is none of your affair. You will leave now."

When Hawkins hesitated, the second guard grabbed him and spun him. He allowed himself to be spread-eagled against the wall.

"Hey, guys! What's going on?" he asked, letting his voice quaver.

The guard who patted him down was a pro. The guy pulled all his pockets inside out and even made him take off his shoes.

When the search was over, he was spun again and pushed back against the wall while the first guard spoke into a handheld radio. When he got his reply, he motioned for the other guard to lead him back to the elevator.

"Don't come back," he said when the doors opened.

"Okay, okay, guys." Hawkins raised his open hands as he stepped backward into the elevator. "I get the message."

When he reached the bottom floor, he walked out to one of the tables on the patio and slid into the chair next to Calvin James.

"I see you got out alive," the ex-SEAL commented.

"This time. I need a beer."

THAT EVENING Gary Manning and David McCarter were both in the hotel's main lounge, but they weren't sitting together. Manning had taken a table by the entrance and McCarter was on a stool at the bar. This gave the two of them complete coverage of the area, and they were unobtrusively watching the other customers as they sipped their drinks.

They were also paying close attention to the whispered conversations at the tables against the back wall where tough-looking men with bulges in their jackets drank beer and watched the women in the lounge. The miniature directional microphones McCarter and Manning were both wearing picked up their words and transmitted them to the van where Katzenelenbogen was translating from several languages.

He was also sending the raw transmissions to Stony Man Farm for in-depth translation and review. So far, all he had was bar talk. The security men for Europe's major gang leaders knew better than to run their mouths in a bar.

Nonetheless, even the most closely guarded individual might slip up once in a while.

CHAPTER SEVENTEEN

Budapest, Hungary

"I sure as hell wish that Gadgets was here to help us with this," T. J. Hawkins muttered as he and Gary Manning tried to position a bulky parabolic microphone in front of the open window of a cramped top-floor room in a small hotel across the river from the Gellert. "He'd have this damned thing set up and running in no time."

Manning grunted his agreement as he fought a bulky lock on one of the tripod legs. It had been dented in shipment from the Farm and refused to lock down properly.

The electronic surveillance phase of the operation wasn't going as smoothly as Katz would have liked. The cellular phone intercepts were working just fine, but they weren't picking up much from them. Apparently Prince Charles's widely publicized cell phone problems had alerted everyone to be careful what they said. Hopefully the parabolic microphone would give them additional coverage by picking up the vibrations from the windows along the top floor of the Gellert.

Everyone might know about the dangers of saying anything indiscreet over a cell phone. But few knew that a normal conversation in a room could be picked up from outside the window glass. It took a special type of microphone to detect and amplify the faint vibrations, but they had secured one through the Farm's clandestine contacts in the Langley labs. Who said that the CIA had never done anything for the betterment of humankind?

"Got it," Manning finally announced. "Now let's fire this thing up and get the feed to Katz on-line."

"It's about time," Hawkins replied. "I'll tell you what. I'll flip you to see who has to take the first shift baby-sitting this damned thing."

"Only if we use my coin," Manning said, grinning. "I know all about your two-headed quarters."

"Bummer. I've got to get a new scam. You want to draw cards?"

"Not with your deck."

CARL LYONS SIPPED his beer and watched as the limousines pulled up to the front of the Gellert. Some of the crime bosses and their bodyguards who climbed in for the ride back to the airport didn't look happy. Some of them, though, had obviously made very good deals with their newly acknowledged overlord. Russian weapons and Afghan hashish were going to become as common in Europe as hamburgers and French fries if Interpol didn't shut it down quickly.

Lyons didn't have to count the passengers to know that three of their number would be going home as cargo, if they went back at all. For the past few nights, he'd taken out three known gangsters in an attempt to even the score for Pol and Gadgets. That was three more he had chalked up on his personal scoreboard, but it didn't make him feel any better. He wouldn't feel that he had done his job until he had his hands around the neck of that Russian bastard Rostoff and squeezed until his eyeballs popped out.

"We're ready to roll," Manning said as he walked up to the table. "Katz wants to get on the road as soon as we can."

"Where're we going next?"

"He wants to go back to the west, France again."

"Whatever." Lyons pushed back his chair and reached into his pocket to leave a tip for the waiter. "Let's do it."

WHILE JACK GRIMALDI drove the van, Katzenelenbogen, Bolan, Lyons and McCarter went over the material they had compiled during their three-day surveillance of Rostoff's Budapest summit. Most of the leads they had picked up weren't very helpful in their search for inside information about Rostoff's organization. The Russian had been very careful about what he had mentioned about his operation. So careful, in fact, that most of their intercepts only pertained to the operations of the European gangs.

New drug markets had been blocked out and assigned, new properties had been designated as storage areas and new transportation routes had been mapped. Each gang had signed up for certain numbers of the small arms that were being made available, as well as the increased hashish production. Put together it was an extensive, comprehensive operation, more than doubling the operations that were already up and running. If these plans were allowed to be carried out, Western Europe would start looking a lot like South Central L.A.

But, as valuable as those tips were, they would be passed on to Interpol or to the national police agencies of the nations involved to deal with. There was one operation, however, that Katz thought Stony Man needed to get involved with immediately.

"This one," he said. "I picked up with the parabolic mike. It appears that our friend Rostoff had to grant a concession to the Marseilles mob to get them to come on board. It was the price they demanded before they were willing to give him a piece of their action.''

''What kind of deal is it?'' Lyons asked.

''There's this French cop, a prison director in northern France, who's got seven of their top boys in his slammer and they want to get them out. Rostoff offered to kidnap this guy's family and force him to transfer these prisoners so they can be freed while they're in transit.''

''Who are the prisoners?''

''Some Marseilles bigwigs and a couple of their best gunmen.''

''That's just the kind of people we like to see back on the streets.''

''That's what I was thinking,'' Katz agreed. ''And, to make it even more interesting, Rostoff's going to use some of his terrorist troops on this one, the IRA.''

''When's this supposed to go down?'' the Executioner asked.

''The day after tomorrow.''

''Is there anything we can do to turn this around for that cop?'' Lyons asked.

''We could deal ourselves a hand in this one,'' McCarter said. ''And it wouldn't be too far off the mark from what we've been trying to do here. Since this is one of Rostoff's plays, anyone we take down will be one of his boys. And,'' he said, shrugging, "the more of them we zero, the better it's going to be for us later when we take him out."

"I vote that we decide to make a play on this one," Bolan said as he looked around the van. "Anyone opposed?"

No one opposed having a chance to take out some IRA killers while freeing a man's kidnapped wife and children. If they could pull this off, it was the kind of operation that made everyone feel good.

"Okay then," McCarter said. "What do we know about the details?"

Katz flipped through the printout of the conversation. "Well, we have both the time and the place as well as the safehouse where the wife and kids will be held."

"Do we have numbers?" Lyons asked.

"It won't be that bad," Katz reported. "Rostoff's assigned eight gunmen to the operation. Three to handle the kidnapping and the rest to take care of the hijacking of the prison van."

McCarter grinned. "Hell, that's only a one-to-one ratio, piece of cake. And they're IRA. I always relish taking them out."

Katz started making notes as he flipped through the papers. "Okay, here's the setup. The hostages are supposed to be taken to..."

CHAPTER EIGHTEEN

Stony Man Farm, Virginia

Yakov Katzenelenbogen had transmitted hundreds of pages of material from the Budapest-stakeout intercepts back to the Farm. Most of the information, however, wasn't very useful. But that was the way that kind of surveillance usually went. It always took hours and hours of watching and waiting before you got those few minutes that made the effort worthwhile. Nonetheless, Aaron Kurtzman went over every last line Katz had sent. There was no way to tell when that one bit would pop out that would make all the difference.

After he had carefully gone through the information, he forwarded it directly to Hal Brognola. Kurtzman had linked a back channel to the computer terminal in the big Fed's office, and he, too, was going over the Budapest material as quickly as it came in. Most of it was what he had expected, useful in the long run, but not very enlightening for their immediate purposes.

That was why he went down to the Computer Room and was there when Katzenelenbogen called to let Kurtzman know that they were going after the IRA gunmen who had kidnapped the French cop's family.

"Isn't that a little far afield from their original mission?" Brognola asked carefully after Katz hung up.

"Not really," Kurtzman answered. "As a tactic to bring Rostoff's men out into the open, I think it fits in well with the rest of what they've been doing."

"If it will help," Brognola suggested, "I have a contact in the French justice department that I could call and let them take care of it themselves."

"But," Kurtzman pointed out, "we don't know if Rostoff has a man in the French government as well. The way Katz has planned it, the guys will come down on them out of thin air and he'll have to know that it's us hitting him again. If he doesn't want his empire to start coming apart before it's up and running, he's going to have to break cover and come after us himself."

"You've got a point," Brognola conceded.

Part of Brognola's proof of his change of heart was that he was letting Katzenelenbogen, Kurtzman and Price run this operation without putting in his two cents' worth every ten minutes. He was a hands on kind of guy, but this time he knew that he really needed to butt out.

"I guess we'll just have to see how it comes out, won't we?"

"From where I sit," Kurtzman replied, "that's always the hardest part of this game. And, if you don't mind, how about disappearing again while I let Barbara know what's going to go down?"

Brognola grinned. "I'm out of here."

France

NICOLE CHAVALL HAD BEEN the wife of a police officer for almost twenty years, and she knew what to expect from her IRA terrorist captors. She was fully aware that her chances of getting out of this situation alive were very slim. She would miss her husband, Chief Inspector Maurice Chavall, and she knew that he would be lost without her. But the two of them could endure it. Before her husband had been promoted to the position of director of the regional prison, he had headed one of France's elite counterterrorist units. Because of that, the specter of death had hung over both of them for many years, and each had prepared to meet it with dignity whenever it came.

She had seen the looks that her kidnappers had given her, and she knew what she was going to have to endure before she died. Though she was no longer young, she knew that she was still a striking woman.

While she could be calm enough about her own fate, she was concerned about her children. She and Maurice had had their children late in life and the girls were still quite young, the oldest not yet twelve. There was no way that they could be anything other than completely terrified, and death would come hard for them. The thought of her two precious girls dying under any circumstances was unbearable. The thought of what they would go through here in this remote old farmhouse put her on the edge of madness.

She knew, though, that the girls' best hope was for their mother to keep her wits about her and remain calm. Falling into panic, weeping and begging, wasn't going to help her or the girls. If she appeared calm, however, and strong, it might help them.

She would be stronger and more calm if she thought that there was any hope of their being rescued. The IRA gunmen, however, had delighted in explaining to her in great detail how unlikely that was.

CALVIN JAMES AND T. J. HAWKINS moved in on the remote farmhouse like shadows. The night was clear, but the moon hadn't risen, giving them the maximum protection of the cover of darkness. The thin light from the windows of the target building gave them more than enough light to see without their night-vision goggles.

A hundred yards away on a supporting position on the hill overlooking the farmhouse, Gary Manning scanned the approaches and the grounds with the nightscope of his silenced M-21 sniper rifle. He usually preferred to use his Remington Model 700 for this kind of work, but in a situation like this where he might have to engage multiple targets in a hurry, he needed the semiauto capability of the military long gun. Supposedly there were only three gunmen inside with the hostages, but he had to be prepared for more.

The rifle's magazine was loaded with Match Grade 7.62 mm rounds, fitted with some of Cowboy Kissinger's special projectiles so that one hit was all it would take for him to bring down his targets. In a hostage rescue situation, you had to put the bad guys down fast.

When James and Hawkins reached their assault positions, they checked over their weapons, silenced H&K MP-5 SDs and flash-bang grenades, standard kit for a hostage rescue. Hawkins's subgun was loaded with the 9 mm Glazer rounds, which had been designed for first round stops without punching holes through the walls. These rounds were loaded with miniature shotgunlike projectiles encased in a plastic bullet. When they struck flesh, the plastic bullet opened up, releasing the multiple pellets like a shotgun's blast. But when they hit a hard surface, they didn't penetrate.

On soft targets, such as humans, the Glazers were deadly, but all a target had to do to be safe was to take cover behind something thin. That was why James's MP-5 was loaded with standard 9 mm hardpoints that would punch through doors and interior walls. The two of them would go in together, with Hawkins taking the primary shots and James backing him up in case someone ducked for cover.

When they were ready, they click-coded back to Manning that they were in place, and he passed it on to Katz. The Phoenix Force warriors had to stay in position until they received a call from Katz that the van had been taken. If the van phase went bad, however, they would still go on their end and try to make their part of the plan work.

Or, if the IRA gunmen made a move on the hostages, they would also go in and hope that they weren't too late.

CHIEF INSPECTOR Maurice Chavall was well aware that he was a walking dead man. Were it not for his wife and daughters, he would go out in a blaze of glory and try to take a few of the bastards with him. But as long as there was any chance at all that his family would be released unharmed, he couldn't risk it. Until he knew that Nicole and the children were dead, he had to do exactly as he had been told in the vain hope that it would somehow keep them safe.

The phone call that had started his nightmare had caught him completely off guard. He had worked counterterrorism assignments for a long time, but he had never thought that his family would ever become targets.

When he got over his shock, he had followed his orders exactly. He had arranged for the night-time transfer of the seven Marseilles mobsters and was riding in the van himself. In the guise of secrecy, the van wasn't marked and he had only a driver with him. His second-in-command had thought that a bit strange, but had obeyed his orders and had sent one of his best men to drive.

The route he had been told to take was off the main highway and ran through the countryside, a perfect route for an ambush. Several kilometers short of the arranged meeting point, Chavall was shocked to see a civilian car blocking the road and a man standing in the beams of the headlights. He didn't know what this was, but he ordered the driver to stop and to remain behind the wheel while he investigated.

"I am Inspector Chavall of the National Police," he told the man. "You must move your car."

"Chief Inspector," the man replied in excellent

French, "I am Agent Johnson of the CIA. We need to talk."

Chavall didn't know what the CIA had to do with this, but he was willing to listen.

"We know that your wife and children are being held captive by IRA terrorists," the American said. "And I know that you are transporting notorious criminals that they intend to set free."

"How do you know this?" Chavall was worried. As was always the drill in these kinds of incidents, he had been told that if he contacted the police the hostages would be killed. Having someone else in on it, anyone, was just as dangerous.

"Let's just say that I have contacts within the organization that set this up. Right now, I have men in place around the farmhouse where your family is being held. When I give them a call, they are ready to move in and free them."

"Can this be done without causing them harm?"

"As you well know, Chief Inspector, nothing is certain in a situation like this. But my men are experts at hostage rescue. If your wife and children can be rescued, we can do it."

Chavall didn't know how these Americans had learned of his dilemma, but this was no time to look a gift horse in the mouth. If he wasn't able to help his family, maybe they could.

"How have you planned to deal with the van hijacking?"

Katz smiled. "You will go ahead as you were instructed, but we will be on hand at the meeting place to make sure that the situation does not get out of control."

"What do I tell my driver?"

"Tell him anything you like, but keep him out of the line of fire when this goes down. We do not want him to get hurt. And," Katz added, "I want you to keep down too. You'll be no good to your family if you get killed. Just let us take care of this."

Chavall still wasn't sure why the CIA was involved with this, but he had to go along with it. "All right."

"And," Katz said, "tell your driver not to go too fast. I am going to be holding on to the rungs on the back of the van and I have only one good hand."

AT THE APPOINTED transfer site, the rest of the Stony Man team lay waiting in ambush. They had been in place for several hours, figuring that the IRA couldn't arrive until the last moment. Not knowing exactly where the IRA would put their roadblock, they had spread out on both sides of the road around the milestone marker Chavall was supposed to stop at. Thanks to Rostoff's careful, down-to-the-last-detail planning, Katz and Kurtzman had been able to ferret out enough information that nothing was being left to chance this night.

Half an hour before the appointed time for the prisoner transfer, they saw the first of the IRA gunmen move into position to set up the roadblock. They, too, had a van to transport the men they planned to free as well as a sedan to take the gunmen away. Their plan was very simple: stop the van, kill the driver and more than likely the inspector, release the mobsters in the back and simply drive away. On their way out, they would radio their comrades to execute the hostages, and all the witnesses to their crime would be gone.

Stony Man, however, intended to ruin Rostoff's carefully laid plans big-time.

When Katz radioed a warning that the police van was approaching, Bolan flashed the warning over the com link.

Lyons had retrieved his Colt Python and had it loaded with Silver Tip rounds. His SPAS-12's magazine was full of Cowboy Kissinger's home brew, frangible Magnum buckshot rounds for maximum killing power. Whatever he fired on was going down, and staying down.

He and Bolan were to take the IRA from a frontal position, while Encizo and McCarter were on each side of the road to take care of anyone who tried to break and run. With Katz arriving on the back of the police van, they had the gunmen surrounded.

The van finally pulled into sight, and when it came to a stop, the IRA gunmen closed in on it. As per Katz's instructions, neither the driver nor Chavall offered resistance. When one of the gunmen approached the driver's door, his AK ready to fire, Lyons drew down on him to take the shot that would signal the ambush.

His first .357 slug took the terrorist in the chest and slammed him on his face to the pavement.

The IRA reacted quickly, racing for the back of the van. But when Katz stepped out from behind it, his Uzi blazing, they stopped in their tracks and turned to fight, their AKs spitting return fire.

Bolan's Beretta 93-R stuttered with carefully aimed 3-round bursts in between the roar of Lyons's big Colt. Caught as they were in the open, the IRA gunmen went down fast.

When one of the Irishmen broke toward the nearby woods, Encizo stepped out and cut him down with a long burst from his Beretta Model 12.

When the last gunmen tried to escape in the van, Lyons was on him in a flash. His SPAS belching flame in the dark, he directed his fire to first the door, then to the windshield.

With Lyons's last shot, silence returned to the French countryside.

CHAVALL PICKED HIMSELF UP from the pavement and looked around. In the light from the headlights, the only men he saw still on their feet were the American commandos. The six bodies on the ground were also wearing dark clothing, but didn't have assault harnesses or night-vision goggles.

"Your prisoners are intact," Katzenelenbogen reported to him. "One of them was wounded, but it's not serious."

"What about my family?" Chavall asked in English. "Can you free them now?"

"Yes," Katz replied. "Now that this has been settled satisfactorily, I don't have to worry about the two groups alerting each other, and we can go now."

Katz took out his radio and keyed the mike. "We're clear here," he told Manning. "You can go ahead."

"Roger," Manning sent back as he click-coded the entry team. "We're moving in now."

"It is being taken care of now," he told Chavall. "It shouldn't be long."

Chavall wasn't a religious man, he had been a cop far too long to have much faith left. But he offered up a heartfelt prayer for his wife and children as well as for the Americans who were going to try to rescue them. He fervently hoped that God was listening.

CHAPTER NINETEEN

At the Farmhouse

When Gary Manning got the call from Katzenelenbogen that the van had been secured, he clicked on his com link to alert Calvin James and T. J. Hawkins that they were cleared for entry to rescue the hostages.

"We're a go," he said. "And I've got one of them in my sights right now."

"Take him out," James whispered. "That will be our cue to enter."

"On the way."

On his hilltop, Manning refocused his scope and put the IRA gunman standing in the open in the crosshairs. He had to shoot through a window, but he was confident that the round would hit within an inch of his target.

Taking up the slack on the trigger, he took a deep breath and let it out slowly. When the last of the air left his lungs and he reached that rock-solid hold, he fired.

A hundred yards away, the 7.62 mm slug drilled through the window and was deflected slightly. But it still caught the gunman high in the chest and spun him, pushing him to the floor, dead.

Hearing the window shatter, Nicole Chavall grabbed her daughters and threw them on the floor, covering them with her body. She didn't know how it had happened, but she knew that someone was attempting to rescue them. "Stay quiet, my little ones," she said. "The police are here."

Taking the shattering glass as their signal, James and Hawkins booted the door and were inside. The two remaining gunmen were going for their weapons, and one of them turned to race for the door to what had to be the back room where the hostages were held. With a shout, Hawkins targeted him first.

A 3-round burst from his H&K subgun drilled into the running man's side and lower back. He screamed and crumpled, effectively taken out of play.

At the same time, his comrade received a sustained burst of 9 mm rounds from James. He crashed onto the table, scattering beer bottles and playing cards and was dead before he hit the floor.

After checking their kills, Hawkins moved to the back room. Carefully opening the door, he shone a light and saw the woman covering her children. He didn't see any blood and figured that they were just doing the smart thing, taking cover.

"Madame Chavall?" he said as he walked in. "I don't speak French, but you are safe now. If you will come with us, ma'am, we'll take you to your husband."

Nicole didn't speak much English, but the calm words and manner of the commando told her that everything was fine now. Getting up, she pointed to her wedding ring. "My husband? Is he alive?"

Hawkins caught her gesture and smiled. "Très bien," he said with a smile. "He is okay."

Since "okay" was the one English word that almost everyone in the world understood, she knew he was alive and she finally burst into tears.

"In here, Calvin," James called over the com link.

While Hawkins awkwardly comforted the woman, James led the two girls outside. He kept their heads turned away so they wouldn't have to see the carnage in the house.

"We're clear here," he reported to Katz once he was outside. "And you can tell the inspector that his family is okay. It doesn't look like they were harmed."

"YOUR WIFE AND DAUGHTERS have been freed," Katzenelenbogen told the French inspector.

"Were they hurt?" Chavall tried to keep the anxiety out of his voice.

"My men say that they appear to be all okay."

Now that Nicole and the children were safe, Chavall could afford to ask the questions that had been forming ever since Katzenelenbogen had stopped the van. "You people are not really CIA are you?" he asked.

"No." Katz shrugged. "And it's a damned good thing for you that we're not, too. If we did work for the Company, this operation would not have worked the way it did. We only had a small window, and we had to move very quickly. Even on a good day, the CIA can't move like we can."

"This means that tomorrow morning, you will have vanished and there will be no official report about this incident, is that not correct?"

"As far as that goes," Katz replied, "we'll be out of here tonight and you'll never hear from us again."

"Good." Chavall reached down and picked up one of the fallen IRA AK assault rifles. Walking around to the back of the van, he opened the doors and faced the seven Marseilles mobsters inside. They saw what was coming and started to beg for their lives, but Chavall wasn't in the mood to listen.

The AK spit flame in the dark as he hosed them down with a long burst, slowly swinging the muzzle to make sure that they all got their proper share of the 7.62 mm slugs.

"What you have witnessed," he said grimly as he turned back to Katz and laid the AK down again, "is what all too often happens in these gang wars. My van was stopped by men from a rival gang who had a grudge against these pigs from the Marseilles mob. My driver and I were surprised and rendered unconscious and when we woke, we found that they had somehow killed one another. It is unfortunate, but this kind of violence is all too often a sad fact of life in the criminal underground."

Chavall straightened. "Now, *monsieur,* if you please. Hit me on the back of the head with your gun butt."

"Are you sure you want me to do that?"

"I am. For my story to be believed, there must be blood and an injury."

"And your driver?"

"Him too, but not so hard."

"Can do."

"One thing first—" Chavall raised one hand "—if there is anything I can ever do for you or your men, anything at all, do not hesitate to ask. Even if you want my life, you will have it. You saved my family, and nothing is too great to ask for that."

"We were glad to be able do it."

"Now," the cop said, "will you hit me?"

"My pleasure," Katz replied as he drew his pistol. "Sweet dreams."

"Thank you again with all my heart."

Katz carefully clubbed him and eased him to the ground.

Stony Man Farm, Virginia

"THEY SCORED AGAIN," Akira Tokaido reported triumphantly to Aaron Kurtzman. "It went down like clockwork and so did the bad guys, eleven of the bastards."

Aaron Kurtzman didn't smile as he mentally added that body count to the results of the European operation so far. The Stony Man team was extracting vengeance for Schwarz and Blancanales bigtime, but the operation still wasn't producing the kind of response he had hoped for. The Russians who had set up Able Team were still fighting by proxy rather than getting involved themselves. For this to turn out right, the Russians had to be sucked in so they could be cut up. And he had an idea how they could do that.

Hal Brognola was sitting beside him, scrolling through Katzenelenbogen's after-action report. Kurtzman's in-house surveillance system was getting a real workout now that Brognola had covertly joined the rebellion. He still had to be kept out of Price's sight. The screen showed that she was tied up with chores right now, so the big Fed could sit in on this one for awhile at least and lend his thoughts.

"I think we need to try to do something a little different next time, Hal," Kurtzman said.

"Something other than what we've been doing, you mean?"

Kurtzman nodded.

"But why? They're doing a real gangbuster number over there. Every time this Rostoff guy turns around, one of his operations has been put out of action. And that includes him losing valuable human assets as well. The way Lyons has been working out, Rostoff's going to start running out of people to implement his plans before too much longer, isn't he?"

"They're getting results," Kurtzman agreed. "I can't argue with that. But it's like we're fighting a hundred-legged octopus. We're just cutting off limbs, and we need to get to the brain of the monster. We have to come up with something that will bring Rostoff himself out into the open."

"What do you have in mind?"

"I want to bait the bear even more. Plus, I want to try to nail down that leak in Vallinsikov's office."

Brognola also wanted to find and fix that problem. "How do you think you can work that?"

"Well, even though you're now one of the revolutionaries, I want you to use your office as the SOG leader and send a report directly to Vallinsikov over your signature block. An operational update as it were. First, I want you to apologize for having been out of touch for so long. You know all of the political crap to smooth ruffled feathers. Then, you'll give him a rundown of everything that's happened and make sure that you give Phoenix Force and the others full credit for the Dresden, Munich and Budapest hits as well as this latest escapade."

"If we're right about the leak, that'll piss off Rostoff, but how's that going to flush him out?"

Kurtzman smiled. "Well, finally you'll tell the minister that Phoenix is going to take a short break from their efforts, a little R and R as it were, after this latest operation. You'll give him the location where they'll be staying, and you'll say that they're going to be there for at least a week."

"Set them up to be hit, you mean?"

"Sure." Kurtzman grinned. "They're big boys, and they can take care of themselves."

"But I still don't see how that is going to flush out Rostoff."

"Well, that's because you aren't devious enough. You have to remember that guy's slick, but he's also pathological. He's going to jump at the chance to get back at the men who've been causing him so much trouble. And, when it turns into a trap, he's going to be really pissed and that's the way we want him.

"Look at it this way," Kurtzman added. "A man like Rostoff thinks that he's a hell of a lot smarter than everyone else in the world. That's why he thinks that he can become the overlord of Europe's criminal underground. He's the man who would be king. And with an ego like that, he hates to be thwarted. If he bites on this one and it turns out to be a trap, he's going to want revenge. To get it, there's a good chance that he'll expose himself."

"I still don't get it," Brognola said, frowning. "Why won't he simply send in more of his terrorists?"

"Since his subordinates will have failed him again, he won't be able to trust any of his people to do it right. He'll want to do it himself to insure that it goes down right the next time."

"You may be right, but I still don't know. It was an ambush that got me in trouble in the first place."

"At least let me run this past Katz," Kurtzman said. "And let's see what he and Striker think about it. If they turn me down, we'll just keep on doing what we've been doing."

"I'll go along with that," Brognola agreed as he glanced at his watch. "But I'd better get back to counting paperclips before Barbara catches me down here with you."

Kurtzman chuckled. "This will be over soon and

then maybe we can get back to what passes for normal around here.''

''I sure as hell hope so. I'm starting to talk to myself.''

''Just as long as you don't start answering.''

Russia

BORIS DETLOV WAS TIRED of bringing his boss bad news, and he was very much aware that Rostoff was equally tired of receiving it. Since the ambush in Prague, there had been too many setbacks, both large and small, to suit either one of them. Regardless of what Rostoff thought about the Americans, Detlov saw their hand in all of this. Someone was running an operation against them and it had to be the mysterious Phoenix Force.

''You do not think that this was a leak from within the Marseilles mob?'' Rostoff asked after Detlov reported the massacre in northern France and blamed it on the American commandos.

''I doubt it,'' Detlov replied. ''I really do. Our associate in Interpol informed me that they do not have an informer in the Marseilles gang at this point in time. Their last one slipped up and ended up in an alley shot in the back of the head. That has always been a difficult group for them to infiltrate.''

''Speaking of our Marseilles associates,'' Rostoff said. ''I will have to get in contact with them quickly and try to see if I can salvage our agreement. I was counting on their input to our enterprises, and, if I cannot draw them back in, we will have a war on our hands.''

''When we find the Yankees, we can offer to let them in on the killing. That might make them feel better.''

''That is something I will suggest.''

Germany

AARON KURTZMAN'S plan to use Phoenix Force as bait for a trap went down well with the team. After freeing Chavall's family, they had gone up into Germany to await the next move in this international chess game.

''I like it,'' Carl Lyons stated. ''We get to sit tight and let the bastards come to us for a change.''

Bolan turned to Katzenelenbogen. ''What do you think?''

The Israeli swept his eyes over the Stony Man Farm fax again. ''Tactically,'' he said. ''I think it's very workable. How it's going to shake out will be up to us, of course.''

''David?'' Bolan asked.

''I'm in.'' McCarter turned to the other Phoenix Force commandos. ''What do you lads think?''

''If we pick the right location, limit the avenues of approach and all that, I'm for it,'' Gary Manning agreed. "Plus, I'll need a good place for a sniper's nest as a backup."

Trusting Katz's instincts, Rafael Encizo simply nodded.

T. J. Hawkins smiled. "It sounds like a fun way to spend a few days."

"I'll call the Farm," Katz said.

CHAPTER TWENTY

Stony Man Farm, Virginia

Later that night after everyone had turned in, Hal Brognola went back down to the Computer Room for another planning session with Aaron Kurtzman. When he learned that Katz had signed off on the ambush proposal, he started having second thoughts.

"This had better work," he said. Now that he was back with the program, at least from Kurtzman's perspective, he was being cautious. The last thing he wanted was to make any more mistakes that got someone killed.

Kurtzman, however, was very confident about this next step. "If Rostoff has a mole in Vallinsikov's office, like we know he has, I know it will. He won't be able to let a chance like this pass him by. Now that he knows Phoenix is the source of his problems, he'll want to take care of them ASAP. The loss of the Marseilles people has to have caused him a problem. He was counting on them, and he won't want anything like that to happen again.''

''I just don't like putting our guys in the crosshairs without knowing how he'll try to attack them.''

''Remember,'' Kurtzman said, ''Rostoff's military, and, more than likely, he'll opt for a military solution like he's done in the past. His Berlin operation was typically military, specifically a commando operation. Show up with overwhelming firepower, hit the objective, do your job and get the hell out. I would expect him to do the same thing this time.''

''But,'' Brognola said, playing the devil's advocate, ''sitting in a static position and playing target isn't exactly Phoenix's style.''

''They won't exactly be sitting targets,'' Kurtzman pointed out. ''Think of it more like they're in a carefully prepared defensive position.''

''But, as who the hell ever said, the best defense is a strong offense. That's always sounded right to me.''

Kurtzman smiled. ''We'll just call this the 'hornet's nest' offensive tactic, then. Instead of being ambushed, they'll be the ones doing the ambushing, and that's about as offensive as you can get. Remember, you can't be surprised if you know the other guy's coming to get you.''

"Are you going to be able to give them advance notice of when it's going down?"

"That's the only sticky part," Kurtzman admitted. "I'm getting some satellite communication interceptions from the Moscow region. But most of the stuff that I think's coming from Rostoff is encrypted. I've got Hunt and Akira working on that, and hopefully we'll break it soon."

Brognola glanced at his watch. "I'd better make myself scarce again before I get caught. What does Barbara think I'm doing with my time, anyway?"

"She thinks that I'm keeping you busy with an elaborate misinformation routine and I'll let her keep on thinking that."

"What misinformation?"

"She wants me to tell you that Phoenix is doing things that they aren't just in case you decide to bend the President's ear."

Brognola shook his head. "I'll be glad when this is over."

Russia

WHEN BORIS DETLOV WALKED into his boss's office he wore a smile for a change. Once more, their agent in the minister's office had come through. However, some of the information she had passed on to him wasn't positive. For one thing, she had been able to confirm his fears that the Americans were still operating against them and that they had been responsible for the latest setback with the Marseilles mob.

Rostoff's plans for Western Europe hinged on keeping his alliance with the powerful French gang. They were one of the largest criminal enterprises in the region and had a small army of their own. He had no doubts that the forces he had at his command would be able to completely destroy them should that become necessary, but the less combat there was, the smoother the process would go.

Since the mission to free several of their leaders had resulted in their death instead, Rostoff had reopened negotiations with the mob. But they weren't going well, and having someone to blame the murders on was very good news. It might be enough to prevent an open war, which had to be avoided at all costs.

The other European gang leaders wouldn't like it if the Russians slaughtered the French players and took over their operations by force. It would be difficult to explain it away, and they would all think that they, too, would be strong-armed at some point in time. For this operation to work the way it had been planned, there had to be honor among thieves. For a while, at least.

"We've heard from our associate in the minister's office again," he announced.

"What did she have to say?"

"The minister received a lengthy communication from the United States that confirms my suspicions that the Americans are still in the game. In fact they never left. They just went even more covert."

Rostoff looked thoughtful for a moment. "I should have listened to you more closely, old friend. It looks like you were right all along. What exactly did the message say?"

"There was an apology for having been out of communication for so long, blaming it on unspecified political problems in the White House. But, after confirming that Phoenix Force was responsible for all our recent losses, including the Marseilles men, the message went on to say that the commandos would be taking a few days off to rest and refit. Apparently a couple of them got nicked in the French shoot-out."

Rostoff's ears perked at hearing that. Hitting a unit when they were refitting was one of his favorite moves. "Did it say where they were going to stay?"

"As a matter of fact, it did. The team will be staying in Frankfurt, Germany, at a small hotel. They will be registered under their cover of being a TV news crew for the BBC."

Rostoff switched into full military mode. "We need to recon that site."

"I am already doing that. I ran a computer check and came up with a map of that area of Frankfurt, and located a floor plan for the hotel. A team from the Hamburg office is on its way there now to do a full on-site recon. They're going to register there and phone in what they find.''

"Good." Rostoff nodded. "As soon as they call in, put together a strike force. I do not want the Yankees to get away this time. And, no blank rounds, either. When it is done, I want photographs of their heads so I can make sure that we have gotten all of them.''

"Who do you want me to use for the job?''

"Since this job is in Germany, why not see if the Irish want revenge for what happened in France. I am certain that if you tell them that they will be going after the men who killed their comrades, they will insist that you give the job to them.''

Knowing how the IRA felt about revenge, Detlov could only agree. Plus, even though they had failed in France, they were still the best field operatives they had.

Stony Man Farm, Virginia

NOW THAT KATZ and Brognola had set the gears in motion for the ambush operation, Aaron Kurtzman still had one important thing left to do. He had to inform Barbara Price what was going down. After all, palace revolt or not, she was still the Stony Man mission controller and she had to know what was happening at all times. Asking the others to take a long coffee break somewhere else, he called her office and invited her down.

"What do you have, Aaron?" she asked when she walked in, pausing in front of the coffeepot to pour herself a cup.

"Well," Kurtzman said, "Katz and I have come up with an operation that we think might force Rostoff out in the open."

"What's that?" she asked as she took a tentative sip from her cup.

Taking a deep breath, he told her.

When he was finished, there was a long moment of silence.

"You and Katz are going to do what?" Price couldn't believe what Kurtzman had told her. "What's wrong with you two? We staged a revolt around here, a mutiny against the United States government, because of a setup just like that."

She shook her head in disgust. "If I didn't know any better, Aaron, I'd say that Hal Brognola had his hands in this. This is something he'd push for."

Kurtzman knew that it was time for him to jump back in before she carried that thought too much further.

"This was my idea, Barb," he said sincerely. "And I ran it past Katz and the team for their approval. As you say, we're freelance now, and nothing's going down that the guys don't get to vote on or whatever they're doing to make their decisions now."

"Whatever is more like it," she snorted. "I think you and Katz have lost your collective minds.

"Or," she added, "is this one of the Ironman's vengeance deals? He wants to suck the bastards in close so he can chop them up, and he doesn't give a damn who else gets chopped in the process?"

She leaned over his wheelchair. "That's what it is, Aaron, isn't it?"

"Barbara, it's not quite as bad as you're making it out to be."

"How bad is it, then?"

Kurtzman knew that this was the time for him to exhibit patience by the bucketful. Lyons wasn't the only one who was still working through the deaths of Schwarz and Blancanales. But Price was dealing with it entirely differently. It had made her even more protective of her men.

"As you know," he started to explain, "regardless of our successes so far, we haven't really got any closer to Rostoff than we were before we first went over there. In fact all we've learned that we didn't know back then is his name. We still don't know where he's operating out of, nor do we know anything about his command structure."

He shrugged. "In all of our operations against him, all we've really done has been to fight his proxies, his minions. We've racked up a good body count against them, that's true. But we haven't inflicted any real damage on him or the core of his operation. To put Rostoff out of action permanently and to extract the price for his having killed Schwarz and Blancanales, we have to get to him directly, and this is a way to try to do that."

Price knew that, like it or not, there was truth in his words. Dangling the bait was an important part of catching the fish.

Like it or not, and she sure as hell didn't, it made perverse sense. She could see that she had no choice but to sign on.

"You say that they're going to hole up in Frankfurt?" she asked.

He nodded, knowing that she was about to get on board. "Katz found a small hotel with limited access routes, but an inviting alley to suck them into. They're going to put the kill zone there."

She sighed and surrendered to the inevitable. "Okay. Just keep me informed and make sure that we're able to respond to anything they need to back their play. At least if this goes down as you two think it will, we'll have even more proof that the Russians can't keep their mouths shut."

"There is that," he said, trying to put the best possible spin on it. "And maybe we could use this second event to convince the President to call this thing off completely and bring them home."

"Now you're jerking my chain, Aaron. You

know that the guys aren't going to come back until they've taken care of this. I wish the damned Russian Mafia had taken over the government completely and we'd never been involved in the first place."

"I think that's what the President was trying to prevent, Barbara," Kurtzman reminded her.

When she left the room, he quickly sent a message to Brognola, who had been listening in through his back door, and told him that the operation was on and for him to make sure to keep out of her way until it was over.

Germany

CARL LYONS WAS TIRED of sitting on his hands and waiting for Rostoff's next move. He agreed that playing sitting ducks was probably a good move, but he had never liked waiting and he particularly didn't like it now. At least when he had been waiting in Budapest he had been able to take out known gangsters.

"We're being eyeballed," he reported to Katz late one night when he returned from one of his recons. "Every time I've gone out, I've spotted the same two punks hanging around. They have a room on the floor below, and they've been keeping close tabs on us."

"I'm not surprised," Katz replied. "I would expect Rostoff to have moved in a couple of his people to keep tabs on us while he sets up the hit. I wouldn't worry about them too much. We'll take them out before we leave.''

"Why wait?''

"We can't afford to act against them now,'' Katz cautioned him. "It would alert Rostoff to the fact that we're not quite as stupid as we appear to be. You're just going to have to be patient with those two as well.''

"But I want them when this goes down. They're as much a part of this as the rest of the bastards.''

"No problem, they're yours.''

Lyons smiled.

CHAPTER TWENTY-ONE

Frankfurt, Germany

On the fourth night after Phoenix Force arrived in Frankfurt, a medium-sized Mercedes delivery van marked with a bakery logo pulled up to the curb by the opening of the alley behind the Regency Hotel. The driver got out of the cab, and, after looking around, walked to the rear door of the truck and opened it. Six men quickly got out and moved into the dark alley like the experienced commando team that they were.

All of the gunmen were ex-Provisional IRA members, and they had undertaken dozens of missions like this before. Even the fact that they were going up against well-armed targets wasn't a new experience for them. The extensive training they had received at a PLO-run camp in the Libyan desert had been as good as any in the world. In the past, they had put that training to good use against both British army troops and armed units of the

Ulster Defense Force and the Royal Ulster Constabulary.

As "freedom fighters" went, the IRA was among the best in the world. But the Provisional IRA had fallen on hard times and had been forced to hire out to the Russian Mafia to raise funds for their continuing "struggle" against British imperialism. Even though peace had been brokered in Ireland, the fight, for some, would continue.

This mission, however, they were doing free. When they had learned that they were being asked to take out the Yankees who had killed their comrades in France, the question of taking payment from Rostoff was quickly put aside. The IRA had a long tradition of avenging their comrades' deaths as a point of honor. These Yankees would die blood for blood.

The Irishmen were also well-armed and equipped for this assignment. One of the advantages of working for Rostoff was that the Russian believed in providing adequate firepower for his operatives. Each of the gunmen carried a 5.45 mm AK-74 assault rifle and a 9 mm Makarov semiauto pistol as his basic weapons. Additionally, some of them also carried demolition charges and concussion grenades. After killing the Yankees, they were going to demolish the hotel.

For personal equipment, they had been given individual radios and night-vision goggles to go with their assault harnesses and black combat suits, balaclavas and rubber-soled boots. They were close to invisible and silent as they moved to their objective.

THE STONY MAN WARRIORS were more than ready to greet their nocturnal visitors. The Irish terrorists hadn't arrived unannounced. Even though Phoenix had lost the services of Gadgets Schwarz and his masterful electronic wizardry, they were not without adequate early-warning devices. The alley was wired, and the raiders had been spotted the moment they stepped out of their vehicle into the street.

Preparations had also been made to insure that the Irish assassins wouldn't get beyond the ambush kill zone in the middle of the alley. Bolan didn't intend to give these men a chance to surrender and be taken into custody. This would be a killing, pure and simple, and its primary purpose was to rid Europe of six dedicated Provo terrorists who had walked the earth far too long. And if taking out this team enraged Rostoff, forced him to show his hand, so much the better.

"The drag has entered the alley," Manning reported on the last man in the group from his rooftop position on the other side of the street from the mouth of the alley.

"Copy," Bolan radioed back.

Now that the targets were all in the kill zone, it

was time to take them out. He clicked in his com link. "Take them down."

Manning centered the crosshairs of his eight power sniper scope on the drag, the last man in the formation. At that close range, the scope had been mounted on his silenced H&K MP-5 SD instead of the sniper's rifle he had been using lately. A short squeeze on the trigger sent a burst of subsonic hollowpoint slugs downrange.

Arching his back with the impact of the 9 mm rounds, the IRA gunman spun and went down, his weapons clattering to the pavement.

Almost as one, the other five gunmen whirled to face the threat, but it was too late for them to do anything except die.

Even with their night-vision gear they had failed to see the M-18 Claymore mines fixed to the walls at knee height and angled slightly upward. The four directional antipersonnel mines were connected with matte-black detonation cord so they would all detonate within a microsecond of one another.

Bolan squeezed the handle of the Clacker firing device and the four Claymores went off as one.

As the blast echoed off the building's brick walls, over two thousand .25-caliber steel balls slashed through the alley like the long Scottish broadsword the mines had been named after.

The alley was wide, but the way the Claymores

had been positioned, there was no place for the gunmen to take cover from the bullet-fast projectiles.

When the smoke cleared, the six terrorists were laying sprawled in the alley. Each of them had soaked up enough Claymore pellets to have killed them several times over. Nonetheless, from his rooftop position, Manning used his scope to put an insurance shot into the head of each of the IRA gunmen.

Neither Bolan nor Manning bothered to go into the alley to check their handiwork. No one could have survived the Claymores, and there was no reason to search the bodies. These men had been experienced terrorists, and they wouldn't be carrying anything of interest. They would have "sterilized" themselves for the mission, and they would go that way to the morgue.

"We're clearing out now," Bolan radioed to David McCarter, who was waiting with Katz in the van, "and heading for the pickup point."

"Copy, we're on the way."

On the way out of the room, Carl Lyons broke off to take care of one last little bit of business they had left undone. He had not forgotten the two thugs who had tailed him on his walks through the neighborhood. They were Rostoff's minions as well, and would be added to the body count tonight.

On the next floor down, he listened for a moment to the excited voices behind the door of room 37.

There was no way to silence something like a Claymore, and everyone in the hotel had been awakened by the blasts. Satisfied that he had the right place, he made his move.

Booting in the door smashed the flimsy lock and sent it flying open. Inside the small room, the two thugs turned from the window as one to see the muzzle of Lyons's SPAS-12 shotgun tracking them. Both had their guns in their hands, but they weren't quick enough.

The SPAS roared once, twice and both men were slammed backward by the blasts of frangible buckshot.

Leaving their bleeding, broken bodies behind, Lyons hurried down the stairs to the waiting van.

Stony Man Farm, Virginia

WITH THE TIME difference between Europe and the East Coast of the U.S., it was day when the attempted hit went down in Frankfurt. Barbara Price was waiting in the Computer Room when Katzenelenbogen came on the line to make his report. It took but a moment to run it through the decryption program to put it in plain text.

"You and Katz were lucky this time," she said after reading Katz's message. "But I don't want to see anymore harebrained plans like that being cooked up without checking with me first."

Kurtz checked his smile. "Yes ma'am."

"Where are they going next?"

"Katz wants to try Berlin again."

She frowned. "I would have thought that they had used up their welcome there with the flak tower job."

"He thinks it'll be okay and plans to stay in the old eastern sector this time."

"Speaking of 'this time,' you'd better keep me informed this time."

"Will do."

Russia

"COLONEL," BORIS DETLOV said after knocking on the open door to Gregor Rostoff's office, "we have a problem."

Rostoff looked up from his paperwork. Detlov didn't call him by his rank unless it was something he couldn't handle on his own.

"The Americans set us up."

"What do you mean?"

"The IRA team we sent to Frankfurt was wiped out without firing a shot."

Rostoff's eyes narrowed. "What happened?"

"Apparently the Americans knew that they were coming and were laying in wait for them. They were making the approach to the target when they were ambushed in the alley behind the hotel with antipersonnel mines, the ones the Yankees call Claymores.''

Rostoff knew the American Claymore mines well. The Muji guerrillas in Afghanistan had used them against his troops. The directional mines fired hundreds of deadly .25-caliber steel balls. Used in an alley, there would be no way to escape them.

''They knew our people were coming,'' Detlov repeated, ''and that may mean that Marina has turned against us.''

''You may be right about that,'' Rostoff said. ''Send Sasha and Vanya to bring her in for questioning.''

Marina Vallinsikov, now the young wife of the minister, had been an attractive, underpaid government secretary moonlighting as a talented prostitute when Rostoff discovered her. Taken by her intelligence, poise and beauty, he decided to make her an offer she couldn't refuse. He introduced her to the minister and ordered her to get close to him. He had never thought that the minister would take her seriously enough to marry her, but when he did, it was even better.

Like many older men who had been able to nab a young trophy wife, Vallinsikov lived with a secret fear that she would someday leave him for a younger, more vigorous bed partner. He knew that he couldn't compete with younger men in the sexual arena, but few men in the new Russia, young or old, could match his personal power. Almost without knowing that he was doing it, he started talking shop with his young wife to impress her, and she became an avid listener of his stories.

She claimed to be fascinated with the petty details of Moscow power brokering and always asked questions about his most recent coups and plots. Sometimes when he was in the middle of a long detailed explanation of something, she would excuse herself to go to the bathroom where she would jot down a few notes before returning to hear the rest of the story. His proud story of how he had been able to enlist the assistance of a covert American action team in his war against the Mafia was particularly interesting to her.

"This doesn't mean that she betrayed us," Detlov quickly spoke up for Marina. Sasha and Vanya had their uses, particulary when it came to questioning women, but he didn't want to see Madam Vallinsikov fall into their hands. For one, she was a nice woman, but mostly she would be difficult to replace. And after the Sakarov twins were done with her, she would be of no use to anyone anymore. "The Americans might have fed the minister erroneous information."

Rostoff's eyes narrowed. "If that is the case, it means that they know of her connection to me, and that is even more dangerous."

"I disagree," Detlov replied. "I think it has become obvious to them by now that there's been a leak somewhere in the minister's office. Even the Americans are smart enough to figure that one out. And Marina did report that her husband mentioned something about his needing to tighten security. I think we should leave her in place and just be more careful with what she reports in the future.''

''If they're feeding us false information to lead us into ambushes, we may be able to turn this against them. We can send a small unit into the next ambush, but have a larger group standing by to ambush the ambushers.

''You remember, Boris, how we used to do that with the Mujis, sending government troops into the trap and then sending in a heliborne strike team to encircle the Dushmen while they were busy killing the Kabul troops. It worked every time back then, and it will work this time.''

''That would work,'' Detlov agreed. ''But who do we use for the goats?''

''Locals only and use our own operatives to spring the trap. Anyway, leave the report and let the rest of the IRA know of their loss.''

''As you wish.''

When Detlov got back to his computer room, he rang up Marina Vallinsikov and informed her what had happened. He also warned her what would happen to her if she wasn't very careful in the future. Though Rostoff had discovered her and she was now married to the minister, he had a very personal interest in her well-being that not even Rostoff was aware of.

GREGOR ROSTOFF WAS a megalomaniac, but that didn't mean that he had lost the skills as a tactician that had made him one of the old Red Army's fastest rising stars before his fall from grace. He could read an after-action report as well as the next man, and he knew that he had been suckered. He had to admit that the man in charge of those Yankees was good.

Even worse was the fact that the timing for this couldn't have been more troublesome. General Belislav had finally gotten his hands on the medium-range SS-22 missiles that were the keystone of his grand plan for a new Russia.

When he launched his coup, the missiles would ensure that none of the other military commanders tried to deal themselves a hand in the game. The general had also managed to acquire the warheads for the missiles and he would use them if he had to. He wouldn't allow anything or anyone to stop him from achieving his destiny as he saw it.

The problem was that since the Yankees had figured out that there was a spy in Vallinsikov's office, they would continue to feed Marina erroneous information, which was dangerous both to him and the general.

After thinking it over, he decided not to inform Belislav of this latest incident. The general had enough to think about.

CHAPTER TWENTY-TWO

Stony Man Farm, Virginia

As soon as the Farm shut down for the night, Hal Brognola went down to the Computer Room to check in with Aaron Kurtzman. He had followed the Frankfurt reports from Katzenelenbogen through his back door, but it was time to start planning to exploit the team's success.

He rummaged around in his jacket pockets, fished out two antacid tabs and downed them before pouring himself a cup of coffee. "That went rather well, I thought."

Kurtzman was all grin. "Didn't it?"

Brognola settled in the chair by Kurtzman's workstation. "Now at least we know for certain that there's a leak in Vallinsikov's office. Since the Frankfurt information didn't go through the Oval Office before it was sent to Moscow, we have proof positive of the leak. Now, all we have to do is convince the minister of the facts."

"Even with what we have that still may be difficult," Kurtzman pointed out. "He just doesn't seem to want to face the facts."

Brognola took a sip of coffee and nodded. "That sure seems to be the case, which is why I've decided to go to Moscow myself to talk to Minister Vallinsikov face-to-face about this. Hearing it from a representative of the President might make a difference."

When he saw the shock on Kurtzman's face, he continued. "I think that this situation qualifies as an emergency. We need to bring closure to this. I'll clear it with the White House and be out of here before Barbara even knows that I'm gone."

"She's going to be pissed."

"Well, what's new about that since this started? Since you'll have to deal with her instead of me, I'll take that chance."

"Thanks a lot, buddy."

"What are friends for, anyway? I'll need you to work up a briefing packet for me, copies of messages going both ways, the team's after-action reports and all that, starting with Prague. And while you're doing that, I'm going to line up a plane at Andrews and talk to the Oval Office. If you can get me the briefing papers soon enough, I'll be out of here at first light tomorrow."

Now it was Kurtzman's turn to be concerned. "Do you think it'll work? There's a chance that

Rostoff's spy will pick up on your visit and he'll have a reception committee waiting for you."

"I know," Brognola admitted. "But I think that I need to try it anyway. If I can convince Vallinsikov of the leak, we can set a trap to deal with Rostoff when he surfaces. It will cut our risk factors down to something we should be able to manage."

That was still the program, and Kurtzman couldn't argue with it. "Good luck."

"I'm going to need it."

Kurtzman could only agree.

Russia

WHEN GREGOR ROSTOFF got word from Marina Vallinsikov of Hal Brognola's pending visit to Moscow, he was glad that he had listened to Boris Detlov and hadn't turned the Sakarov brothers loose on her. Now that he knew the Yankees were feeding him false information, he would simply be more careful before responding to it.

But a visit from the mysterious leader of Phoenix Force couldn't be a trap. It was, however, an opportunity that he would have to take advantage of. And he would also inform General Belislav of this development.

As a general rule, Belislav was completely paranoid about anything that had to do with Americans. He had lived the life of a committed cold-war warrior for almost fifty years and the experience had left him little choice but to think that way. So, when he heard about Brognola's secret visit, he ordered Rostoff to bring his two captives to his dacha for further interrogation.

The general's plans for his coup were almost complete. There were still, however, a few major military units that were holding out, units that he would like to have on his side. The Americans getting even more involved at this critical juncture could prove dangerous for him. He had to learn the reason for Brognola's visit, and he figured that Blancanales and Schwarz would know what it was.

Stony Man Farm, Virginia

BARBARA PRICE WORE a frown when she walked into the Computer Room early the next morning and confronted Aaron Kurtzman. "Where's Hal?" she asked. "I heard the chopper take off."

Kurtzman turned in his wheelchair to face her. Damn Hal, he had taken the easy part of this gig and left him to deal with her. "He's on the bird and he's heading to Andrews to catch a flight to Moscow."

"Moscow? He didn't say anything to me about going to Russia. When was that arranged?"

"Well, since you two haven't exactly been close

lately," Kurtzman explained, "he talked to me about it and I agreed that he should go."

"I didn't expect that from you, Aaron," she said. "I thought that we had agreed to cut him out of this operation until it is concluded."

"We did," he agreed, "and it seemed like the right thing to do at the time. But since then, he and I have had a chance to talk and we came to a couple of conclusions."

"Such as?"

"Such as he says that he's going to tender his resignation as the director of SOG as soon as this mission is over, whatever 'over' is going to look like this time around. And since this is going to be his last time out..."

"That's crap, Aaron. Hal's been in this game too long. He doesn't know how to do anything else."

"That's very true, but he still remembers that he has a family and he says that he wants to spend some time with them before they completely forget that he exists. He thinks that it's time for him to move on and leave this to someone else."

Price was confused. "Then why is he going to Russia? What does he think he can do in person there that we can't handle from here?"

"He says that he wants to see if he can do something to bring this to a conclusion without any more of our guys getting bushwhacked. He figures that if he can plug the leak in Vallinsikov's office, Rostoff will have to come out of the bushes himself and we'll be able to whack him instead."

"Does the President know that he's making this little visit?"

"Yes, but that's about all he knows. Hal gave him some typical political doubletalk about needing closer liaison with the Russians on the mission and conferencing with their officials. The Man apparently bought it, and he sanctioned the trip."

Kurtzman saw the look on her face and quickly added, "Hal's on our side in this now, Barbara, he really is. And since this is going to be his last mission, he wants to try to make up for the screwup in Prague. He really does blame himself for what happened."

She shook her head slowly. "I see your fine hand in this, Aaron Kurtzman. This is one of your famous backdoor operations, isn't it?"

"No," he answered honestly. "He came to me with this idea all on his own."

"Is he going to have any cover or backup while he's over there?"

"No, he's going in open. But he should be okay since he'll be picked up at the airport and he won't be leaving the ministry."

"Wonderful, he's over there and I'm stuck here waiting for him to come back so I can get permission to go to the little girls' room."

"That's not exactly the case, Barbara." He

paused to sweep his eyes from one end of the room to the other. "Hal signed all of this over to you as his successor while he's gone. He even filed a copy of it with the Oval Office so you can operate in his name while he's gone. You're the interim leader of SOG and liaison to the Oval Office."

That gave Price pause. For Brognola to have done that on his own authority meant that he really was going to hang it up. She also knew that it meant that he wasn't too certain that he was going to come home. Signing the Farm over to her would make a transition easier in case anything happened and he didn't make it back.

"I think we may have misjudged him, Barbara," Kurtzman offered.

"Dammit, Aaron," she said sharply, "don't you go soft-headed on me now. I don't want to have to put you out to pasture too."

"You can put me out to pasture whenever you like," he replied stiffly. "But until such time as you do, I still have a job to do here. If Hal can find the leak in Moscow, we can wrap this thing up and call our people home."

"To do what?" she asked. "We're finished here as soon as the President realizes what has happened."

"That's then," he replied. "And I'll worry about that when it happens. Right now, however, since we're still running a mission, I would like to respectfully suggest that you get back to controlling the damned thing.''

"Okay, Aaron, you win this one. But if this doesn't work out, I'm going to kick your butt all the way to the retirement home."

"And here I thought that we were going to go to a chicken farm in Arkansas."

"Get back to work, and get me a briefing paper on Hal's mission to Moscow ASAP. If I'm running this place now, I need to know what in the hell is going on around here."

"Yes, ma'am."

Going back to her office, Price got on the satcom link to talk to Katzenelenbogen in Berlin. Since Brognola had gone in without backup, if anything went down, Katz would need to be prepared to send in Phoenix to bail him out. She was still angry at him for doing this behind her back, but as long as she was running the show, she wasn't going to let the big Fed swing in the wind. Not as long as Stony Man had muscle on the ground in Europe.

Russia

GADGETS SCHWARZ and Rosario Blancanales were passing the time in their cell playing word games, when they heard the sound of footsteps coming down the hall. Since it wasn't mealtime, they both tensed for whatever was coming their way.

The man they had come to know as Rostoff's second-in-command opened the door. Even though the two Able Team commados hadn't offered any resistance since being captured, two hard-eyed guards holding assault rifles always flanked Detlov.

"I have brought you new clothes," the Russian said. "Get dressed. You are going on a trip."

"Where're you taking us?" Blancanales asked.

"That is not important for you to know."

The clothing they were given wasn't the expensive European threads they had been wearing when they were ambushed in Prague. Apparently the clothing had been ruined by the dye in the blank rounds that had hit them. This clothing was the cheaply made, shapeless stuff usually associated with Soviet government officials.

As Schwarz stepped into the too-short trousers he had been given, he had an idea. Holding up the chunky shoes the Russian had handed him, he said, "These things don't fit well. Do you still have the shoes I was wearing when I came in here, the American cowboy boots?"

Detlov translated and one of the guards left the cell. When he came back, he was carrying a pair of tan cowboy boots.

Blancanales was careful not to look at his partner when Schwarz slipped into his old Dan Post boots. Finding that they hadn't been spirited away and sold on the black market was more than a stroke of luck in their favor for a change. It might be their salvation.

Apparently Rostoff's men hadn't discovered the emergency signaling device in the boots, or they wouldn't have brought them. Now all they needed was one of Kurtzman's borrowed NRO satellites in the vicinity and they could send a message that they were still alive. It should at least get the Farm to think about them again.

"How do I look?" Schwarz asked.

Blancanales grinned. "You look like a Bulgarian skating team coach who's been touring in Texas."

"That good? Wow!"

As soon as the two men were dressed, the guards put blindfolds over their eyes and led them through what seemed like endless echoing corridors until they reached the open air. Then they were hustled into the back of a van and their hands were cuffed behind them with plastic restraints.

When the van's door was closed, Schwarz listened but didn't hear it being locked and hid a smile. This might turn out even better than he thought.

CHAPTER TWENTY-THREE

Russia

With the blindfold securely in place over his eyes, Schwarz was relying on his other senses to tell him where they were being driven. He realized that his plan, if something thrown together with almost zero chances of succeeding could be called a plan, was pure desperation.

He had to wait until the right time, though, before he tried. Jumping out of a speeding vehicle wasn't going to make it any easier for him. He couldn't get very far on a sprained ankle or a broken leg.

After what he figured was an hour spent on fairly open roads, he felt the van slow as if they were entering more congested traffic. In another few minutes, he heard the sounds of other vehicles and honking horns as the van apparently stopped at traffic lights.

"I think I'll take a powder soon," he said to Blancanales. Since the guards spoke English, they had kept silent so far. But using a little archaic slang might confuse the issue.

"Do you think this is it?"

"It floats my boat," Schwarz said as the van came to a stop again.

"*Uno, dos, tres,*" Blancanales said softly.

On three, Blancanales lunged for the guard seated beside him on the bench in the back of the van. The man was caught off guard, and the two ended up fighting on the floor.

Turning on the bench, Schwarz reared back and slammed both of his feet against the van door. When the latch popped, he leaped out. With the blindfold still in place, he stumbled, falling to the ground. Ducking his head, he rubbed it against the ground, pulling the cloth of the blindfold out of position enough to see out of one eye. He had landed by a curb next to a sidewalk half full of pedestrians who were turning away their eyes. Even in the new Russia, it was best not to see certain things. Getting to his feet, he took off running.

Even with his hands cuffed behind him, he was making good time. There was what looked like a street market about two blocks away and if he could make it there, he might be able to lose himself in the crowd.

He heard authoritative shouts in Russian, and the sounds of someone running behind him. The people, though, weren't trying to stop him; they simply made way for him and his pursuers. Being good Russians, they knew better than to get involved in any way.

Hearing the sound of a vehicle, he glanced over his shoulder and saw the van coming after him in reverse. Only on streets as deserted as Moscow's could a vehicle do that.

When the vehicle drew close to him, the second guard jumped out and tackled him.

Since he couldn't use his arms to break his fall, he hit hard, his face scraping the concrete. The guard followed him down and had his Makarov in action before he stopped skidding. With the muzzle of the pistol drilled into his ear, Schwarz had no choice but to go quietly.

Stony Man Farm, Virginia

AARON KURTZMAN WAS still chasing Rostoff's old Red Army buddies when Hunt Wethers called to him from his workstation across the room. "Aaron, do you remember the emergency beepers Able Team was wearing when they went to the Prague meeting place?"

Kurtzman frowned. "Yes."

"Well, the recon bird over Moscow just picked up one of them squawking. It's the right frequency and the right coded pulse."

"Check it again."

Kurtzman didn't see any way that emergency beacon could have gotten all the way from Prague to Moscow. Schwarz and Blancanales were dead, Lyons had confirmed it.

"It checks out," Wethers replied. "What do you want me to do about it?"

"Nothing. It has to be a mistake."

Under different circumstances, he might have notified Price and Brognola about this. But with everything that was going down now, he didn't want to distract anyone's attention from the tasks at hand.

Schwarz and Blancanales were dead, and that was that. No amount of wishful thinking was going to change that.

"Log it with a note that we need to change the beacon's signal in the future."

Russia

SCHWARZ LAY on the floor of the van, trying to catch his breath. He hadn't stayed on the street very long. But he had been able to activate the signal, and he might have been free long enough for the emergency signal to be heard.

Their blindfolds were off now, and both of the guards had them covered with their Makarovs while the driver shouted over the radio in rapid-fire Russian. When he hung up, he said something to the guards and turned the van.

Neither Schwarz or Blancanales bothered to ask where they were being taken now.

GREGOR ROSTOFF DIDN'T look amused when Schwarz and Blancanales were dragged in front of him.

"Do not think that you have escaped being questioned," he told the two Americans. "All you have done is insure that the questioning will be done here. And, actually, that is easier for me. I am afraid, however, that it will be rougher on you."

He turned to Schwarz. "And since you instigated this, you will be questioned first."

Schwarz smiled slowly. "Great, I always liked being first."

"We'll see about that."

As Schwarz was taken away, Blancanales was led back to his cell to wait.

HAL BROGNOLA'S INITIAL meeting with Minister Vallinsikov hadn't gone as well as he would have liked. It hadn't been a complete failure, but he hadn't been able to make headway against the man's rock-hard belief that his ministry was free of moles.

After flying the polar route from Washington, D.C., to Moscow, as he requested, his plane had been met at the airport by Vallinsikov's security men and he had been driven straight to the ministry.

The minister had turned out to be a congenial man in his late sixties, and his English was good enough that they had been able to conduct their meeting without having to go through an interpreter. That had been the first and only thing that had worked out well. Things had quickly gone downhill from there.

Even with all the evidence Brognola had brought with him to back up his theory about the leak, Vallinsikov had steadfastly refused to be convinced. In fact he had resented Brognola even bringing up the topic.

Brognola knew that part of the Russian's vehement denial was simply national pride. It had cost the Moscow government much of their "face" when they had been forced to call upon the Americans to help them get control of this Mafia mess. Admitting that they had an internal spy was out of the question.

But Brognola also considered himself to be a good reader of character, and he realized that there was more to the minister's steadfast denial than merely bruised national pride. The man really believed that his people had done everything they possibly could do to provide airtight security for the joint operation. He was equally convinced that Vallinsikov was dead wrong and knew that the spy, whomever he was, was under extremely deep cover.

So deep, in fact, that not even the Russian intelligence service had been able to ferret him out.

More and more he was understanding Barbara Price's viewpoint about the Russians, and he sincerely wished that he had listened to her earlier. It really had been ill-advised for Stony Man to have taken on this task, and he should have done more to insist on stronger safeguards before agreeing to it. This was the one time that he should have gone to the wall with the President and refused to take on the mission until the Farm could work up its own intelligence sources and cut the Russians completely out of the loop.

Where this all left him now, he didn't have a clue, but he wasn't about to give up.

Since he had gone directly from the airport to the meeting in Vallinsikov's office, he was still fighting jet lag and he needed to rest before he even tried to think that far ahead. Another meeting had been scheduled in the morning, and maybe if he was fresher, he'd be more convincing. If he wasn't, he would have no choice but to return to Washington and lay the whole mess on the Man in the Oval Office. Along with his resignation from SOG, of course.

While Vallinsikov had balked at accepting that there was a mole in his office, he had been very interested in the Farm's identification of ex-Red Army Colonel Gregor Rostoff as the mastermind behind the Russian Mafia. A quick check with army records had given him information about the disgraced colonel's Afghan drug operation and his disappearance from a military prison during the disruption of Gorbachev's resignation. He thanked Brognola for that tip and promised to start an investigation of Rostoff's whereabouts and activities immediately.

At least that part of the operation had worked out. If he was forced to ask the President to pull Stony Man off the job, at least the Russian would have that much to follow up. Why they hadn't been able to come up with the man's name on their own was beyond him. He knew that their intelligence apparatus was better than that.

Brognola was being lodged in the ministry's own safehouse, and it had all the amenities of a modern hotel, including a modem line. The first thing he did when he got settled into his room was to plug in his laptop, boot up the e-mail and type out a short report to Kurtzman. Since he expected the line to be tapped, he used one of the Farm's open-line codes to tell Kurtzman the results of the first meeting, as disappointing as they were.

What Barbara Price's response would be, he didn't wait to know. As with so much else involved here, he'd deal with that later.

After that chore had been taken care of, he took a long shower and called down to order his dinner.

He wasn't very hungry, but he knew that he would need the energy in the morning. Fifteen minutes after finishing his meal, he was dead asleep.

A LITTLE BEFORE MIDNIGHT, a well-dressed woman wearing a long fur coat drove up to the guardhouse in front of the ministry safehouse. She seemed to be known by the agent on duty and engaged him in conversation. While his attention was diverted, two men in black combat suits slipped in behind her.

The guard caught a glimpse of movement, but before he could react, one of the men fired a silenced pistol twice. Both rounds took him in the face, and he slumped back into his guard shack.

After buzzing herself through the security gate, the woman proceeded to the front door of the house. There, she buzzed again and slipped her hand into her purse. When the door was opened, she greeted the man behind it by shooting him in the chest with a small pistol.

As he fell back, the two men in black rushed past her, their silenced pistols at the ready. Minutes later, the safehouse was secure.

HAL BROGNOLA SLEPT the sleep of exhaustion, but the alarms in his subconscious mind were going off, telling him that someone was in the room with him.

He was struggling to come awake when he felt a pain in his arm and he went into blackness again.

"He'll be out for the next several hours," one of the men in black told the woman as he pocketed the syringe he had used to give Brognola the injection.

"Good," she replied. "Put a coat on him and get him down to the garage immediately."

One of the men pulled Brognola's limp body out of bed and held him upright while the other one worked his arms into his overcoat. Once dressed, they supported him on both sides and walked him out of the room and down the stairs.

In the garage, Brognola was dumped into the back seat of a Mercedes sedan. The woman walked back to the security gate, and, after letting the sedan through, closed it behind her. Walking back to her own car parked at the curb, she got in and quickly drove off in the opposite direction.

She didn't want to be late for her social engagement. It would be her alibi to her husband.

ROSARIO BLANCANALES knelt beside Gadgets Schwarz's cot. He had taken off his shirt, moistened it and was washing the sweat from his friend's face. Rostoff had really worked him over this time. His pulse was seriously elevated, and he was twitching uncontrollably from the aftereffect of the nerve induction machine. Another session like that would probably kill him.

"Pol?" Schwarz's voice was weak and rough from shouting his pain.

"It's me."

"I did it."

"I know." Blancanales cursed not being able to talk to him without being overheard. Had he been able to speak with him, maybe he could have talked him out of trying something like that with so little chance of survival. Like Gadgets, he hated doing nothing, but if that's what it took to keep them alive, it was worth it.

"I can't move my arm." Schwarz reached out with his left hand to see if his right arm was still intact. "It's there, but I can't make it move."

"Your nerves have been burned out," Blancanales said. "It should wear off in a little while. Go back to sleep, and I'll wake you when they feed us again."

"Do you think the Farm heard me?"

"I don't know," Blancanales answered honestly. "I really don't."

Schwarz's eyes rolled back in his head as he passed out.

CHAPTER TWENTY-FOUR

Stony Man Farm, Virginia

Aaron Kurtzman was working late again. Brognola's report from Moscow was disquieting to say the least. If the big Fed couldn't convince the Russians that something was wrong in the ministry, this was really going to blow up in their faces and really bring an end to the SOG. No one, no matter what had gone down, really wanted to see the end of Stony Man Farm.

From the lowest ranking blacksuit to Hal Brognola himself, every man and woman involved with the SOG had devoted their lives to their work. Their dedication was total to even the exclusion of old friends and family. That was why so many of them were single or divorced and didn't have families of their own. The Farm was like a monastery in that working with SOG was a calling that took precedence over what other people would call normal life.

Brognola had to succeed in Moscow, or they would all be lost.

But, for that to happen, everyone involved had to do everything that they possibly could to make it happen. And, for him, that meant going into the electronic world that was an extension of his existence, and surfing the web until he found the key that would unlock the information they so desperately needed.

One of the things that made Kurtzman so good at what he did was that he approached the science of gathering information from cyberspace as if it were an art. Rather than charging straight into it using A plus B equals C linear logic, he liked to approach his goal in what he liked to call a poetic manner, a cyberZen, as it were.

Somewhere out there, specifically somewhere in Russia, was the man who was running one of the world's largest criminal enterprises, ex-Colonel Gregor Rostoff. Something that big had to leave a trace of its activities somewhere. Just as a battleship left a bigger wake than a rowboat, something as big as Rostoff's operation had to be making major cyberwaves. He just had to keep on surfing until he bumped into one of the waves. Then he would turn and follow it back to its source.

He instinctively knew that Rostoff's military service was the connection that would finally pay off. The question was, in a nation where almost every able-bodied male had done some kind of military service during his lifetime, where were the links? Of those millions of ex-servicemen in Mother Russia, who was Rostoff in contact with? Who was helping him put together his criminal empire? Deciding to start from the top down, he went into the web to track high-ranking officers.

He was working the list of the generals Rostoff had come into contact with during his service career when he was jerked back into linear logic. The icon at the top of his screen was announcing that he had a top-priority, emergency message from the office of Minister Vallinsikov.

After reading it, he punched the button to Barbara Price's bedside com line.

"Yeah?" she answered.

"Hal's been kidnapped out of Vallinsikov's safehouse in Moscow."

There was silence on the other end for a long moment. "I'll be right down."

A RUMPLED BARBARA PRICE walked into the Computer Room almost immediately. "Where is it?"

"On the screen."

"Maybe now he understands what I was trying to tell him," she said as she read the dispatch from Vallinsikov. "If he'd listened to me in the first place, this wouldn't have happened. And, why wasn't he staying at the American Embassy? That's why we spend good dollars to build embassies in foreign countries. They're a safe place for government officials to stay when they visit so they won't get snatched.''

"I guess he didn't want to turn down the minister's hospitality and make matters even worse.''

"Now what am I supposed to do?'' She frowned. "Do I have to tell the Man that he's been grabbed?''

"Since he left you in charge,'' Kurtzman reminded her, "I guess that's your call. Tell him now or tell him later. I don't see that it really matters at this point. But having the President jumping up and down isn't going to get Hal back any faster, so I suggest that you wait.''

"You have a good point,'' she said.

"Okay,'' he said, "what do you want me to do first about getting him back?''

"I want you to reestablish complete communications with the team and get Mack and Katz in on this full bore. I want them to go to Moscow immediately and represent us with Vallinsikov. Now that I'm the boss, I want to have all of our best brains working on this together. Then call the minister and let him know that they're coming. And since it was your bright idea to send him over there, you're not going anywhere until this is over. I'm even going to have your meals brought to you in here.''

"But," Kurtzman groused, "this was Hal's idea. Really it was."

"Then you should have told me about it earlier so I could have stopped him from going."

"Right. How were you going to do that, tie him up in the supply room?"

"I'd have thought of something."

Germany

BOLAN AND KATZENELENBOGEN were taking their turn monitoring communications in the van while the rest of the team stood down in Berlin. The reunited city was a great place to spend dead time. They had taken rooms in a small hotel in the old Communist sector where people still didn't ask too many questions, and they could park their now unmarked van in private.

When the incoming-message bell rang, Katzenelenbogen took it. "We need to get our gear packed ASAP, Striker," he said, turning to Bolan. "We're going to Moscow this afternoon."

Bolan lifted his eyes from the report he had been reading.

"Hal was snatched during the night by Rostoff."

"I thought he was supposed to be staying at the ministry safehouse?"

"He was. But apparently someone broke in, wiped out all of the staff and snatched him."

Bolan t~~~'~ ~ ~~moment~~ to marshall his thoughts. He and Katz hadn't been happy to hear that Brognola had gone to Moscow in the first place. They understood his reasons for wanting to make the trip, but knew the risks and didn't think that they were worth taking.

If Rostoff was able to pull off a stunt like this, the situation was worse than any of them had thought. Nonetheless, now they had a real focus for their efforts. Moscow.

"We'd better get Carl and David in here too," Bolan said. "If we're going after Hal, we're going to need them with us."

"At least the Ironman will love it."

"He's been wanting to get at the Russians ever since this started."

Russia

MINISTER VALLINSIKOV was seriously considering suicide as his only way to get himself out of the mess he had created. That the American, Hal Brognola, had been kidnapped out of his ministry's own safehouse wasn't the sort of mistake that any politician could ever recover from.

However, rather than killing himself right away, he would first take vengeance on the woman who had got him into this situation, his own wife, before he ended his life. Damn that woman! But, damn himself double for being an old fool and marrying her.

When he had been younger, he had made fun of older men who fell for the charms of women who were so much younger than themselves, then married them. There was something ludicrous about a fat, balding, old man with a woman on his arm young enough to be his daughter. The young ones were good to have for mistresses, but to marry them, that wasn't dignified. And, if nothing else, an old man needed to keep his dignity.

But, when he ceased being a young man—and he had no idea when that pivotal event had happened—he stopped thinking that way. In his case, though, he hadn't dumped a fat old wife his own age to seek a younger replacement. His first wife had died, and, since he was a man who always enjoyed living with a woman, he started to look for a new wife.

Actually, if he was honest, he knew that he hadn't found Marina, she had found him. And, had he not been such a blind old fool, he would have asked himself why she had been so eager to give her sleek young body to a man twice her age. He liked to think that he was too smart to fall for a trap like that. But the facts were in now, and he was a fool. It was apparent that she had been planted on him to be the spy in his office that Brognola had tried to convince him existed.

According to the one guard who had survived the massacre at the safehouse, the raiders had been led by his wife. The man had met her many times, and there was no doubt that the identification was correct. He also said that she had fired the shot that had almost killed him. That she could have been duplicitous really didn't surprise him; he believed that was a legacy every woman was born to. That she could kill, though, shocked him. He hadn't expected that. He hadn't even known that she knew how to shoot a gun.

He would soon know how all of these things had come to pass, though. In less than an hour his wife would show up at the front door of the ministry. He had invited her to lunch with him, a social occasion with some of his fellow ministers and their wives. But instead of showing off her wardrobe and jewels to envious wives, Marina would find herself in one of his basement cells, minus her expensive clothing and jewelry. And the only eyes on her would be the cold, hard eyes of his most trusted men.

He would have the answers to his questions, and he didn't think that it would take long for him to get them. The Russian people were good at many things, and one of the things they did best was ask questions. What would be left of her after all his questions had been answered wasn't something that he wanted to think about right now. But he would have his answers.

WHEN HAL BROGNOLA awakened, he found that he was in a windowless cell. The ache in his head and the scummy taste in his mouth told him that he had been drugged. He remembered half waking in the night, but that was all. He forced himself to try to figure out what had happened. He had no doubt about the why, though. The Mafia spy in the ministry had passed on word of his visit, and Rostoff had acted quickly to take him out of the game.

He had to admit that the ex-colonel was fast on his feet and willing to take chances. That fit with everything else he had done so far, so the big Fed shouldn't be surprised. He was looking forward to meeting this mystery man, and he didn't think that it would be long in coming. He had spotted the video camera in his cell and knew that his captors would know that he was awake.

ROSTOFF WATCHED the monitor screen as Hal Brognola tried to make himself presentable. He didn't have much to work with, just a rumpled set of pajamas, but he was combing his hair with his fingers and tucking his pajama tops into the bottoms.

"Take him clothing," Rostoff told Detlov, "and bring him into the conference room."

"Yes, sir."

"MR. BROGNOLA," Rostoff said, stepping forward, his hand extended in greeting. "I am Gregor Rostoff, the man you have been looking for. Welcome to my headquarters."

Brognola was enough of a politician to know that he should take the Russian's hand. Considering that he was a prisoner, angering the man wouldn't be a good move at this point. Particularly not with four armed hardmen standing in the corners of the conference room he had been led into. Getting strong-armed wasn't going to help him right now.

"Please have a seat." Rostoff motioned to the only other chair at the table.

"Can I get you a cup of coffee?"

"Coffee would be nice, cream and sugar please."

Rostoff's eyes took in Brognola's shapeless army-surplus fatigue uniform. "I am sorry that my men did not bring your luggage from the minister's safehouse, but I will see what I can do to get more suitable clothing for you."

If Rostoff was expecting gratitude for his gesture, he was sadly mistaken. "Since I'm your prisoner," Brognola said flatly, "these will do well enough for now."

When the coffee came and a cup was put in front of him, Brognola let it sit.

Rostoff filled his own cup and took a sip from his cup before continuing. "Now that you've been taken out of the game, as it were, who will take over the Farm for you, Barbara Price?''

"You don't really expect me to answer that, do you?"

Rostoff laughed. "You will answer my questions, Mr. Brognola, never fear. I just wanted to give you a chance to answer on your own, a courtesy, if you will, from one professional to another.''

Brognola had had about all of this phony bastard's "courtesy" he could stomach. It was simply part of the interrogation process designed to gain his trust and to make him think that Rostoff knew more than he did.

He had to admit, however, that the man obviously knew more than he really should. He knew better than to think that Rostoff had access to anyone who worked at the Farm. Not in this lifetime or any other. But the question remained, where in the hell was he getting his information?

That was a question he would work on later. Now it was time to end this charade.

"You might be a professional," Brognola countered, "but you and I aren't quite in the same profession. As far as I'm concerned, you're just another low-life, cheap hood who's working to destroy his mother country. You've obviously got your hands on a nice place to work from, but that doesn't make you anything other than a scumbag like the rest of the world's criminals.''

The smile didn't leave Rostoff's face. "I am sorry that you think that way, Mr. Brognola. I had hoped that we could conduct our business without animosity, but obviously not."

"We don't have any business to conduct. I'm your prisoner and that's the end of it."

"Oh, but we do have business. You just don't know it yet."

Rostoff motioned for the guards. "Take Mr. Brognola back to his quarters."

Brognola pushed back his chair, stood and waited for the guards to close in.

CHAPTER TWENTY-FIVE

Russia

As soon as Hal Brognola was led back to his cell, Boris Detlov joined Rostoff in the conference room. "So much for trying to do it the easy way. Do you want me to alert the medical staff?"

"We have lots of time yet," Rostoff replied thoughtfully, "so I don't want to hurry this. I want to give our Mr. Hal Brognola a while to think about his situation first. A soft man like him, a politician, will not have the strength that a soldier has. His own fears will do most of our work for us.

"Don't worry," Rostoff continued when he thought Detlov was going to say something. "I'll get everything we need out of him. And, to help the process along, I want him to witness our next session with Mr. Schwarz. That should go a long way toward convincing him to answer my questions."

Detlov would have rather started working on his

latest captive immediately, but he knew better than to cross Rostoff. The colonel had his ways, and he didn't like to be second-guessed.

"As you wish."

"Has Marina checked in yet?" Rostoff asked, changing the subject.

"Not yet," Detlov replied. "But with the ministry in an uproar, she will have to be very careful."

"Let me know as soon as she calls."

"Yes, sir."

WHEN YAKOV Katzenelenbogen and Bolan arrived at the Moscow airport they were met by openly armed, uniformed guards from Minister Vallinsikov's office. After being escorted through the terminal, they were driven away in an armored van. Having lost one American, Vallinsikov wasn't taking any chances this time. Additional troops and armored personnel carriers surrounded the ministry when they drove up. Only after showing their ID were they allowed through the security screen.

Vallinsikov was waiting in a small office, and he stepped forward when the two men were shown in.

"I am ashamed to admit," he said without introducing himself, "that Hal Brognola was correct about Gregor Rostoff having a spy in my office. I am even more ashamed to have to say that the spy was my own wife, Marina. I didn't know it, but he arranged it so that I met her right after my wife died and I was particularly vulnerable.''

''I am very sorry, Minister.'' Katz read the anguish in the older man's eyes and felt his shame. ''But it sounds like it wasn't your fault. How could you have known that your wife was working for him?''

''I am afraid that it really is my fault,'' Vallinsikov replied honestly, ''in that I had a habit of talking to her about everything we do here in the ministry.''

The minister shifted his eyes to look out the window for a long moment. ''She is quite a bit younger than I am, and I thought that she would love me more if she knew how important the work I do here is. She always listened intently and asked me many questions. Like a fool, I thought that she was truly interested in my work. I acted like a schoolboy, and there is no excuse for it.''

Katz and Bolan could only agree with the minister's accurate assessment of his own behavior. It was the oldest story in the book of spy tricks, and it had doomed more than one good man. But it was irrelevant now. The only thing left for them to do was go into damage-control mode and hope that they weren't too late to limit the damage.

''Is your wife available for questioning?'' Bolan asked bluntly. ''Brognola might still be alive and she may be able to lead us to him.''

"She is available." Vallinsikov's eyes were cold. Husband or not, he was enough of a professional to know what had to be done. "And she is being questioned as we speak. I will take you to her."

The minister led them to the elevator that descended below ground level to the building's holding cells. Every government building in the old Soviet empire had had such cells in the basement, and there was no doubt that many of them were still in use, as they were here.

In one of the interrogation rooms, a young, blond woman stood in front of a table where three men sat. The men stood to attention when Vallinsikov walked in and quickly briefed him in Russian.

Even somewhat battered and wearing a shapeless prison uniform, Katz saw that Marina Vallinsikov was a stunningly beautiful woman. Now that he had seen her, he better understood how the minister had fallen into this "honey trap" and been seduced to betray his operation. It was a stupid thing for a man in his position to have done, but as long as men were men and women were beautiful, the story would be repeated many more times.

"What have you learned so far?" Bolan asked the minister.

"We now know where Rostoff has his headquarters."

"Where is that?"

"At Mother Site Eight."

Bolan and Katz exchanged glances; that wasn't a Russian military term they were familiar with at all. "What is a mother site?" Katz asked.

"It is a heavily defended, ballistic missile launching complex outside Moscow. It was designed to withstand both air and ground attack while it served as a control center for other launch sites. It appears," he added, "that even though Rostoff had been disgraced in the Red Army, he still had many friends in the military. Maybe some of these men had been in with him on the Afghan drug-smuggling scheme. We do not know all of the details yet.

"Anyway, when we removed the missiles from our launch complexes in accordance with our treaties with your country, we sold off the empty structures to anyone who wanted to buy one. Someone bought Mother Site Eight. We are working to find out who that was right now. Somehow it ended up in Rostoff's hands."

Vallinsikov met Katz's eyes squarely. "The worst part is that we believe that this particular mother site was not properly demilitarized before it was sold. It appears that the inspectors were bought off."

Bolan didn't like the sound of that. "What do you mean?"

"Unfortunately it means that this site still has its full defensive capacity intact—ground defenses, air defenses—and we think it's still capable of launching nuclear missiles.''

"Does it have any missiles?'' Katz asked. Rogue nuclear missiles were one of the greatest threats any nation could face in the modern world.

"To be honest with you, we do not know at this time.''

He glanced back at his wife. "But we intend to find out very soon.''

NOW THAT THE AMERICANS had been shown that Vallinsikov had the situation well in hand, he took them back up to his office.

"What is your next move?'' Katz asked.

"We are assembling a force to try to take the mother site right now. Since we have the details of the defenses, it will be a little easier for us to defeat them.''

"Can you hold off the assault until I get the rest of my team in here?'' Katz asked.

Vallinsikov looked surprised. "I thought that you would want to move immediately to free Mr. Brognola.''

"Hal's tough,'' Katz stated. "And I'm confident that he can hold out a little while longer. If possible, I'd like to use my own people so there are no mistakes.''

"But of course,'' Vallinsikov replied. At this point, he wasn't in any position to protest.

"But," Katz added quickly, "if this place is as bad as you say it is, we'll be glad to have any help you can provide to go in with us."

"Like I said," the minister replied, "I am putting together a team of specialists in this kind of operation and they will be happy to have you and your men join them."

UPON BEING RETURNED to his cell after his first meeting with Rostoff, Hal Brognola had laid on his narrow bunk to husband his resources. There were no doubts in his mind that his stay here, however long or short it might turn out to be, wasn't going to be a Club Med experience. He was going to need all of his strength to deal with what was coming like a man. And that meant conserving his strength, because he was going to need it later.

He was old enough to be fully aware that he wasn't going to live forever. In his line of work, he had come to that realization much sooner than men who lived safe, quiet lives; it went with the job.

He had also learned that how one died was just as important, if not more so, than how one lived. He had few regrets about how he had lived, and he wanted to have none about how he was going to die. He knew that pain was the great leveler, but he vowed that he would try his best to remain true to how he had lived his life, no matter what Rostoff did to him.

He also knew that was an easy vow to make, but not an easy one to keep.

An hour or so later, he was ready when he heard footsteps outside the door of his cell.

Detlov entered, flanked by two of his hardmen. "Please come with me, Mr. Brognola."

Taking a deep breath, he went calmly.

ROSTOFF WAS ALL SMILES again when Brognola was taken to him, and he acted as if their previous conversation hadn't taken place. Rather than reassuring the big Fed, however, it put him on alert. He knew never to trust a man who changed his mind so easily. He was surprised, however, when the Russian said that he wanted to take him on a tour of his facility.

"Since I feel that I know so much about your 'Farm,' as you call it, I thought that you might like to see my operation."

After being taken past a control center that Rostoff immediately identified as a missile-launch facility, he was taken to a war room that Rostoff bragged controlled an elaborate defensive system. "This facility was designed to withstand the final war," he said. "We can fight off an armored division if it comes down to that."

If, Brognola thought, he had the manpower. So far, he had seen only a couple dozen people all told and even with automated defenses, he would need more help.

"Now, I'm sure you will want to see my computers," Rostoff said as he led him into a large room, its walls lined with computer equipment.

"I have three Grodonov mainframes," the Russian said proudly. "And I am told that they are of a slightly higher capacity than the Crays you have at the Farm. Now that I know more about your security systems, my people are working to break into your cyberspace communications. As you well know, when that happens the game's over."

Even with the powerful mainframes Rostoff had, Brognola was confident that there was no way that he could crack Kurtzman's home-brew cybersecurity systems. The computer expert played with cybercryptology the way a grand master played chess. The only time the Farm's computer security systems had ever been breached had been when another wild card, genius hacker had temporarily overcome Kurtzman's gate guards. And, even then, it hadn't lasted very long.

Even so, Rostoff apparently thought that he had enough information to make the attempt. Which, of course, brought to mind the question of where he was getting his information. Brognola's capture proved that he had a spy in Vallinsikov's office, but the Farm had been careful how much information had been passed on to the minister. There had to be another answer to how Rostoff knew so much about the Farm's operations.

"Before we go back to my office to continue our conversation," Rostoff said, "I want to show you something that I'm sure will hold your interest."

Wondering what was coming next, Brognola followed as Rostoff led him to a window looking into what had to be a medical facility. A man was strapped in a chair while technicians in white coats attached what looked like electrical equipment to him.

When they moved his head to face the window, Brognola couldn't believe his eyes. Gadgets Schwarz was alive!

"What is he doing here? Schwarz was supposed to have been killed in Prague."

"He wasn't killed. He was captured."

"But how? We had a witness to his death."

"It was child's play to capture him," Rostoff bragged. "After luring your so-called Able Team into the factory, we staged a shoot-out and Mr. Lyons was forced to flee as we wanted him to, and he obviously told his Phoenix Force friends that his two teammates had died."

"You bastard," was all Brognola could say.

"My parents were married," Rostoff replied calmly. "But I know what you are trying to tell me. You must have blamed yourself for their deaths. You thought that the information you passed on from Vallinsikov's office was responsible for the ambush, and in that you are correct. But, of course, you had no way of knowing that the information originated from me.''

As Brognola watched, the technicians made adjustments to their equipment and Schwarz visibly reacted in pain. The room had apparently been soundproofed, but he could see Gadgets open his mouth in a scream and lunge against the restraints.

''Why are you doing that to him?''

''I'm afraid that Mr. Schwarz has proved to be somewhat of a problem for me,'' Rostoff admitted. ''He is stubborn, so I have had to resort to what I am sure looks like a barbaric means of getting the information I need from him. Rest assured, however, that he will have no permanent damage. The nerve induction interrogation is painful to be sure, but it has no lasting effects. He will recover just fine.''

Schwarz's back arched and his mouth opened in an unheard scream as another jolt of electricity coursed down his ulnar nerve. After looking like he would break his own back in his agony, he fell limp against the restraints.

''He has passed out again,'' Rostoff said. ''That's unfortunate. Now I will have to question Mr. Blancanales instead.''

''Rosario is alive, too?''

''But of course. Do you think that I would kill

him before I complete my interrogation? That would be a waste of a good source. Russians know how to care for our sources of information. With the three of you, I will learn everything I need to know to insure that your country never meddles in Russian affairs again.''

Brognola knew that he was being put through a full court press. Being shown that Gadgets and the Politician were alive and that they were being tortured was a calculated tactical move, one carefully crafted to break his will and soften him so he would talk freely instead of being put through that torture himself. Rostoff wanted to make him afraid of what he would do when it came his turn to go under the machine. But that wasn't the way his mind worked.

With him, it was the unknown that was fearful. The known, no matter how bad, wasn't to be feared, but simply to be endured. Now that he knew what he was facing, he could deal with it and wouldn't break.

He almost wanted to thank the Russian for giving him this information. After that, of course, he wanted to tear the bastard's throat out with his teeth for what he had done to Schwarz and Blancanales.

"We're going to get you for this," Brognola said calmly. "You realize that, don't you?"

Rostoff almost laughed. "You think that Carl, the Ironman, Lyons is going to come bursting through the door with his guns blazing like an actor in one of your movies? Or, do you think that Phoenix Force is going to drop on me from out of thin air?

"This is not one of your fanciful films, Mr. Brognola, where the good guys, as I think you call them, arrive at the last moment and achieve a dramatic rescue. Although I really do wish that your Phoenix Force would try to come after you and your friends. It would save me the trouble of sending my operatives after them later."

Just then, Boris Detlov walked in and whispered something to Rostoff in Russian. Rostoff's face registered shock, and he barked an order to the two guards.

Without saying another word, the two Russians hurried off while the guards closed in on Brognola to take him back to his cell.

CHAPTER TWENTY-SIX

Russia

Hal Brognola would have given anything to know what had put Rostoff off his stride. The bastard had sure lost his superior smirk fast. It looked like the ball hadn't exactly stopped rolling yet, nor was it in Rostoff's court as he wanted it to be. The Russian had enjoyed a good laugh at Phoenix Force's expense. But no one knew better than Brognola how dangerous it could be to underestimate those men. Most of the others who had made that mistake were worm food now.

He knew that Barbara Price was furious at his having put himself in a position where he could get captured, but he also knew that, as much as she wanted to, she wouldn't leave him swinging in the wind. Lyons, Bolan and Phoenix Force would be coming for him, and Gregor Rostoff had better make sure that he had his affairs in order.

He laid on his cot to rest and tried not to think about what he had seen being done to Schwarz.

Rostoff had also laughed at the concept of Lyons breaking down walls to rescue his friends, but he didn't know how close that was to being a reality. If there was any way that he could let the Ironman know that his teammates were being held prisoner here, he'd chew through the concrete to get to them.

As he drifted off to sleep, the image of Lyons's familiar look of grim determination kept coming into his mind. That a man like him was out there somewhere looking for him was a comforting thought. Regardless of what Rostoff thought, this was a long ways yet from being a done deal.

THE NEWS THAT HAD interrupted Gregor Rostoff's session with Hal Brognola had been a report that Marina Vallinsikov had been arrested by her husband and had disappeared into the depths of the ministry. It took awhile for him to confirm the report and, when he did, he was concerned. The effect that her capture might have on his operation wasn't lost on him.

Now that the minister had finally figured out that his marital pillow talk had been his downfall, he wasn't going to be happy about it. The only question that remained to be answered was how fast Marina could be made to tell what she knew and he had no doubt that she would talk. Her husband was an old fool, but he wasn't enough of a fool not to put her under interrogation.

The first thing he had to do was to inform General Belislav of this development. The general had known about Rostoff's access to the ministry, but he had never been comfortable about who the spy was. Being the conventional man that he was, he hadn't liked the idea of using women as agents. But it had been done, and now they had to work with it. The fact that he had nabbed Brognola, though, would go a long way to mollify the general.

When he dialed the private phone line to Belislav's dacha, it was picked up on the first ring. "Belislav."

"It's Colonel Rostoff, General, and I have some news."

Rostoff quickly briefed him, first on the capture of Brognola and lastly of Marina's imprisonment.

"I must know why the Americans sent Brognola to Moscow immediately," the general insisted. "We are not ready to move yet, and I must have advance warning if they have decided to get involved to a greater extent."

"Brognola will be able to answer those questions," Rostoff assured him. "And I will have those answers for you as soon as possible."

"Has there been a response from the Americans to his disappearance?"

"I have no way of knowing," Rostoff replied.

"Now that Marina Vallinsikov has been captured, I have lost my inside line to the ministry."

"I warned you about the dangers of using her."

"She knows nothing about my connection to you," Rostoff reminded him. "So if she talks, all she can do is give away details of my operation. And as you well know, I can take care of myself here as long as you can keep the military from attacking me."

After receiving assurances that the general would use his not-inconsiderable influence to ensure that no Russian military forces would be used against Mother Site Eight, Rostoff hung up and turned his mind back to the problem at hand.

He regretted that he hadn't placed a second agent within the ministry. Marina had worked out so well that he had ordered Detlov to stop trying to recruit another member of the staff. Recruiting efforts always carried a risk of being turned against you, and he hadn't wanted to take that chance. Now, though, he was without a way to silence Marina.

Losing his eyes in the ministry made him blind, but it hadn't doomed him. He still had Belislav's influence to protect him from the military.

Stony Man Farm, Virginia

BARBARA PRICE FROWNED as Aaron Kurtzman went through the data Katzenelenbogen and Bolan had forwarded from Moscow. "What's this 'mother site' business?" she asked. "It sounds like something out of a made-for-TV horror movie about an invasion of giant cockroaches."

"It might as well be science fiction," Kurtzman explained. "With the exception of the National Command Center at Cheyenne Mountain, we don't have anything like their mother sites. When we started targeting the Russian's command centers and individual ICBM launch sites with our first strike multiple-individual-reentry-vehicle weapons they came up with this concept to counter that. Basically the mother sites are mininational command centers that can take over if the national command center has been taken out and direct a retaliatory nuclear strike."

"That's just common sense. What's the big deal about that?"

"Well," Hunt Wethers said, stepping in with the results of his research, "being Russians, when they designed the eight mother sites, they kind of went overboard like they always do. Not only are these independent command centers, they're also fortresses designed to withstand both conventional ground and air attack. They have complete, full-spectra ground surveillance systems, minefields, automated defensive bunkers, both low- and high-altitude antiaircraft missiles and millions of tons of concrete.

"The general consensus is that a mouse can't get into one of them without being spotted and blasted out of existence. That's why they were first on the list of Russian sites to be dismantled in the SALT II talks. With them out of commission, we both went back to having only one national command center. The fear was that one of them would fall into unfriendly hands. And, apparently," Wethers concluded, "that's exactly what happened."

"And you say that the Russians are providing an assault force?" Price asked Kurtzman.

"Yes. Vallinsikov is having problems with the army not wanting to get involved, but he has got a company of their special forces who have been specially trained in this kind of combat. They will make the initial assault and Stony Man will go in after they have breached the defenses."

"What if they can't break in?"

Kurtzman shrugged. "Apparently the Russians don't consider that to be an option."

"I don't know if that's good or bad."

"All it means is that Vallinsikov has vowed to take that place out no matter what it takes."

"But Hal's probably being held somewhere in there."

"I know."

Russia

ROSTOFF WASN'T CONTENT to just sit and wait for the situation to develop around him. Nor was he going to leave his security solely in the hands of General Belislav. He expected the Americans to try something and when they did, he would be ready for them. No commando team, no matter how good, was going to be able to crack the defenses of Mother Site Eight. The bunkers and heavy weapons positions could chew up anything short of an armored battalion.

"I want all of our foreign associates brought into the site and put in the bunkers," he told Detlov.

"You mean the terrorists?"

"Our associates," Rostoff insisted. "They have been on the payroll for some time now, and it is time that they earned their money."

"We may have some trouble bringing in the Afghanis," Detlov said. "You know they don't like living in the same quarters with Christians. They are worried about religious contamination."

"They will go where they are ordered or they will die," Rostoff snapped. "And you will see that they do one or the other."

"As you command, Colonel."

The last thing Detlov needed was to start a religious war between the various factions of his forces. But Rostoff was right. If they were attacked, they would need every man they could get in the bunkers. Much of the mother site's defenses were automated, but the kind of automation that controlled them required a warm body at the sensors and firing controls.

Stony Man Farm, Virginia

WITH THE SPEED in which the Moscow situation was developing, Aaron Kurtzman had had little time to spare to continue his background check on Gregor Rostoff. Plus, now that they had located the elusive bastard, it hardly seemed necessary. Nonetheless, he had put one of his database search engines on autopilot to work on the problem, then he promptly forgot about it.

One of the things that made Kurtzman so good at what he did was his ability to know when to quit a particular line of inquiry and when to keep at it to the exclusion of everything else. But when he dropped a topic, he dumped it from his personal short-term memory as well.

When the Look At Me! icon on the upper-left corner of his screen started to flash, he automatically clicked on it to see what was demanding his attention. For a moment, he didn't remember what he had logged into this particular search engine, the one he had tagged Bulldog. And then it clicked in his mind.

Bringing it up, he saw that his search had revealed that there was one particular ex-general of the Red Army who'd had a long association with ex-Colonel Rostoff. Paval Belislav had cycled in and out of Rostoff's military career many times, both as his commanding officer and his military mentor. In fact the general had testified on Rostoff's behalf at his court-martial, thereby saving the drug smuggler from a firing squad.

Even more interesting, though, was the fact that Belislav had been the officer in charge of demilitarizing the ICBM launch sites to comply with the SALT II Agreement. That could go a long way to explaining how one of Russia's most heavily defended military installations had ended up in the hands of the man who ran the Russian Mafia.

It also made him wonder what else the general had passed on to his old protégé. Maybe a nuclear missile or two to go in the silos at the launch site? Rogue Russian missiles had long been a world-class problem, and having such weapons fall in the hands of criminal elements was a possibility that concerned everyone in the western world.

Reaching out, Kurtzman activated the satcom link to Minister Vallinsikov's Moscow office. This was one piece of information that might prove very useful to them.

Russia

WHEN MINISTER Vallinsikov received Kurtzman's message about the Belislav connection, he finally and fully understood the chain of events that had put Gregor Rostoff where he was today. General Belislav was on a long list of ex-Soviet military officers who were kept under surveillance as being dangerous to the survival of the new republic. There wasn't a man or woman in Russia who didn't look to the military as the nation's last defense against chaos. It was equally no news that many of the old Red Army officers weren't in favor of the new democratic reforms that had reduced their power to control Russia's destiny.

But if a man like Belislav was backing Rostoff, it could only mean that the dissident officers were purposefully creating chaos in the form of the Mafia to bring themselves back to power, and it could only mean that a military coup was in the making. Such a military takeover had been feared for a long time and, since the fall of the Communist Party, several attempts had been averted already. Some of them only at the last possible moment.

Deciding that he needed more information, Vallinsikov went to question his wife. Marina hadn't yet mentioned anything about a Rostoff-Belislav connection, but that could be because she hadn't been asked the right questions. He, however, now knew exactly what to ask, and he knew that he would get answers.

WHEN VALLINSIKOV left his interrogation rooms several hours later, he was convinced that Marina knew nothing about General Belislav. Beyond having heard his name as a hero of the Afghan War, she had no idea who he was.

He was disappointed, but he should have expected that. One of the first tenets of trade craft was to not let the left hand know what the right was doing. Plus, there would have been no reason for her to know; she had merely been a dupe for the conspirators. A willing dupe, true, but a dupe nonetheless, and not even a highly valued one at that. Rostoff hadn't even done her the courtesy of giving her a means of killing herself to escape interrogation in case she was caught.

He, however, had corrected that oversight. He was now convinced that she didn't know anything else of interest. She was wrung as dry as a husk and had no further value to him. It wouldn't even help to put her on trial. And even though she had betrayed him, he didn't want to see her suffer any longer.

Her evening meal would be her last. Her body would be taken out and buried in an unmarked grave in the Moscow cemetery that was reserved for enemies of the state. The documents that he would sign would indicate that she had died of a heart attack while in custody. Death while in custody was an old story in Russia, and, sadly, one that showed no signs of ending. As long as malcontents continued to attempt to overthrow the government, whichever government it was, such medical accidents would continue to happen.

Even knowing that he had been betrayed, he would miss her, which was why he had decided not to witness her execution as was customary. It was also why she would be given the easy out. No pistol shot in the back of the head while she knelt on the concrete floor for her. She would simply go to sleep and never wake up. He hoped that her last dreams would be happy ones.

Shaking off those thoughts, the minister went back to his office. He still had a rebellion to put down and a nation to save. In the process, he hoped that Hal Brognola would be rescued intact. But his primary mission was to put Rostoff and Belislav in the same cemetery that Marina was destined for, and concern for the American's fate would have to take second place to that. He was sure that Brognola would understand.

PHOENIX FORCE WAS MET at Berlin's Schoelfeld airport by a Russian AN-22 heavy cargo plane. Looking like a pumped-up C-130 Hercules, the big turboprop aircraft was more than large enough to take the team's van with its weapons and commo gear inside. Vallinsikov had arranged for in-flight food service and sleeping accommodations for the team so they would be rested and ready to go to work when they arrived in Russia.

CHAPTER TWENTY-SEVEN

Russia

When Mack Bolan and David McCarter walked into the briefing room at the military compound next door to the ministry, the eighty Russian soldiers waiting for them stood to attention. From the blue-and-white-striped jumpers they wore under their khaki jackets, Bolan recognized them as the famed Spetsnaz, the Russian equivalent of the U.S. Army Special Forces and Rangers combined.

These were Russia's elite, and they were as good a unit as any nation had ever produced. He had worked with them before, although not on Russian soil, and he knew that they would do the job.

An officer with the pips of a major on his shoulder boards stiffened as well, and saluted. "Major Yuri Bagdonivitch at your service," he reported in flawless English.

Bolan replied, using one of his field personas.

"I'm Colonel Rance Pollock. Please have your men take their seats, Major."

At the major's command, the Spetsnaz sat.

After showing his visitors to their seats in the front row, the major went to the podium and snapped on a slide projector. An aerial view of a large, camouflaged military complex filled the screen.

"This is Mother Site Eight," he said, "the traitor Gregor Rostoff's command post. This missile launch site was supposedly decommissioned in accordance with the SALT II Agreement between our two governments and was put up for sale. Somehow, Rostoff came to possess it and, we believe, all of its military equipment as well."

"Including the missiles?" McCarter asked.

"That we do not know yet," the major answered. "Since the documentation for this site has proved to be phony, we cannot count that possibility out."

This was a factor that Bolan hadn't expected to have to deal with. But if it was true, the stakes of this game had just gone up yet another notch.

He turned to McCarter. "Have Katz contact Kurtzman and ask him to make a full-spectrum recon run over this place. If he still has missiles in there, the warheads might show up on one of the radiation scans."

"Will do."

"What are the site's defensive positions?" Bolan

asked next. Since this would be a commando raid, the ground defenses were the first problem they would have to overcome.

The slide changed and a diagram flashed on the screen. Bolan didn't know Russian military symbols as well as he did the American, but there was enough similarity for him to take pause.

"Are those ground-to-air missile positions?" he asked when he spotted a familiar symbol.

The Spetsnaz major nodded. "They are SA-7s, and we have just learned that those missiles are still in their launchers."

"That bloody well nixes a chopper air assault," McCarter commented. "How about we just bomb the place."

"If Hal wasn't in there, I think I would talk to them about doing exactly that."

"You really think he's still alive, don't you?"

"Until we see the body," Bolan replied, "we have to assume that he is. Rostoff wouldn't have gone to the trouble of kidnapping him if he just wanted him dead. I think it's more likely that he's being questioned."

"Next," the major said, flicking his pointer across the site's perimeter, "you can see that there are a series of automatic sensing machine-gun positions. They are controlled by a central command unit located in..."

AFTER GOING OVER the defensive positions and the interior floor plan of the complex in great detail, the major switched off the screen. "Are there any questions, gentlemen?"

"What's your fallback, Major?" Bolan asked. "What happens if your men can't fight their way inside?"

The major stiffened slightly. "Should we fail to take the objective, Colonel," he said seriously, "the minister has arranged for the complex to be taken out by a surface-to-surface missile."

"Nuclear-tipped?"

"Of course," the major said calmly. "The mother site is much too large to neutralize quickly with chemical explosives. The population of the local area will be cleared of course," he hurried to add.

"Of course," Bolan replied dryly.

"But," the major continued, "I do not expect that it will come to that. My men will be able to handle a criminal gang no matter how well it is armed."

"There is," Bolan informed him in case it had slipped the minister's mind, "also the possibility that Rostoff has terrorist units on hand as well as his Russian renegades."

"What do you mean by terrorists, Colonel?"

"Twice in the past few weeks, Rostoff has used ex-IRA members to attack us in Western Europe.

We also have reason to believe that he has recruited other ex-Communist terrorist groups from all over Europe into his private army. People like the Red Brigades.''

"That may make things a little more difficult," the major admitted, "but it will not change the outcome. Ex-Communist terrorists or not, they are not Spetsnaz."

Bolan well understood the major's enthusiastic esprit de corps and just hoped that his optimism wasn't misplaced.

Picking up briefing packets for Lyons and each of the Phoenix Force commandos, Bolan and McCarter went back to the rooms they had been assigned in the Spetsnaz compound.

WHEN BOLAN AND MCCARTER returned from the briefing, the rest of the Stony Man team was well into its mission-prep phase. A call to Stony Man had gotten them a priority shipment of some of the Farm's specialized weaponry, and they were surprised to see that John Kissinger accompanied the shipment.

"You're a long way from home, lad," McCarter commented when he saw the weaponsmith.

Kissinger grinned. "Since Hal got himself knocked on the head and stuffed into a bag," he said, "things have got so tame around the ranch that I was sitting twiddling my thumbs. So I thought

I'd baby-sit the shipment and make sure that you guys haven't forgotten how to use this stuff.''

Hawkins laughed. ''You lie like a rug on the floor, man. You just wanted to get out of Dodge before the excrement hit the ventilation.''

The weaponsmith shrugged. ''You got that right,'' he admitted. ''But I thought that I might be of some small use over here. You know, play water boy, pick up after you, that sort of thing.''

''Did you bring an extra Kevlar vest with you?'' McCarter asked.

''I brought my entire kit,'' Kissinger replied.

''And do you know how to shoot an RPG-9?''

''I've never even held one,'' he admitted of the latest Russian bunker-busting, rocket-propelled grenade launcher. ''But I'm a quick study.''

''You'd better be, because you're our new RPG gunner.''

''It's nice to be needed.''

''And,'' McCarter added, ''you're also the assistant demo man. Once we're inside, we'll need you and Manning to take down any locked doors we come across.''

''Good. I brought several rolls of linear-shaped charge and det cord as well as a few two-pound shaped charges. When do we leave?''

EARLY THE NEXT MORNING, the trip to Mother Site Eight was made in the Spetsnaz's armored personnel carriers. As the major had explained, with the site's antiaircraft defenses intact, a heliborne assault was out of the question. Even in the armored vehicles, they started taking long-range fire when they were still half a mile from the outer perimeter.

From a distance, the mother site didn't look all that formidable. Most of it was underground, and the topside structures had all been camouflaged to blend in with the trees. When they got closer, however, Bolan started to spot the camouflaged bunkers through his field glasses. They were positioned to give covering fire to the bunkers on either side.

This wasn't going to be an easy task for the Spetsnaz. But, with the detailed plans Vallinsikov had provided, they already knew where each bunker and heavy weapon was located. All they had to do was to take them out.

Halting the armored personnel carriers in hull-defilade positions a quarter mile from the perimeter, the Spetsnaz major sent several of his vehicles forward under the cover of suppressive fire from the rest.

"The approaches to the outer perimeter are mined," the major explained, "but we are going to cut paths through them with the minefield-clearing devices on our tracks."

With every on-board weapon firing as fast as it could, the single tracks halted two hundred yards in front of their assigned bunkers and triggered their mine-clearing devices. Trailing dirty white smoke, small rockets shot out over the open ground pulling small explosive blocks linked together in a chain behind them.

When they settled to the ground, the explosives were command-detonated and the shock of their explosion detonated the mines buried for several yards to each side. A twenty-yard-wide lane erupted in smoke and dust as the mines went off. Several paths were cleared through the minefields at the same time to confuse the defenders as to which one would be the main avenue of attack.

Before the smoke of the detonating mines had cleared, the rest of the Spetsnaz armored personnel carriers roared forward, their weapons blazing. The bunkers returned fire and scored minor hits on several of them, but they charged on.

When the first track was knocked out, they all halted, dropped their rear ramps and the Spetsnaz stormed out in six-man teams. As they took cover on the open ground, their tan, green and brown camouflage uniforms blended in with the earth and the light brush that had foolishly been allowed to grow up around the perimeter.

With the heavy weapons on the tracks firing over their heads, they charged the bunkers.

IN THE ARMORED PERSONNEL CARRIER that had been assigned to Phoenix Force, Bolan and Mc-

Carter both watched the battle from a safe distance through periscopes. The plan called for them to wait until the outer perimeter had been breached and Katzenelenbogen monitored the Spetsnaz radio transmissions, giving them a running commentary.

From the beginning, it was apparent that the Spetsnaz major had quickly discovered that his commandos had encountered fierce resistance. Going up against Rostoff's defenses wasn't turning out to be an easy task. Even with the plans of the complex in hand, his troops were having to fight their way from one bunker position to the next. Rostoff's men were criminals, but too many of them were veteran soldiers as well, so this had turned into a fight for the honor of the Russian soldier.

Seeing one of his assault teams falter, the major ordered in his last reserve team to help them. Everything was committed now, and the outcome was in the hands of God.

"Is there anything we can do to help those poor bastards?" Hawkins asked as he watched the battle through one of the vehicle's open firing ports. "They're getting their butts kicked out there."

"Not yet there's not," McCarter replied. "But as soon as they can take out two adjoining bunkers in the outer ring, we can try to punch through the inner defenses."

"Get ready," Katz told their Spetsnaz driver.

"The major said that bunkers Eight and Nine have been knocked out."

"Do you think you can get us past those knocked-out bunkers?" McCarter asked the driver.

"Can do."

Switching on the microphone, Katz quickly told the major what they were going to try to do and asked if he could provide a little suppressive fire. When the answer came back, he turned to Bolan. "Let's do it."

BORIS DETLOV WAS at the mother site's command center conducting the fight. The video cameras and surveillance gear gave him an almost godlike view of the battlefield. The Spetsnaz were taking terrible casualties, but true to their code, they weren't backing off. As he watched, the Russian commandos threw themselves again and again at the storm of fire from the interlocking bunkers.

The attackers were slowly eliminating the positions one at a time, but at such a heavy cost that he didn't think many of them would survive. Though he had been with Gregor Rostoff since the Afghan War days, in his deepest heart he was still a Russian patriot and it hurt him to watch the Spetsnaz die so bravely.

Nonetheless, even though they were winning so far, most of Rostoff's security force weren't doing very well. Even after calling in all of Rostoff's so-called associates, he wished that he had more men on hand. The site's defenses had been designed to be manned by a full company of infantry, some 120 men, and he had only seventy.

What was even more critical than the numbers was the quality of the defenders. Over Detlov's objections, the colonel had placed great faith in his ex-terrorist units, but they weren't proving to be as tough as their press. Like most of the terrorists he had known, they lacked the discipline needed to stand against dedicated fighters like the Spetsnaz, and they were proving to be the cowards that he had always thought them to be. Killing helpless women and children with car bombs wasn't the same as standing against armed men who were intent on taking your life.

The Afghan War veterans of Rostoff's old Guards Regiment were holding up much better, but too many of them were past their prime. It was one thing to have fought the Mujis in the eighties and entirely another to try to get back in that frame of mind after a decade of peace. Ambushing drug gangs and extorting money from businessmen wasn't the same as cold, hard combat against men who were willing to die for what they believed in.

As yet, he hadn't seen any men he could identify as the vaunted American Phoenix Force. They could be wearing Russian uniforms, but he didn't think that they would do that. From everything he had learned about them, when they came, they would come in as Americans and wouldn't hide behind the Russian troops for protection.

CHAPTER TWENTY-EIGHT

Russia

Phoenix Force's Spetsnaz driver let out a movie-cowboy yell as their armored personnel carrier shot toward the gap in the defensive line. The instant it started to move, the track drew fire. Even with bunkers Eight and Nine knocked out, they were still in the fan of fire from the positions on either side of them and the entire secondary line of defense.

The Russian driver jinked the vehicle from side to side while it still drove full bore, seeming to magically sidestep everything that came at them. Almost every time he turned, the track was rocked by a near miss.

Small arms rounds were spattering all over the personnel carrier's armor, but no 7.62 mm bullet was going to stop them this day.

David McCarter was in the command turret for the wild ride behind the firing controls of the track's autoloading 57 mm high-velocity gun. The cannon was loaded with a mix of sabot and plastic HESH bunker-busting rounds. Even with the gyrostabilizer on the gun mount, with the vehicle bouncing all over the place, it was difficult to bring the cannon to bear accurately.

He managed to score a direct hit on the firing aperture of a bunker of the second line that was directly blocking their path. They had to luck out every now and then. A huge gout of flame blew out both the front and back of the bunker along with chunks of what at one time had to have been men.

The track also had firing ports along both sides so the men inside could have something useful to do while they were waiting for the big one to knock out their vehicle. Not being men who liked to wait, Phoenix Force was taking advantage of that armored design.

Hawkins was at a firing port on the left side with his H&K MP-5. The subgun was a bit short-ranged for that kind of work, but anything that could keep the bad guys' heads down was helpful. Spotting an RPG team in the underbrush, he gave them a full magazine squirt and was rewarded by seeing the unguided antitank rocket miss them by a wide margin. He gave them another long burst as they flashed by so they wouldn't want to try it again.

Kissinger had one of the track's top hatches open and was teaching himself how to shoot the unfamiliar RPG-9. With Manning loading for him, he was firing at anything that came into view. His first two shots didn't hit what he had been aiming at, but he felt that he was starting to get the hang of it.

"One more!" he yelled down to Manning as he handed down the empty launcher.

When the Canadian handed him a loaded RPG, Kissinger swayed with the movement of the vehicle as he locked a secondary bunker in his sights. Seeing a flat piece of ground coming up, he waited until they reached it before squeezing the trigger.

This time, the RPG rocketed out of the launcher on its prop charge, and an instant after the main motor kicked in, it impacted right in front of the bunker. With the rocket motor still burning, the antitank round bounced and flew in through the bunker aperture before detonating. Again, a gout of flame blowing out both sides marked another direct hit.

"Do it again!" Kissinger called down to his loader. "Hurry!"

Seeing Phoenix Force make its run, the Spetsnaz major extorted one more heroic effort from his men to take the defenders' minds off that one particular track. Only half his men were still on their feet, but they could still put out a lot of firepower. Two of his tracks also charged the perimeter, their 57 mm cannon hammering. One of the tracks took a direct hit from an RPG that punched through to the fuel tanks. The armored personnel carrier erupted in a ball of flame.

The second vehicle broke through the ring of bunkers before an RPG round hit it broadside and tore one of the tracks loose. Even immobile, though, the crew inside continued fighting from the side ports and top turret.

With the Spetsnaz assault confusing the defenders, Phoenix Force's track drove past the defenses and charged for the main building.

"Over to the right," McCarter shouted over the intercom to the driver.

Locking his right track, the driver turned the vehicle and they shot off in the new direction.

"Stop at that building on your left," McCarter called out. The driver locked his treads and brought the track to a skidding halt a few yards from what looked like a concrete loading dock. When the track's rear ramp dropped, the Phoenix Force commandos sprinted out, keeping to the cover behind the armored vehicle.

His engine still running, the driver repositioned himself in the commander's turret and prepared to use the 57 mm gun to cover his crazy passengers while they tried to break into the mother site.

FROM A COMMAND and control van safely parked twenty miles away, Minister Vallinsikov was monitoring the fight through the Spetsnaz radio transmissions. He didn't have communications with Phoenix Force, but the Spetsnaz major reported that they had penetrated the mother site's inner defenses and should be on their way inside.

How much eight men would be able to do against it was yet to be seen, but he had to admit that they had been successful so far. Should they falter, however, he was prepared to carry out his threat of using a tactical nuclear strike to eradicate the mother site and everyone in it. In fact the SS-9 rocket on its mobile launcher was parked five hundred yards from his van, and its crew was busy bringing it up to firing status.

One way or the other, Mother Site Eight would die today.

He was also monitoring the radio transmissions of another Spetsnaz unit that was closing in on the dacha of General Belislav. They, too, were meeting resistance, but nothing like what was going on at the mother site. And, unlike the troops at the mother site, they had orders to make sure that the general survived the assault even if they had to take extra casualties to keep him alive.

Now that Marina was dead, he had a vacancy in his interrogation room, and it was reserved for Belislav. He could afford to leave Rostoff to American vengeance if he had the general in his basement, because he would know the name of every other traitor in Mother Russia. As long as he was cleaning house, he would clean it all the way up to the rafters and down to the cellar.

THE SKILL OF THEIR Russian driver and the sacrifice of the Spetsnaz got the Stony Man team close enough to try to force an entry. The plans they had been given listed the building they were at as a service-area annex. What that meant they had no idea, but the plans had also shown two short corridors leading from there to the main building.

Normally they would have taken a more direct approach, like the front door. But the plans had also shown that the main doors of the launch complex were hydraulically operated, steel-faced, concrete blast doors that weighed tons and there was no practical way to breach them.

In the middle of the concrete wall in front of the service-area loading dock was a huge door that looked like it belonged on a bank vault. It was formidable, but the plans had shown that the doors of the service-area annexes, while large, were merely steel. And steel gave way in the face of the proper explosives.

Had they been going for a silent entry, a door that size might have presented a problem. But with the battle raging all around them, who would notice another small explosion or two?

While the rest of the team stood guard, Manning and Kissinger pulled a roll of linear-shaped charge from the demo pack and quickly ran a smaller loop of it all the way around the face of the door. As Kissinger held it in place, Manning pressed it against the surface to activate the adhesive strip on the back.

Taking a two-ounce block of C-4 plastic explosive from his pack, Kissinger molded it around the line charge and stuck it to the door. Manning had the electronic detonator ready, stuck it in the C-4 and backed away, unrolling the firing wires.

Line charges don't have much back blast, and the men didn't have to move far out of the way before hitting the switch. The steel rang like a bell under the blow of the plastic.

When the smoke cleared, a smaller opening had been cut in the door and blown back inside to lay on the floor of what appeared to be an air lock. Considering that the site had been designed to withstand a nearby nuclear attack, that wasn't surprising. Even the service areas would have to be sealed from possible contamination.

When the inside door turned out to be locked as well, Manning put a two-pound shaped charge over the center of the locking mechanism and backed out of the chamber. When that charge blew, it punched out the lock on the inner door and blew it open.

When the smoke cleared, Calvin James and T. J. Hawkins hurried forward, tossed grenades into the corridor beyond and stepped back while they detonated. As soon as the shrapnel stopped singing through the air, they charged through the opening.

WHEN BORIS DETLOV SAW the indicator light for one of the service-area doors come on, he instantly knew that he had been outflanked. Somehow, the Americans had got through the bunker line and blasted their way inside the mother site. Calling up the diagram of the complex, he immediately saw which door they had forced. It was an air lock, rather than a blast door, and was made of twenty-millimeter-thick steel. But, as he well knew, even steel that thick could yield to explosive persuasion.

They had blasted their way in, but they were still in the service area, the annex to the main building that provided the kitchens, the storage rooms and other service-and-supply functions when the mother site wasn't at war. The area had been designed to be cut off when the complex went on alert, and if he could keep them confined there, he could move in troops to take care of them.

Reaching for his controls, he hit the switches that locked the access doors to that area. Since they were concrete blast doors, he felt secure and turned his attention back to the Spetsnaz.

IT TOOK but a few minutes for the Stony Man commandos to sweep through the service area and find it empty. They also found that the corridors leading into the main building were closed with more concrete blast doors.

"Damn!" Manning muttered as he examined one of the massive slabs. "I'm not sure that I have enough charges to even crack this sucker, much less move it out of the way."

"Is there an emergency override?" Kissinger asked.

"There's some kind of control panel over here," Encizo called out, "but it's all in Russian."

"Bag that," James said. "I think that there's some kind of small air-lock door over here. From the wheeled dumb boxes parked around it, I think it's some kind of garbage chute."

Garbage chute or not, if it led inside the mother site, they would use it.

A small explosive charge peeled the round door back, revealing a metal-lined tunnel a few yards long that ended with another hatch.

"I'll get it," Manning said, pulling another charge and detonator out of his pack.

DETLOV WAS SURPRISED to see yet another one of the indicators on the master security panel light up. Reading the legend beside it, he saw that it was the inside door to the trash chute to the annex. He hadn't realized that it opened into the main corridor, and that meant that the Yankees were inside.

He hadn't told Rostoff about the Yankees getting

into the service annex, but he had to inform him about this. Maybe he could move in some of the reserve forces to trap them and finally kill them.

ROSTOFF WAS WEARING a set of his old Afghan War fatigues and had a faded sweatband tied around his forehead. A 9 mm Stechin machine pistol was strapped on his waist belt, an AK-47 assault rifle was slung over his shoulder, and he had a Czech Skorpion subgun in his hands. It was time for him to go to war again.

He hadn't expected Detlov's report that the Yankees had broken in somehow, but he wasn't going to go down without a fight. He had tried to put a call through to General Belislav, but had found that the phone line wasn't in operation. Considering the state of the general's communications equipment, that could only mean that Vallinsikov was moving against him as well. It was apparent now that he had seriously underestimated the minister. He should have used Marina to assassinate the old bastard while he'd had the chance. Even so, all wasn't lost yet.

He had come so far that he didn't really need Belislav anymore. In fact he had been coming to the conclusion already that he would be better off without him. A Russia dominated by the military might actually hamper his criminal enterprises rather than give him free rein. Before he worried about that, though, he had to deal with the immediate threat.

Detlov was still defending the mother site against the Spetsnaz commandos, so it was up to him to take on Phoenix Force. That was actually the way he wanted it. These men had brought him trouble, and he intended to give it back to them in full measure.

Walking into the separate barracks room Detlov had assigned to the Afghanis, he saw that they were ready to go into action. But rather than send them outside to finish off the faltering Spetsnaz, he would use them against the Americans.

"Come," he said to them in Afghani. "The infidels have broken in and I need you to kill them for me."

"Which infidels?" one of the Afghani leaders asked. "You are all infidels in this country."

"These infidels are my American enemies, and they have come from the Great Satan across the ocean to try to bring an end to our very profitable association. I will give a bonus in gold for each of their heads you bring me."

That brought cheers. In a culture that didn't allow men to drink alcohol, they easily became drunk on gold. Though Rostoff was a Russian infidel, the Afghanis respected him as a warrior. He had killed hundreds of their countrymen, but then so had they. So many, in fact, that they had been outlawed in their own country and had to sell their services to men like him.

NOW THAT THEY WERE inside the complex itself, the Stony Man warriors split into teams to search for Hal Brognola and Rostoff. With Kissinger working with Phoenix Force for the duration, that gave them four two-man teams so they could cover the underground maze that much faster.

Bolan was teamed up with Lyons again, as he had been since Prague. This was payback time for the Ironman, and Bolan wanted to make sure that he came out of it alive. What he would decide to do once this was over, Bolan didn't have a clue. With Schwarz and Blancanales gone, maybe he would finally hang up his gun and retire. But to reach that decision point, they had to clean out this place first, and that was something Lyons was good at.

CHAPTER TWENTY-NINE

Russia

The minute that he stepped into the main complex, Carl Lyons was well aware that this could be the day he died. But it was going to take a lot of killing to put him down, and he didn't think that any of the Russians were tough enough to get the job done. He wasn't going to let anyone keep him from getting his hands on, and his knife into, Gregor Rostoff.

During the briefing, Vallinsikov had said that he wanted prisoners taken so he could put them on trial, but the minister didn't understand the realities of fighting under these conditions. Unless someone just happened to fall into their hands when they weren't busy, their chances of taking prisoners were slim to none. Rostoff, in particular, wasn't ever going to stand trial. Not as long as Lyons had anything to say about it.

JAMES AND HAWKINS MADE their way through a wide corridor, pressed against the opposite walls. So far, they had encountered only two Russians; one had fled and the other died before they moved on. Their map of the complex had been translated into English, and they were now headed for what was listed as the Command Prime. They had no idea exactly what that was, but it sounded important.

They were nearing a T intersection when they heard voices. Halting, they tried to pinpoint the sounds, but the metal walls echoed and it was difficult to hear which way they were coming from. James signaled for Hawkins to move forward and see if he could hear better.

Crouching, Hawkins made his way along the wall, halting at the corner. Putting his ear to the floor, he heard voices coming from his right, and they weren't speaking English. Signaling his intentions to James, he pulled a fragmentation grenade from his assault harness and pulled the pin.

James got ready to back his play, and on a silent count of three, Hawkins heaved the grenade down the right branch of the corridor. The detonation served as a signal for both of them to step from cover and unload a magazine from their H&Ks down the hall.

When his bolt locked on an empty magazine, Hawkins ducked back to reload. "This is T.J.," he called over the com link. "Calvin and I have a bunch of them cornered in the corridor leading to what we think is the control room."

"Keep them busy," McCarter radioed back.

KISSINGER AND MANNING were headed for what was listed as the power generator deck. Since they had night-vision goggles, fighting in the dark wasn't a problem for them, but it might confuse the enemy. Coming to a juncture in the corridor, Manning stopped to check around the corner. They hadn't run into any opposition so far, but he knew the enemy was somewhere.

Peering around the edge of the wall, he spotted half a dozen men spread out to cover the door they needed to go through. The gunners were dressed in standard Russian army battle dress, but they all wore turbans.

"They're mujahideen," Manning told Kissinger. "Rostoff is pushing Afghani hash, and it looks like he brought his business partners with him."

"David," he transmitted, "we've come across what looks like mujis guarding the generator deck."

"We've run into them too," the Briton responded. "Take them out and get on with it."

"I heard the man," Kissinger said. "And I've got just the thing to send them to God—one of my monsters."

He dug into his demo bag and came out with two one-pound blocks of C-4 studded with what looked like roofing nails. He put a standard grenade fuse between the two blocks and slapped a couple wraps of back tape around them to hold the improvised grenade together.

"Get ready," he said as he pulled the pin on his monster grenade and cocked his arm back to throw. "Now!"

Manning stepped out, his H&K hammering to cover Kissinger as he lobbed the explosives down the corridor. The detonation brought screams as the roofing nails cut through the air. Those the grenade left alive quickly went down to Manning's subgun.

FAINT NOISES BROKE through to Hal Brognola and brought him out of a light sleep. Over the background mechanical sounds of the forced-air ventilation system, he thought that he heard the unmistakable sound of automatic weapons' fire.

There! He heard it again.

Swinging his legs to the floor, he looked around his Spartan cell one more time, but he didn't see anything more than he had seen the first two-dozen times he had surveyed his stark surroundings. There was absolutely nothing in the cell he could use as a weapon.

The gunfire had to mean that Phoenix Force had figured out where he was being held and were coming for him. He vowed that if Rostoff's men got to him first, he wasn't going to go down easy; he was going to fight. He quickly took off his shirt, twisted it into a bulky rope and held it in his hands like a garrote. If he could get it around someone's neck, he could take at least one of the bastards with him.

As the gunfire sounded louder and closer, he took his place behind the door, his makeshift garrote ready. But when he heard the muted thud of rubber-soled boots coming down the hall, he turned to look out the barred window of his cell. Rostoff's people all wore hard leather on the soles of their shoes, so this had to be the cavalry.

"Striker!" he called out through the bars. "Here!"

"Hal?"

"Down here!"

Bolan and Lyons quickly appeared and punched the button to open the cell door. "You don't look too bad off," Lyons commented.

"Gadgets and Rosario are someplace in here too," Brognola told him.

"They're dead," Lyons snapped. "I saw them die."

"No, they're not," Brognola insisted. "Rostoff staged their deaths, and they were captured and brought here. He let me watch while Gadgets was being tortured."

"Do you know where they're being held?" Bolan asked.

"No, but they've got to be somewhere close. I saw Gadgets yesterday."

"Striker, you take care of Hal," Lyons said. "I'll go find them."

"I'm not staying here," Brognola said. "Give me a gun and I'll come with you."

"We have to get you out of here alive," Bolan stated, "and that means keeping you out of the line of fire."

"Just give me a damned gun!" Brognola growled. "I can take care of myself."

Bolan drew the Beretta 93-R from his shoulder rig and handed it to the big Fed.

"You got the extra magazines for this?"

The Executioner handed him the two spare clips from the pouch on his harness and Brognola stuffed them in his left front pocket. "Let's go."

Back in the hall, the trio heard bursts of automatic weapons' fire coming from the left. Checking in on the com link, Bolan told everyone that Brognola had been freed and advised them to be on the lookout for Schwarz and Blancanales.

"They're alive?" Encizo asked in amazement.

"I'll explain it later," Bolan replied. "Just keep an eye out for them."

"If they're in here," James cut in, "we'll find them."

"And save Rostoff for me," Lyons added. "I want that bastard."

ROSARIO BLANCANALES had also heard the sounds of gunfire echoing through the complex. His partner, however, was still unconscious from Rostoff's last interrogation session. Schwarz had been in bad shape when the guards brought him back. His body was jerking as if he were having seizures, and his heartbeat had been erratic. He seemed more stable now, and Blancanales knew that sleep was good for him.

He was going to the door to see if he could see anything in the corridor outside when Lyons burst through the door with Brognola and Bolan at his heels.

Lyons stopped cold, not believing his eyes.

"It's about time you showed up," Blancanales quipped. "We were beginning to think that you'd split for Hawaii or something."

Lyons closed his eyes for a moment. "I thought you guys were dead. I saw you get shot all to hell."

"That's what Rostoff wanted you to think. They shot us with tranquillizer darts."

"What happened to Gadgets?" Lyons asked when he saw that his teammate hadn't moved from his bunk.

"He's been tortured pretty badly," Blancanales replied. "Rostoff used a nerve induction machine and kept asking him questions about Hal, wanting to know why he had come to Moscow. Of course Gadgets didn't know anything, so they kept zapping him until he passed out."

Lyons kneeled beside the narrow cot and checked his pulse. "Dammit, Gadgets," he muttered, "you'd better not die on me, you bastard."

"Carl?" Schwarz's eyes opened, and he tried to lift his head.

Blancanales hurried to Schwarz's side. "How're you feeling?"

"Help me up," he told his teammate as he struggled to sit. "I'm coming with you guys."

"You two are going to stay right here," Lyons said as he stripped off his com link and handed it to Blancanales. "Use this to call for help if you guys get in trouble, but I want you to keep out of this. We'll get back to you when this is over."

"Hal," Bolan said, turning to his old friend, "I want you to stay here too while we secure the rest of this place. I know you want to get at Rostoff, but I think Carl has a prior claim. So, if you don't want to have to tangle with the Ironman as well, I think you should stay put here."

"You've got a point," Brognola agreed, hefting the borrowed Beretta. "I'll stay and guard them."

"Good man," Lyons said with a grin. "I promise you that I'll take care of Rostoff."

Now that the missing men had been located, Bolan made a call over the com link. James and Hawkins were still working on getting into the control room, but Kissinger and Manning had secured the generator room. "Do you want me to cut the power?" Manning asked.

"No," Bolan radioed back, "we need to keep the ventilator system, but stand by there."

"Roger."

BORIS DETLOV WAS TRYING to follow the battle inside the mother site, but the Americans were smart enough to shoot out the video cameras each time they came across one. From what little he could see, though, the battle wasn't going well. Outside, the Spetsnaz had taken heavy casualties, but they had managed to roll up half of the defenses. And for all of Rostoff's combat experience, he wasn't performing well this time, either.

He could see the defenders starting to flee their bunkers, and it had become very clear that it was time for him to abandon his post in the command center and try to save his life as well.

He knew that Rostoff would stay and die, but he had no intention of going down with him. Picking up his AK-74, he headed for the door. Opening the soundproofed door, he heard a firefight going on around the corner. That wasn't something he wanted any part of, so he closed the door and locked it.

He walked over to the elevator and punched the button for the next floor down. When the elevator door opened, he waited to see if there was any gunfire, but it seemed that this section of the complex was clear.

With his AK at the ready, he raced down the corridor to one of the emergency air locks that led outside.

HAL BROGNOLA HEARD the sounds of hard leather-boot soles running toward their cell. He had disabled the lock, but had swung the door shut for their protection. Looking through the barred window, he saw one of the Russians racing down the corridor. He started to back up when he recognized who it was—Rostoff's second-in-command.

Waiting until the last moment, he slammed the door open and stepped into the man's path, the borrowed Beretta in his hand switched to 3-round-burst mode.

Detlov jumped back as the door swung open and was bringing up his AK when Brognola shouted "Hey! Scumbag!" and triggered the pistol.

The three 9 mm parabellum rounds took the Russian in the chest. He staggered back, only to take three more hits, then crumpled to the concrete.

Brognola pulled the door shut behind him as he stepped back into the room. "One more for the good guys."

ROSTOFF WAS DOWN to only a handful of Afghani defenders. Even with his extensive knowledge of the complex, the Yankees were proving to be more than his men could handle. Every time they had tried to ambush them, it had been turned around on them. Too late, he realized that it had been too long since he had come up against real professionals.

Keying his radio, he called to Detlov in the control room. "Boris, come in."

When there was no answer, he called again, "Boris, answer me, dammit!"

When a third call went unanswered, he realized that Detlov was either dead or had run out on him. But he still had his few Afghanis, and they could fight their way out. As long as he was alive, his empire was intact and he could run it from anywhere in Russia.

The Afghani on point suddenly gave a shout of warning and spun, swinging his AK to cover a side corridor. A burst of fire stitched him across the torso, and he went down. The other Afghanis dived for cover as a firestorm erupted in the close quarters. One by one, the Afghanis collapsed to the floor.

When his AK locked on an empty magazine, Rostoff frantically dumped the magazine, and was reaching for a fresh one when he realized that his ammo pouch was empty. At the same time, he saw that he was the last man standing, and that several submachine guns were aimed at him.

"Don't shoot him!" Lyons shouted. "He's mine!"

CHAPTER THIRTY

Russia

Seeing the invaders relax, but not pulling their weapons off target, Rostoff slowly bent to lay his empty assault rifle at his feet. Since he wasn't dead yet, this wasn't over.

When the Yankee who had shouted for the others not to shoot put down his shotgun, Rostoff realized that he had to be the so-called Ironman.

The Russian's hand went down to his boot top and came up with a Jumbiyah, the curved dagger of the Arabic world. He had killed more men than he could remember with the blade, and he would send this American down to hell with him.

"Come on, Yankee," he beckoned with his other hand.

Lyons smiled as he drew his Tanto fighting knife from his harness. The Russian's curved dagger was a good slashing weapon, but the chisel-pointed Tanto was better for what he had in mind. All he would have to do was block the Russian's slashes until he could get close enough to gut him.

Rostoff liked seeing Lyons's smile; it told him that the American was a little too confident. He had never seen a straight-bladed knife like the one the Yankee carried, but it didn't look that fast. And it was single-edged, so it was no good for a back slash. Since this was going to be his last knife fight, he might as well put all he had into it.

"Come to me, big Yankee."

Unlike in the movies, a knife fight is usually a very short affair, and the guy who best knew what he was doing always won. This time, however, the two opponents were equally matched. Rostoff made the first move, a slashing attack from left to right with a nasty back slash at the end of it.

Lyons pivoted to miss the attack, but when he rolled back, the Jumbiyah's back slash caught him across the top of his left forearm. The razor-sharp blade sliced the heavy cloth of his combat jacket as if it were tissue paper, and the blood welled up from the shallow, but long cut.

Rostoff smiled when he saw the blood and stepped forward for a second attack. Again Lyons turned to miss the blade, but he didn't step back as Rostoff expected. Instead, as the back slash passed his belly, he moved into his opponent, the Tanto held low with the edge upward.

Rostoff slashed down to parry, aiming for Lyons's knife arm, but the big ex-cop used the bottom of his left forearm to deliver a stunning blow to the top of Rostoff's wrist, knocking the curved dagger off target.

The second half of his move drove the Tanto fighting knife all the way to the guard in the pit of Rostoff's stomach, the chisel-shaped point severing his aorta.

The Russian's eyes grew wide at the sudden loss of blood. But before he could die, Lyons ripped the knife upward, gutting him.

The last thing the Russian saw was his intestines spilling out of his belly.

Lyons retrieved his knife, wiped off the blood on Rostoff's uniform and sheathed it.

"Now we can go home," he said as he picked up the SPAS from the floor.

EPILOGUE

Stony Man Farm, Virginia

Hal Brognola found the War Room packed to the walls when he walked in. It had been a week since he had returned from Russia, and since this was expected to be the final gathering of Stony Man Farm crew before the expected presidential ax fell, everyone who could find a seat or a place to stand was in attendance.

"First off," Brognola stated right away, knowing better than to keep this crowd waiting too long, "Gadgets Schwarz is going to be okay. The neuro people at Walter Reed say that no permanent damage was done to his arm. I gave him a couple of weeks off, R and R as it were, but he'll be back to duty right after that."

"Did he say where he was going on leave?" Rosario Blancanales asked. The least Schwarz could do was let him and Lyons know where he was going to be.

"He said something about trying to look in on the abalone festival in the British Virgin Islands."

Blancanales and Lyons exchanged grins. Their partner was headed for one of the Caribbean's finer cathouses, the Abalone Shell on St. Thomas. As soon as this meeting was over and they had received their walking papers, they'd join him there for a well-deserved rum punch or three.

Brognola glanced down at his paperwork. "As most of you know, Gregor Rostoff and most of his henchmen are dead and the Russian Mafia is in complete disarray. It's gone back to being a collection of petty gangsters without any central guiding hand, and they'll be a lot easier to deal with. To keep after them, Minister Vallinsikov has been appointed the new head of the Russian Justice Department, and they will be working closely with our government."

Even though that news didn't affect the United States directly, it was still good news. No one wanted to have to live with a resurgent Russia in the hands of the mob.

"Equally important, the planned military coup of General Belislav has been put down, as well. There will be no military rule in Russia for a while at least."

Again, that was good news.

"The intercepts Katz made in Budapest have been turned over to Interpol, and they are conducting massive sweeps in Western Europe. So far, they have been getting good results and expect them to continue.''

This was more good news, because many of the European gangs had established U.S. connections, and the last thing America needed was to find itself awash in Afghan hashish.

''And lastly, Barbara,'' Brognola said, looking directly at her, ''your little revolt here didn't happen.''

''Say again?'' She looked puzzled.

''I said that nothing out of the ordinary happened here at the Farm during the last mission.''

''How in the hell did you manage to pull that off, Hal?'' Lyons asked.

Brognola smiled like a Cheshire cat. ''Well, as it turns out, Minister Vallinsikov and I had this plan in place to find the leak in his ministry, and it included having Katz and the field teams fade out of sight for a while. That forced Rostoff to have to expose himself more and more until we were able to get a hook into him and shut him down.''

Price was stunned. ''I've heard a lot of bullshit in my day, Hal Brognola,'' she said, ''but that's the biggest crock I've ever heard.''

''Isn't it just?'' Brognola looked very pleased with himself. ''I thought it was a rather clever crock, as well.''

"Are you trying to tell me that the President bought that story?"

"Of course he did," Brognola replied seriously. "All politicians like to hear bedtime stories with happy endings. It lets them sleep at night without worrying. And since the story came on the minister's own letterhead, it's a classic example of the new spirit of cooperation between our two governments. Letters of commendation from the Russians with endorsements from the White House have been placed in all of your files."

"Are you telling me that it's over?" Price asked. "That's all there is?"

Brognola nodded. "You can unpack your gear now and go back to work."

"I'll be damned," Kurtzman said softly.

"You will be if you ever try anything like that again," Brognola promised. "One free revolt per lifetime is all you get. The next time any of you people try to pull something like that, I'll be all over you like white on rice."

He reached into his briefcase. "Oh, yeah. There is one more thing."

"Here it comes," Kurtzman muttered loudly enough for everyone to hear. "Grab your ankles."

"This cooperative effort worked so well that the President wants you to look into assisting the Red Chinese with putting down the Hong Kong Tongs. Now that China's taken over the city, the Tongs have become a real problem. It seems that they have a new leader and he's become more than they can deal with.''

Price shook her head in disbelief and looked over at Kurtzman. ''Since we're still packed up and ready to go, Aaron, you want to drive over to that chicken farm and get settled in?''

Kurtzman unlocked his wheelchair and started to back away from the table. ''Let's get the hell out of here before they chain us to the floor again.''

James Axler

OUTLANDERS™

HELLBOUND FURY

Kane and his companions find themselves catapulted into an alternate reality, a parallel universe where the course of events in history is dramatically different. What hasn't changed, however, is the tyranny wrought by the Archons on mankind…this time, with human "allies."

Book #1 in the new Lost Earth saga, a trilogy that chronicles our heroes' paths through three very different alternate realities…where the struggle against the evil Archons goes on….

THE
LOST
EARTH
SAGA

BOOK 1

In the Deathlands, power is the ultimate weapon....

JAMES AXLER

DEATH LANDS.

Starfall

Ryan Cawdor and his warrior survivalists jump into Montana territory, where they are joined by members of the Heimdall Foundation, an organization of whitecoats that investigates the possibility of alien visitation on earth.

Their paths cross with those of a Baron's sec men, who are searching for valuable debris from an abandoned space station that fell from the sky—the same "fallen star" that intrigues the Heimdall members.

While Krysty tries to fend off a telepathic mind assault, Ryan and his companions must find a way to deal with the sec men....

Desperate times call for desperate measures. Don't miss out on the action in these titles!

#61910	FLASHBACK	$5.50 U.S. ☐
		$6.50 CAN. ☐
#61911	ASIAN STORM	$5.50 U.S. ☐
		$6.50 CAN. ☐
#61912	BLOOD STAR	$5.50 U.S. ☐
		$6.50 CAN. ☐
#61913	EYE OF THE RUBY	$5.50 U.S. ☐
		$6.50 CAN. ☐
#61914	VIRTUAL PERIL	$5.50 U.S. ☐
		$6.50 CAN. ☐

(limited quantities available on certain titles)

TOTAL AMOUNT	$
POSTAGE & HANDLING	$
($1.00 for one book, 50¢ for each additional)	
APPLICABLE TAXES*	$ _____
TOTAL PAYABLE	$ _____
(check or money order—please do not send cash)	

To order, complete this form and send it, along with a check or money order for the total above, payable to Gold Eagle Books, to: **In the U.S.:** 3010 Walden Avenue, P.O. Box 9077, Buffalo, NY 14269-9077; **In Canada:** P.O. Box 636, Fort Erie, Ontario, L2A 5X3.

Name: _____

Address: _____ City: _____

State/Prov.: _____ Zip/Postal Code: _____

*New York residents remit applicable sales taxes.
 Canadian residents remit applicable GST and provincial taxes.

GSMBACK1